Slowly, the wooden door moved . . .

. . . and with each precious movement Mary prayed for deliverance from her confinement. A faint light drifted in the cell as the door continued to open and bid her freedom. But she cautiously waited; her captors could be tormenting her and laying a trap. She kept her silence and watched, her heart thudding wildly in her chest as the door came to a halt half open.

She heard the hint of a shuffle and moved deeper into the protective arms of the darkness.

Mary watched, her eyes widening as a dark figure suddenly filled the partially open doorway. The faint light framed his silhouette. There was a slight hunch to his form, yet preciseness in his movement. He was shrouded completely in black, a hood draped over his head concealed his face, black gloves covered his hands that lay pressed together against his stomach. His black robe covered all but the tip of one boot.

"Your father sent me," he said in a harsh, grating voice and held out his gloved hand.

Other **AVON ROMANCES**

DONNA FLETCHER

DARK WARRIOR

AVON BOOKS

An Imprint of HarperCollinsPublishers

This is a work of fiction. Names, characters, places, and incidents are products of the author's imagination or are used fictitiously and are not to be construed as real. Any resemblance to actual events, locales, organizations, or persons, living or dead, is entirely coincidental.

AVON BOOKS
An Imprint of HarperCollins*Publishers*
10 East 53rd Street
New York, New York 10022-5299

Copyright © 2004 by Donna Fletcher
ISBN: 0-06-053879-1
www.avonromance.com

First Avon Books paperback printing: November 2004

Avon Trademark Reg. U.S. Pat. Off. and in Other Countries, Marca Registrada, Hecho en U.S.A.
HarperCollins® is a registered trademark of HarperCollins Publishers Inc.

Printed in the U.S.A.

10 9 8 7 6 5 4 3 2 1

For my Mom and Dad,
with love

Chapter 1

Thus shadow owes its birth to light.

JOHN GAY, *"The Persian, Sun, and Cloud"*

Mary ran for her life in woods that once offered sanctuary.

Low-hanging branches scratched at her arms in an attempt to impede the escape, and familiar tall trees became as angry sentinels blocking her at every twist and turn. Gray storm clouds rushed overhead, keeping pace with her; a fine mist of rain fell, dampening the linen shift and tunic she wore. Her soft leather boots crushed the fresh spring growth as she tried to increase the distance from her pursuers.

Their angry warning shouts were meant to frighten her, but she did not think she could be any more frightened; she had been running for the last ten years.

The ground trembled from the pounding of running feet as they gained on her. She hastened, but the rapid pace brought on a growing fatigue that soon would impede her flight.

She silently encouraged herself. *Keep going. Keep going.*

She ran and she ran and she ran. Her heart pounded, breathing turned rapid, and the voices behind grew louder.

Do not turn around. Keep running.

The pursuers taunted her with their laughter, playing with her, letting her know they were so very close to capturing her. She refused to let them intimidate her and refused to surrender. She would run until she breathed her last breath.

Her determination gave her renewed speed; she heard a string of violent oaths spewed from behind as she moved beyond their reach.

The wet ground made her footing difficult. She slipped and righted herself, but not quickly enough.

Hands suddenly shoved at her back and she tumbled face-forward to the ground, her breath knocked completely out of her. Given no time to regain her senses, the man roughly turned her onto her back, straddling her and grabbing her neck in his large, thick hand.

"Run from me will you?" He snarled between panted breaths, sounding like an enraged animal about to tear his prey to pieces. "You're not going anywhere. Decimus wants you."

Mary grabbed at his hand, fear racing through her. He was choking her; she could not breath. She pulled and clawed at his wrist, his arm, but he squeezed even harder. Her vision blurred, shouts sounded around them.

She struggled and fought, and knew she was dying.

No breath. No breath. No—

Mary woke with a start, her hand going immediately to her neck. She cringed from the pain. Total darkness surrounded her, and she curled up into herself in the tiny prison cell.

It had been a full day since her capture, at least she thought it had been. Being deprived of light made for the absence of time. It was as if darkness was a void where time did not exist or matter.

She gently moved her fingers over her neck, determining that it was bruised nearly from ear to ear. She had attempted to give answers demanded of her captors' questions after the strangling ceased, but her throat was so pained that speech was barely possible.

This angered them even more, and the one who had choked her shoved her in disgust to the wet ground. She was already wet and muddied; this only added to her miserable condition. And now she sat in a cell, the mud having dried and caked on her garments, in her long blond hair, streaking her face. She knew she must look a sight.

She laughed softly. What did her appearance matter? She sat alone in the dark cell, her life in danger. Her thoughts should be on more important matters, but then what chance was there for her to escape? And being released? She shook her head at the absurdity of the wishful thought.

A faint noise in the corner of the cell caught her attention. She listened as the scurrying of tiny feet rustled the straw serving as the cell's floor-covering. No doubt mice or rats looking for a morsel of food. She tapped her feet together to frighten the rodents off. She heard an anxious scurry of feet and then sudden silence. They had made their escape, while she remained a prisoner waiting for . . . ? Mary shook her head and huddled in the corner of the cell, a chill causing her to shiver. She hugged herself tightly.

Decimus had finally caught her after all these years.

She shivered again, gooseflesh prickling her soft skin at the mere thought of the man and his infamous reputation for hunting, capturing, and punishing heretics. It was said that he gained extreme pleasure from inflicting pain on his prisoners, and the only escape from him was death.

She shook her head slowly at the memories that had brought her to this tiny cell. She had lived a quiet, uneventful life since her parents' friend Magnus, or as most knew him the "Legend," had brought her to sanctuary in the woods in the northeast of Ireland far from her native Scotland.

Her parents were good people, though their beliefs were a mixture of pagan and Christian. The village of Muir where she had been raised was not a common village. It was a place of pagans and old beliefs, and had once belonged to an old hermit who had grown tired of his solitude and encouraged travelers to remain on his land. The people worked hard alongside each other growing their crops, tending to the needy, sharing laughter and singing songs. They remained to themselves, unnoticed by authorities until her father's reputation as a teacher had grown.

Tears slipped down her cheek in remembrance of her parents and all they had done to help people. They believed people had the right to worship as they chose, to think, to question. Questions were not encouraged by the authorities or the Church; obedience and submission were the rules and they were to be obeyed without question.

Her father taught men and women to rely on their instincts and their own thoughts; that thoughts brought forth ideas and knowledge, and knowledge brought forth questions. Good, honest questions that made a man think, but a thinking peasant was a dangerous one.

She had listened endlessly to her father's teachings. He had a soft voice and an understanding nature. She could not remember him growing upset over anything. He would see reason in all there was to see; an astute observer, he could accurately predict people's reactions to any given situation, making him a man much sought after, especially by those who saw him as dangerous.

She missed talking with him and hearing his soothing voice. Many insisted her own tender ways were inherited from her father, her beauty and kindness from her mother. She also felt she inherited their courage, and was glad of it. Without this courage she did not know how she would have survived.

And she would have lost her life to Decimus, as her parents had done, had Magnus not rescued her from the same fate. Magnus had been a student of her father's and was nearly done with his studies when the trouble began. It was learned that Decimus was investigating her father. There was little doubt that her father would soon be taken to Decimus's fortress of hell to answer questions of heresy. Few left the fortress alive, and then only by escaping. A torturous death was often the only means of departure.

Following her parents' deaths the Church claimed she was the daughter of heretics and had been soiled by their heretical beliefs. She required cleansing, even if it meant death. Magnus had seen to her escape and had taken her away from her homeland, brought her to Ireland to live in peace for the past twelve years.

But had she run from an inevitable fate?

A single tear was the only one she would allow herself to shed. Crying served no purpose and would only cloud her thoughts. She needed a clear head to aid in solving her problem.

Suddenly her head snapped up. Her eyes widened. Mary thought she heard a noise, a shuffle of sorts, like the whisper of a garment hem when it brushes along the ground, though the dark was too dense to see through. Did someone approach?

She strained to hear but silence greeted her efforts.

Had she imagined the noise in the hope that someone had come to rescue her? She sighed and her shoulders sagged with the weight of her troubled thoughts. She had been taught to keep hope alive forever in her heart, but what hope was there of escape?

It would take days for Magnus to learn of her abduction and by then . . .

She shuddered at the thought of the torture she would suffer. But if she could survive, would Magnus arrive in time to free her? Her father had told her that Magnus was not only his best student but also a true friend who could be trusted. Through the years, he had always been there, watching over her, making certain she remained free of danger and Decimus's discovery. Magnus was a good, caring man, though many thought him a warrior to be feared.

She turned her head sharply, certain this time she had heard a sound.

Footsteps?

She remained quiet in her thoughts, listening and hoping.

Seconds crawled by yet she remained vigilant. She could only detect a faint crackle from the torches lining the narrow hall to the dungeon's entrance.

Then a distinct sound interrupted the heavy silence. *The cell door is opening.*

Slowly the wooden door moved, and with each precious movement Mary prayed for deliverance from her confinement.

A faint light drifted in. The door continued to widen and bid her freedom. But she cautiously waited; her captors could be tormenting her and laying a trap. She kept her silence and watched, her heart thudding wildly in her chest as the door came to a half-open halt.

She heard the hint of a shuffle and moved deeper into the protective arms of the darkness.

Mary watched, her eyes straining as a dark figure filled the partially open doorway. The faint light framed his silhouette. There was a slight hunch to his form, yet preciseness in his movement. He was shrouded completely in black, a hood draped over his head concealed his face, black gloves covered his hands that lay pressed together against his stomach, and his black robe covered all but the tip of one black boot.

"Your father sent me," he said in a harsh grating voice and held out his gloved hand.

Mary was too stunned to move. The message was from Magnus, the very words they had agreed upon if someone other than himself should come for her. The words guaranteed her safety.

"We have little time."

She attempted to stand but stumbled, her body having yet to heal from the punches and kicks her captors had enjoyed inflicting on her.

The dark figure reached out to her and she recoiled, his shrouded appearance intimidating. She quickly regretted her reaction and eased forward to offer an apology.

"I—I—" Her hand grabbed at her throat, the intense pain rushing tears to pool in her eyes. She shook her head to let him know speech was not possible.

"They have injured you?"

She nodded.

"You cannot speak?"

She shook her head, and was prepared to escape.

This time he would not give her a chance to recoil for he swept her up into his arms. She tensed at being held with such familiarity in a stranger's arms.

"You will be safe shortly."

His harsh voice sent a shiver through her. She could only hope he spoke the truth for she had no choice but to trust him.

Chapter 2

After what seemed like an eternity moving through unlit, dank corridors, a risky flight up a stone staircase, and a chilling journey through a secret, narrow passageway, they finally made their escape. The dark night greeted the couple as they left Decimus's stronghold. Mary breathed deeply of the fresh air in an attempt to rid her nostrils of the dungeon's stench, then lowered her head near to the stranger's chest as they entered the woods to keep her face from being hit by leaves and tree branches.

With darkness as their ally, they fled in silence, his footfalls barely detectable. He was a shadow among shadows blending with his surroundings. She wondered over their destination. Though her rescuer's familiar words should have reassured her, she remained concerned for her safety.

She grew tired, her battered body not having time to fully recover. Her eyes began to drift closed, she forced them open. She had to remain alert and prepared to walk no matter how painful her legs.

"Sleep."

His harsh whisper sent a shiver through her, causing him to hug her tightly. Could she expect to be carried much farther?—she was not a small woman, gentle in curves with fullness to her breasts and hips. And she was more than capable of taking care of herself.

"Sleep. We have a distance to travel and you need rest."

His words were a faint rumble in his throat, but she clearly heard them. They blended with the steady rhythm of his heart, which had not faltered or sped up in fear. He was confident and comfortable in his task as though assured of success.

She thought to tell him to put her down so that she could walk on her own, but that would not be a wise decision. She needed to rest and grow strong so that, when the time came, she could keep pace with this shrouded stranger.

She did not recall her eyes closing. His whispers woke her and she saw that dawn had peaked on the horizon. They had come upon a dilapidated building long abandoned by people and animals but embraced by the woods surrounding it. Vines and brush had claimed the sorry structure, closing it off from the world as if in protection.

He bowed his head to clear the doorway and his warm breath fanned her face. She detected a hint of a familiar scent. What was it? Her weary mind needed rest; perhaps then she would be able to distinguish the scent.

"Can you stand for a moment?"

She nodded, wanting to test her aching legs.

He lowered her feet to the ground and tenderly braced her against the wall. "Give me a moment and I will have a pallet for you to rest upon."

She wanted to tell him that this was not necessary, the hard earth floor would serve her well enough, but her painful throat would not allow her to speak. She reached out, her hand grabbing his arm as he turned away.

He turned back, her hand dropped. She almost cringed but stopped herself. His dark garb was ominous, not an ounce of flesh showed and she wondered what he was hiding.

"Your injured throat needs healing, you should not speak. I will have you to safety shortly and when you heal, we can talk."

He walked away, gathering dried brush that lay scattered over the floor and piling it in a shadowed, secluded corner. He then left the structure.

A quick glance confirmed her suspicion that this place was no cottage; it lacked a fireplace for warmth, which meant it was a storage shed at one time. She wished to explore the small space if only to see if she was strong enough to walk, but her instincts warned her against it.

He returned with an armful of fresh brush and laid it on top of the dry brush. He then walked over and reached out to lift her in his arms.

She held her hand up and shook her head, instead placing her hand on his arm for support to let him know she wished to walk with his assistance.

He obliged her, though after taking two steps he slipped his arm around her waist for further support.

He lowered her gently, then joined her on the pallet and slowly moved closer.

She tensed.

"We will need each other's warmth for the night will grow more chilled."

He was right. Her meager tunic and shift were not sufficient garments against the cool spring air. She shifted her body nearer so that their sides would touch. That was all she could bring herself to do, for lying more intimately with a stranger would not be appropriate.

She was curious about this shadow of a man she was about to sleep with, and she gently tapped his arm. He turned his head.

She stared at the black void and realized that his face shroud was of different material than his robe and made visibility possible for him, though she could only make out a faint outline of a face, nothing more.

She patted her chest, then turned her hand over and with her finger slowly wrote the letters of her name on her palm.

"Aye," he said. "I know your name is Mary."

She was elated by the fact that he could read, at least then she could communicate while her throat healed. She tapped his arm with her finger.

He understood her question. "My name is unimportant."

She shook her head and patted her chest to make him understand that his name was important to her. A name gave someone an identity and she needed him to have an identity.

He seemed to understand and paused as if in search of a name. "Michael, call me Michael."

She nodded and once again wrote on her palm—*Magnus*. She then pointed at him and back at her palm.

"You wish to know how Magnus and I know each other?"

She nodded eagerly. She had to be certain Magnus had sent him.

"Our paths have crossed on occasion and we have become friends."

She continued to stare, waiting to hear more.

"Do not look for answers I cannot give you. It is safer for you to remain ignorant of me. Know that Magnus sent me to see you to safety and that is what I will do."

She shook her head to let him know his answer would not do. She wanted something more to prove Magnus had sent him.

"I spoke the words Magnus told me to speak to you so that you would know he sent me. Trust that it is so and know that he would have come himself if his bride-to-be Reena was not in danger."

Excitement and worry gripped her all at once. She was happy that Magnus would marry but was concerned for his future wife. She squeezed Michael's arm wanting so badly to ask him dozens of questions.

"I understand your concern. Reena, though pint-sized, is courageous; Magnus will allow no harm to befall her."

Suddenly a hard shiver racked her body. He moved closer and draped his arm over her. She did not tense this time; his warmth was much too welcome and warded off the intense chill.

"I can give you but one day to rest, no more. Decimus searches for all escaped prisoners with a vengeance. He puts the fear of God in his men so that they will obey him without question, which means he will order them to find you no matter how long it takes. I must get you to a temporary place of safety as quickly as possible."

She shivered with the reminder of Decimus's relentless thirst for revenge. Stories abounded of his cruelty, some so absurd that Mary could think them nothing more than tall tales. She would, however, only need to see a vision of her parents' horrible fate to know that Decimus was capable of the unspeakable.

Would there ever be a place of safety for her? She had been lulled into a false sense of security in the last couple of years. She had thought herself safe from the evil that hunted her, and she had begun to think of life without fear of capture. She had wrongly assumed Decimus searched for her no more, or perhaps she had hoped that he had lost interest in her. She had been barely eleven when her parents died. What harm could she have done him? Or had her escape been a wound to his reputation that had festered and putrefied with the years?

She fell into a troubled slumber, Michael's protective presence a haven from her fears.

Daylight was fading when she woke to find herself alone. She grew anxious over Michael's absence, then realized how foolish her thought. He would not abandon her; he had entered into an agreement with Magnus to see to her safety. She could rely on him at least for now. Eventually she would have only herself to rely on and she would survive. She could not allow Decimus victory over her, not after all this time and all the heartache he had caused her.

She noticed an old bucket near the pallet that had not been there the night before.

Fresh water.

She scooped up the cool liquid and drank. The chilled water eased the pain in her throat and she sighed with relief. She thought to wash her face, she must certainly look frightful, but if this was their only drinking water she did not wish to waste it. Her face would just have to remain dirty.

"Drink your fill."

She jumped, startled by Michael's voice, not having heard him enter.

She nodded her thanks and again took a handful to quench her seemingly relentless thirst. Perhaps it was the awareness that it might be some time before water would again be available.

Michael sat beside her and unfolded a part of his robe that he had bunched together and used like a sack. Berries and edible roots spilled out.

She smiled and patted her stomach.

"I thought you might be hungry."

Mary nodded and reached for some berries.

"I cannot chance a fire or we would have feasted on meat."

She scooped up a fat root and grinned wide. *This meal is fine.* She detected a laugh but was not certain of it. She thought under all that darkness must lie a *hint* of light.

She pointed to the food and then to him.

"I must confess I ate while I gathered."

She finished the root and all of the berries, sighed her contentment.

"Your throat," he said, raising his gloved hand slowly, careful not to frighten her. "Does it continue to pain you?" He gently stroked the bruised area with a lone finger.

She sat very still, hiding her fear of his faint touch, but her startled, wide eyes alcrted him to her discomfort.

His removed his hand slowly; they sat quietly for several minutes until he ended the awkward silence.

"We will leave tomorrow night."

She nodded.

"You should rest. We have much land to cover."

She wished to know their destination. She pointed to him then herself, then walked her fingers across her palm and shrugged.

"Northwest, to a small village where I have friends who will shelter us," he answered.

Another matter that needed attention was a quick walk in the woods. She would prefer to go alone but with night having fallen, no voice to cry out for help, and unreliable legs, she knew his company was necessary.

She pointed to the door and once again she walked her fingers across her palm and pointed to herself.

He understood and helped her to stand. "Your legs will hold you?"

She shrugged and nodded simultaneously, indicating she was uncertain but without choice.

They walked a short distance into the dense woods, his firm arm around her waist. He released her gently and made certain she remained steady on her feet before bending down to snatch something off the ground. He handed her two stones.

"I will leave you to your privacy and be only a short distance away. If you should need me, throw the one stone and I will come to you. When you are finished toss one stone then the other and I will come to you."

She acknowledged with a nod then saw to her needs. Her legs pained under her full weight. When she finished she did as he had said, she tossed the first stone then the second. He appeared before her like a phantom materializing out of the night, giving her a start.

His arm quickly circled her waist. "I startled you; I am sorry."

She shook her head and, with hand motions she hoped made sense, attempted to let him know that in time she would adjust to his strange manner.

He spoke as they walked. "You will grow accustomed to me."

She nodded vigorously, pleased he understood.

"I think it wise if you carry a few stones with you. They may prove helpful if we are ever separated and you need me."

Need him.

She did not want to need him. Need brought dependency and possible harm to the person she needed. The couple who had taken her in, and cared for her like their only child, would have been in jeopardy had she not taken flight as soon as she had discovered that men who hunted her were nearby. She could not cause another harm; it was a belief she had been taught and one she intended to live by.

She took a few steps and stopped abruptly in front of the doorway. Mary stuck her chin up and, with rapid hand motions, did her best to convey her confidence in taking care of herself.

He stepped closer, until their bodies almost touched. "You may think you are capable of seeing to your own safety, but you are wrong if you think you can defend yourself against Decimus. That is what I am here to do, keep you safe from him, and I will do that. No matter what it takes, I will keep you safe."

His forceful words impressed her. She realized then why Magnus had chosen him for the task. He had no intentions of failing. He would see to her safety even if it meant his life. And she wondered if perhaps he hated Decimus as much as she did.

"We both need rest for our journey." He took hold of

her arm and guided her gently into the shed, walked her to the pallet. "Sleep."

She lay on her back. The aches and pains tormented her and the cool night air had begun to creep under her meager garments, sending a chill through her. Would he join her again tonight and keep her warm? She hoped he would; she was cold and needed his warmth. Though he was a stranger, he had proven that he knew Magnus and would protect her.

Soon he lowered himself down beside her. "Cold?"

She nodded, eager for the warmth of his body.

He moved up against her, his arm wrapping around her. He draped his robe over her legs and she shifted closer to him.

"At the moment we have only each other."

He was right and, to let him know she agreed, placed a gentle hand over his. They fell asleep and soon were wrapped together like lovers.

"Wake up, Mary," a harsh voice whispered in her ear. "Wake up now."

She thought she was dreaming, feeling snug in her warm cocoon and not wanting to leave it. She bristled as the arm around her squeezed tighter.

Something is wrong.

Her eyes opened wide, daylight had just broken, the night inching back into the shadows.

"Someone approaches."

She listened but heard nothing.

"I need to see who it is. You must remain here and not make a sound."

She squeezed his arm in response. As he left their shelter, she quietly moved closer to the door so that she could see if the intruders approached. She could not leave her safety completely in his hands. What if something happened to him? She had to be ready to defend herself and to flee if necessary.

The sun continued to rise, chasing the night away along with the shadows that so often haunted the woods. She wondered about Michael's safety. The night was his friend, the daylight his enemy. Where would he hide?

She thought she heard a rustle of leaves and saw a movement in the thick brush. She remained still and listened then heard it again.

Someone is out there.

Her heart beat wildly, fright sent gooseflesh racing over her body. She feared being returned to Decimus. His insidious reputation as an inquisitor caused dread among the innocent and guilty alike, his power coming from on high—the Church.

She did not fear death, her father's beliefs having taught her it was a beginning not an end. It was the senseless suffering that Decimus inflicted on his victims that frightened her.

The rustle of bushes and sudden appearance of a man had her catch her breath and hastily place a hand to her pounding heart. She recognized him, tall and hefty, with a face that would win no hearts; he was the man who had caught her in the woods and choked her.

He approached the shed quietly and apprehensively, casting cautious glances around him. He kept his hand firm on the hilt of his knife in the sheath secured to his belt.

Mary kept a steady watch on him, wondering where Michael had gone. She grew nervous as the man inched closer to the shed, not certain of what to do should he attempt to enter. She could not cry out but remained helpless. She looked around for a weapon when a movement outside caught her eye.

Michael appeared without warning, had the man down on his knees and his hands around his neck. Where he had come from she could not say. It was as if he appeared magically from out of nowhere. The thought made her shudder.

The two men exchanged words and then suddenly the captured man reached out and, with one swift blow to the leg, took Michael to the ground.

Mary watched horrified as the two men rolled and punched and fought like vicious animals ready to kill. One minute Michael seemed the victor, the next minute the other man would have the upper hand, and so it continued until Mary thought it would never end. Then in one instant the man reached for Michael's mask and tore it aside.

Mary could see only the man's reaction, as Michael's back faced her. The man grew pale, his eyes widened in horrible fright, and his mouth dropped open as though he was ready to scream for mercy, but then, as though he gave it second thought, he lunged for Michael.

With swift hands Michael deflected his attack, grabbed him around the neck and with a quick jerk broke it.

Chapter 3

Mary was stunned silent. She had seen death through illness, but never had she seen one man take another man's life. And never had she seen a man kill to protect her. She shuddered, her stomach quivered, and she closed her eyes, offering a quick prayer for both men.

With her eyes open again, the shock and horror on the man's face when he looked upon Michael played before her eyes. She could not imagine what caused this terrifying reaction, and the thought that she was dependent on a stranger who brought such fear made her shiver. Had she placed her safety in a savior or the devil's hands?

Michael rushed through the open door. "We need to leave now."

He reached down to where Mary crouched on the floor, grabbed her arm, yanked her to her feet and out into the bright sunlight. Mary saw no signs of the man's body as Michael hurried her into the woods, but then he would not be foolish enough to leave the dead man in plain sight.

A few feet into the woods, Michael stopped and snatched up several stones.

"Keep these with you in case we are separated." He shoved them into her hand. "We must move quickly and put as much distance as possible between Decimus's men and us."

She nodded vigorously to let him know she understood, placed the stones in the hem of her sleeve. They would need to keep a steady pace and probably continue on into the night. She had to remain strong whether she had the stamina or not.

He stepped in front of her to lead the way, hesitated a moment and turned his shroud-covered head to her. "Your legs, are they strong enough?"

She responded with a faint smile; she was not at all certain if her weak legs would hold her.

"No harm will come to you." His voice was harsh and confident.

He turned and walked ahead, his strides powerful yet silent. As Mary followed behind him, ignoring the pain in her legs and back, she realized he moved like a shadow, weightless and fearless of his surroundings, avoiding the bright sunlight as much as possible, choosing instead the dense part of the woods where sunlight fought to penetrate the thick, leafy canopy. He was at home here, the shadows welcoming friends who embraced and protected.

Michael seemed intent on keeping their arduous pace; he showed no signs of fatigue. She wondered how his black garb did not become burdensome when the sun pierced the heavy foliage and grew more potent with the day.

She wished she could call out to him to let him know she needed water and food. A sprinkle of perspiration marked her forehead. If she could pin up her long hair, pull it off her back and neck, it would be a welcoming relief. And rest—oh, how she wished she could rest if only for a moment.

He stopped suddenly and Mary almost collided with him. He stood still and listened, and she did the same, hoping to hear what had caught his attention, praying it was not footsteps.

It took a moment but she heard the familiar sound and smiled. It was faint but distinct—a brook or stream. She wanted to run fast, cup handful after handful of water to drink and splash on her face. She eagerly turned, ready to find the stream.

Michael took hold of her arm. "We must be careful. Any who travel will look for water to refresh themselves and we must not be seen."

They made their way cautiously toward the sounds and, after Michael made certain they were alone, walked to the stream.

Mary immediately dropped down, cupped some water and did not stop drinking until her thirst was quenched. Then she proceeded to wash her face. The water felt refreshingly cool against her warm skin.

From the corner of her eye she saw Michael scoop water into his ungloved hand and drink. This was the first time she caught a hint of flesh. She was surprised to see that his skin was warm in color, not pale as one would expect, as he spent his days completely shrouded from the sun.

He finished quickly, reached for the glove beside him on the ground, and stood. "I will find food."

She nodded eagerly and returned to rinsing her face

with the cool water. When she finished she combed her tangled hair with her fingers as best she could. Mary then looked for a twig; picking one off the ground, she twisted her hair up onto her head and threaded the sturdy stick through the knot. She retrieved from the loose hem her stones, then fashioned a pouch with the corner of her tunic, knotting it to keep the them in place. She tucked one stone in her belt, ready and handy to use when necessary. She felt refreshed.

Michael was standing beside a tall tree. He stood perfectly still and seemed as focused on her, or perhaps his attention was on something in the distance, beyond Mary.

She turned but saw nothing, and when she glanced back to Michael she jumped; he stood beside her. She held her palm out, walked her fingers across it then pointed to her ears and shook her head.

"Silent steps are necessary for me." He held out his cupped hands filled with berries.

Mary took a handful and savored their sweet juice.

"We will rest for only a few moments; we have a distance to go and cannot waste time."

Mary nodded, walked to the water's edge to sit and give her weary legs rest. Michael joined her, offering the remaining berries. A tender smile showed her appreciation and she reached out, gently brushing the berries from his hand into hers. She stared at his glove-covered hand realizing that strength and tenderness rested there. He could pick delicate berries without crushing them, and yet the same hand could snap a man's neck. He was a contrast of shadow and light and she could not help but wonder what had created him.

She wished she could speak, ask him questions. A sudden thought struck her and she looked around excitedly, reached for a stick nearby. Then she wrote in the dirt in front of them.

Why?

She pointed at him, her finger going up and down the length of him.

"Why do I conceal my identity?"

She nodded.

"If people could look upon the Dark One, he would be dark no more. And he could help no one."

Why help?

He did not answer immediately. He turned his head away and answered harshly. "I have no choice." He stood and held his hand out to her. "We must go."

She dropped the stick and took his hand. She had touched on a subject he did not wish to discuss, did not wish to reveal. Strange, they were so much alike. They both hid. She from Decimus, but who did he hide from?

Her thoughts were soon directed to her footsteps, the terrain having grown more difficult. Small hills, fallen trees, large stones that needed to be climbed, avoided, or walked around slowed their pace, as did her tired aching muscles. Just before nightfall they stopped briefly to eat roots collected along the way. Mary wished for any bed, even the hard ground to rest upon, but it was not to be. They continued on, darkness closing in around them. Mary tripped several times, unable to clearly see the path. Finally, she almost tumbled to the ground but Michael quickly caught her. She dropped her head tiredly to his chest.

He wrapped his arm around her for support. "I know you are worn out, but there is a cave a few more miles ahead and we can rest safely there."

It felt good to rest her weight against him, if only for a moment. But she had to remain independent, reliant on herself, no matter how exhausted she was. She reluctantly eased herself off him. Then they continued, Michael at a hardy pace, she keeping up—surprising for two people who had been walking since daybreak. Neither uttered a word, focusing all their energy on steady and persistent footsteps.

Nearly two hours passed before they arrived at the cave. It was small, dark, and cold. Mary shivered. She rubbed her arms, longing for a fire to warm her bones. Michael cloaked his robe around her. "I will not take a chance and light a fire, though I do not think anyone has followed us this far; I will not risk it."

Mary fought against dropping against him to rest again, but since she had not an ounce of strength left, it took only seconds for her body to betray her. She slumped against him, surrendering with her entire weight.

"Sit and rest while I go find soft brush to fashion a bed," he urged. "We must sleep and have much land to cover tomorrow." Then he lowered her exhausted body to the ground.

Mary's aching legs were grateful for the reprieve. As she rubbed the sore muscles she gave thought to Magnus. Would he join them soon or were she and Michael completely on their own?

Michael returned shortly with an armful of pine branches to find Mary writing in the dirt floor. He laid out the brush, then looked to see what she had written.

Magnus here soon?

Michael explained. "I am to see to your safety until I can contact him. He will then decide what is to be done with you. He is a good friend and cares very much what happens to you."

Mary hung her head, her shoulders slumped, and she sighed heavily.

Michael bent down in front of her, slipping his glove-covered finger beneath her chin and lifting it gently. "Magnus will make certain that you have a safe place to live."

She shook her head. As long as Decimus lived she would not be safe. She stretched out on the bed of pine.

"Your fatigue brings disillusionment. You will feel stronger in the morning." He lay down beside her.

Strength. Her parents' death had given her strength. One night she was a young girl with a loving family, the next night she had no one and faced torture and death. She remembered how she had cried when Magnus told her they were dead, that she would have to leave her village, go far away. She had cried until there were no more tears to cry, and then she got angry. She swore that one day she would make Decimus suffer for what he had done, but that was a young girl's hurt and pain speaking.

How would she make him suffer? Perhaps she has been, by eluding capture. The thought gave her comfort.

"Sleep, Mary," Michael said and turned on his side to drape his cape over her. "I will let nothing happen to you."

She sighed softly, pressed her fingers to her lips and then pressed them to his lips, an innocent gesture of gratitude.

And as she drifted off to sleep she thought she smelled a familiar scent again, one she could not identify but which seemed to be the key to a special memory.

Chapter 4

They slept well into the next morning and it was not until midday that they continued their journey. Clouds hurried overhead only minutes after they began walking, and Mary hoped the rain would wait; a muddy path made travel all the more difficult.

A good night's rest had helped and her legs felt strong today. Michael had told her that if they kept a steady pace they could reach their destination after nightfall. There they would have hot food and a soft bed. The thought gave her strength and she was determined to keep pace with him.

He was agile for a man who appeared burdened with heavy garments and a mask. If she was not aware that the face-covering was of a thin material, she would have wondered if it were magic that allowed him to walk the road so confidently. And his harsh voice allowed for no insight into his true nature, and often fostered fear.

He hid his identity well. There was no telling who

this man was, even his true height went undetected; a
slight hunch always with him.

Yet Mary could not help but wonder over her rescuer's identity. Were his facial features also harsh? Was
he so hideous that people recoiled in fear?

She knew nothing of him and attempted to piece together what she could. He was brave and unselfish,
placing himself in danger to help her. But he was also
confident in his ability to protect her. She wondered
how often he protected the innocent and if it was a service he provided for a fee. Keeping his identity hidden
was a wise choice, for then he could walk freely among
the masses without fear of capture. He could actually
live two separate lives, unless of course this shroud
concealed a badly scarred face and body.

Michael turned suddenly, startling her. "Men and
horses nearby." He took her hand and dragged her off
the path. He found an area dense with shrub and forced
his way in, pulling her in behind him. It was a tight
squeeze with little room. They huddled together between thick branches, the thorny leaves poking at their
arms, legs, and faces. One pricked like a fine bone needle at her neck. The riders were closer now so she knew
she could not move. She remained as she was and soon
felt the first drop of blood drip down her neck.

She could hear the men grumbling as they guided
their horses over the rough terrain. She wondered if
they searched for her or if they were thieves who preferred a trail less traveled.

It seemed a very long time before their voices drifted
away; even then she did not move. There was no telling
if men straggled behind. She and Michael remained as
they were, bodies pressed against each other. She realized she was growing accustomed to their closeness.

She knew it was not proper for a man's body to be so close to hers unless of course it was her husband's. She recalled when she was young how she and the other young girls in the village would giggle over the lads' attempts to impress them. Those giggles had ceased when she had been brought to Ireland. She had been too fearful of strangers to share in the village activities so she had kept herself, isolated from people. As she matured she made a few friends, but mostly with people who could teach her things—the bowman, the healer, the metal smith. She had felt the need to protect not only herself but also the aging couple, James and Nona, who had so generously opened their home to her.

Michael stirred and she was quickly brought out of her musings. It was time for them to go and he parted the thick branches for her.

She stepped out and placed her hand to her neck to see to her wound.

"You are hurt."

He sounded angry as he examined her wound but gently wiped away the blood, his glove-covered finger lingering on her neck. This tenderness was in such contrast to his harshness. A touch barely detectable, a faint whisper across her skin. Gooseflesh raced over her.

She gently pushed his finger away and shook her head, letting him know it was nothing to be concerned with, then pointed to the direction where the men had disappeared.

"We must change our course. We cannot risk meeting those men along the trail. It will delay our arrival time by several hours and the terrain will prove burdensome at times."

She shrugged; she understood there was little choice.

"Think of the food and soft pallet you will rest upon tonight; it will be the impetus that keeps you going."

Was that a note of teasing in his harsh voice? She hoped so, for it made him more human.

Several hours later she fought tears and exhaustion. There was no trail to follow. They climbed hills, scaled rocks, descended into valleys and climbed out of them. She barely felt her legs, and her arms ached from pushing away branches and grasping them to help her climb. She had thought she ached before but never like this, never had she felt so compelled to drop to the ground and give up.

"A short distance more."

He had encouraged her with those words time and time again, but now they only meant more endless walking and climbing. And when she thought things could not get worse, night fell and darkness rushed around them.

The barely visible path was now impossible to see, nor could she see Michael, his black garments blending with the night. He finally stopped and, standing on the edge of a slope, he pointed down into the valley.

She wished she could cry out with joy when she saw the small village, lights glowing from the cottage windows.

He took her hand and helped her descend into the valley. As they got closer she caught the scent of roasting meat and heard laughter and children playing, and she wanted to run and join them, leave her fears behind.

By the time they reached the first cottage her mouth was watering from the delicious scents. She was exhausted in body and mind. They were greeted with enthusiasm, almost as if the villagers were expecting him.

They were ushered into a cottage, the children

shooed away while the adults busily saw to getting them food.

Mary grabbed for the pewter tankard offered her, the smell sweet. She relished the pleasure of the brew's thirst-quenching taste and the way it soothed her sore throat.

A short, stout woman introduced herself as she replenished Mary's tankard. "I am Glenda and it is pleased we are to have you here."

Mary quickly drank more of the soothing brew, her eyes turning wide in appreciation.

Glenda patted her shoulder. "We know you cannot speak. Rest your voice and do not worry. You are safe here with us."

Mary eagerly reached for a thick hunk of dark bread to dip in the pot of stew placed in the center of the table. The delicious aroma made her salivate and she wanted to sigh at the exquisite taste.

"Rabbit stew," Glenda said. "Enjoy, there is plenty, and when you are finished I will help you wash up if you would like?"

Mary was quick to nod her head. Tired as she was she wanted to rid herself of the dirt and grime and climb into bed clean and refreshed, ready to begin anew.

She looked over to Michael talking with a man in the corner of the cottage. The man looked old and worn though Mary could not say it was from age. His long red hair held not a hint of gray, his body appeared strong but weary. The curve of his shoulders showing he once carried heavy loads. He was worn out and worn down as though stamped on repeatedly until it was impossible for him to stand up.

She looked at Glenda and the other woman helping her, Patricia someone had called her. The two women possessed the same worn looks as the man, as though life had been harsh on them, especially Glenda. Deep lines and wrinkles intruded on a pretty round full face and bright blue eyes; a scar marred the right side of her jawbone. She may have been young in age, but she had been aged by life.

Mary sopped up the stew with piece after piece of bread, Glenda and Patricia encouraging her to eat as much as she wished.

Michael joined her at the narrow table and ate sparingly. He was quick to excuse himself explaining he had matters to attend to. Mary waved her arm to let him know she would be fine. She was enjoying the food and was not ready to stop eating. She looked forward to feeling clean again and a bed, a real bed with a warm blanket— Her thoughts had rushed to a halt. Michael would not be sleeping beside her tonight. She needed his warmth no more, but the safety and comfort of his arms was a different matter.

Michael hesitated at the door. "Glenda and Patricia will see to your needs."

"Aye, she will be fine," Glenda said, her smile generous.

Patricia agreed with a nod and Mary noticed how thin and pale the young woman looked, almost as if it had been some time since she had last eaten.

Glenda must have thought the same for when Michael left along with William, the man he had been speaking with, she encouraged Patricia to eat.

"You barely touched your meal; share the stew with Mary."

Mary nodded eagerly and held out a hunk of bread to the thin woman.

Patricia hesitated until Glenda nudged her to take the bread and sit at the table.

"We will all share the meal and enjoy the delicious brew Patricia made," Glenda said, filling tankards for them all.

Mary held up her tankard, smiled, and nodded to let Patricia know how much she enjoyed the drink.

Patricia gave a meek smile.

"Herbs and flowers," Glenda said. "She does not share the secret of her mix with us, but she is generous in preparing it for everyone."

Glenda continued to do most of the talking and Mary tried not to yawn between mouthfuls, but fatigue was fast overpowering her and soon she would not have the strength to lift her goblet.

"Patricia, go see if you can find a nightdress for Mary while I help her wash." The young woman hurried off.

Glenda soon had the table cleaned and a bucket of water and cloth brought in for Mary's use. She did not ask permission to help, she simply took charge and in minutes had Mary out of her tunic and shift with a blanket wrapped around her. Mary was grateful for her assistance, but tired as she was she could not let someone else see to her needs. She had to rely on herself; it was important for her to know that. She took the cloth from Glenda with a tender smile of appreciation and began to wash herself.

"You should know this is a special place."

Mary had a feeling it was and listened as Glenda explained.

"The Dark One has saved everyone here. Patricia was being starved and abused by her manor lord and then he accused her of heresy. She found herself in one of Decimus's dungeons." She paused, rubbed her scarred jaw, then seemed to garner strength and continued. "I was in the same dungeon, accused of practicing the black arts because of my healing skills. I heard Patricia's every scream as she did mine." She touched her scar again. "I thank God for the Dark One's courage every day. He brought us here to safety and it is here we help him in his task of securing safe places for all those he rescues."

Mary scrubbed the dried dirt from her skin while Glenda's every word reinforced her fear of Decimus and inflamed her anger. He inflicted punishment on people without care to the truth.

"The Dark One is a good man. We trust him and care for him." She stuck her chin up. "And it matters not what lies beneath his dark garb for his intentions are pure."

Mary realized then that Michael took no fee for his services. He unselfishly rescued the innocent, but why? Why was he a savior to so many? The more she learned about Michael the more intrigued she became with him.

"We are a village of discards; no one wants us or cares what happens to us, no one, that is, except the Dark One. He cares and sees that we are kept safe." She lowered her voice. "There is nothing that he would not do for us or we for him."

She suddenly beamed, a smile that lighted the whole cottage. "The Dark One even found me a husband. He rescued Terence from Decimus last year and brought him here after his hand was cut off under torture." Glenda's eyes filled with tears and she had to clear her throat to finish her tale. "The Dark One carried him into the village, brought him right to me and told me to look after him, that he needed my smile to make him well."

Mary grew nauseous over the horrific pain and suffering experienced by all three. She could not imagine how anyone with a heart or soul could do such a thing. Only pure evil was capable of such horrendous torture. Decimus was surely the devil's own.

"We were wed three months ago and Terence told everyone that when he looked upon my face, he knew he would be well because an angel was taking care of him." Glenda wiped a tear away as Patricia quietly entered the cottage.

"Put the nightdress on the bed and come help me wash Mary's hair, if you will, Patricia." Glenda said, then looked to Mary. "That is if you would like our help?"

Mary nodded and smiled. She felt as if it had been forever since her hair had been clean and she was simply too tired to wash it herself.

Patricia spoke softly, but Mary heard. "Clean hair feels so very good."

Mary nodded vigorously just before both women set to work.

It took a bit of time to wash away the dirt and grime then comb the tangles out, but Glenda and Patricia were patient and by the time they were done Glenda exclaimed, "My lord, you have beautiful blond hair."

"I have never seen such a stunning color," Patricia said and touched the long strands. "It is an angel's color for sure, pure and light."

The door opened slowly and Michael walked in.

Glenda, with Patricia's help, hastily rid the cottage of any mess, turned back the soft blue wool blanket on the straw mattress, and after a quick blessing for a good night's sleep, the two women closed the door behind them.

Michael made no move; he remained near the closed door staring at her.

The silence grew uncomfortable, Mary wondering if there was a problem. Exhausted and fearing it might be necessary to continue their journey without rest, she turned wide, questioning eyes on him.

He walked over to her. "Nothing is wrong. It is just that you are so very beautiful."

She never felt comfortable when someone commented on her beauty. She did not think herself any different than other women, but since she could remember people, men and women alike, commented on her beauty. It was a neverending litany she attempted to ignore, feeling her looks common enough.

Strangely this time she felt different with the compliment coming from Michael. It pleased her.

She wished she could thank him for the compliment and tell him that she thought him a brave and unselfish man. Instead she displayed her deep gratitude with a significant gesture, she pressed her fingers to her lips then pressed them to his lips, the black shroud feeling coarse against her fingertips.

They both stood rigid when the implications of her actions settled in. She had actually expressed her feelings with a kiss and the thought startled her.

She stepped away realizing her actions inappropriate, but he reached out and gently captured her wrist. "You are grateful for my help."

She nodded vigorously.

"I understand and I am glad to be of service to you."

Service. She had to remember he worked with Magnus to protect her, *nothing more*. He rescued her and she was grateful, *nothing more*. There would be *nothing more* for her in life than keeping free of Decimus.

"We will rest here for a few days while your final destination is determined."

She nodded and forced a smile; a yawn followed.

"You will sleep peacefully tonight. There is nothing to fear; you are safe here."

She reached out to him but stopped before touching him, her hand suspended in air between them, uncertain what to do. Her gesture displayed a need for him. She did need his protection, but she desired his comforting touch. She liked the feel of his arms wrapped around her. She did not feel so alone, so isolated from the world with him beside her.

He took hold of it and drew her slowly into the safety of his dark embrace. They stood for a moment in silence, an odd pair joined together, shadow and light. Then Mary yawned again, her eyes grew heavy and her head drifted down on his shoulder. He scooped her up into his arms and carried her to the bed. He gently laid her on the overstuffed straw mattress then slipped in beside her.

He pulled the blue wool blanket over her as she snuggled against him, closed her eyes and slept.

Chapter 5

Michael sat on a decaying stump in the woods near the village. It was a secluded spot partially encircled by oak, birch, and elm trees. Birds chirped, squirrels raced up and down the trees in play, and rabbits sat feasting on freshly sprouted blades of grass. A new day had dawned, the brilliant sun chasing away the shadows of the night, but he was a shadow not easily chased away.

He removed his black leather gloves, rubbed his hands together and pressed a thumb to each palm, kneading the skin. It was his way of reminding himself he was flesh and blood. A man, not merely a shadow.

The kneading slowed until he stopped completely and touched his fingers to his lips.

A kiss.

He recalled Mary's fingers on his lips after touching her own. The pressure of her warm flesh had tingled his lips and sent a quiver through his body, undetectable to

Mary, for he had displayed no response to her innocent gesture of gratitude.

He quickly dropped his hand from his mouth. He did not need to linger on nonsense. She was appreciative of his help and expressed in action what she could not express in words.

And yet . . .

He stood slipping his gloves on. She was so very beautiful, her long hair the color of honey, her face that of an angel with gentle blue eyes. A man could drown in this shapely body that felt so right in his arms.

He shook his head to chase away his dangerous thoughts. He could not allow himself to think of Mary in such an intimate manner. He was here to help her and see her to safety, yet he felt a compelling need to remain by her side. The thought of walking away from her when all was done caused his stomach to wrench.

He had helped many women, men, and children to safety. Each one was special in their own way, but Mary was different. He knew she would be when he first saw her, covered with dirt and grime and sitting in the shadows of her cell. His heart had reacted then.

He paced, attempting to make sense of his odd reaction. He had empathy for those who suffered the fate of torture. Those who inflicted such cruelty were certainly ignorant, spineless creatures.

But it was not empathy he felt when he first looked upon Mary.

She did not cry or grasp at him; she hesitated uncertainly and then with strength she attempted to step forward, though she was obviously in pain and fearful of him. With courage she accepted him and made her escape. He admired her tenacity, her bravery, and her beauty.

He shook his head. What was wrong with him? What foolish thoughts was he thinking? He could not allow himself to care too much and there definitely was no place in his life for love. He had forgotten what it was like to love, or perhaps he did not want to remember. He had hardened his heart after senselessly losing his mother and sister, the hurt too painful; he had replaced it with a thirst for revenge, and that thirst had turned to a hunger too ravenous to satisfy.

He sat again on the stump. He required focused thoughts to accomplish his mission. He had made a promise to himself and had sworn to allow no one to stand in his way. He had made a vow and would not break it. There was still so very much to be done and time was of the essence.

What would she say once she is able to speak to him?

He stood again, annoyed that his thoughts controlled him. Now was not the time to succumb to foolish musings. His mission needed his full attention. Thoughts of Mary in any way other than needing his help could not be given consideration. He had to make certain all was planned and timed perfectly so that Mary's escape would be permanent and she need not worry about being hunted ever again.

It would be necessary to confer with Magnus on the final plan. He had been the one to see to her safety after her parents' death, and he was certain to care for her as long as was necessary. Magnus and Michael's path had crossed through the years and they had become comrades more than friends. Each had their own pursuits and purpose, and while their lives paralleled each other they had kept their distance, until Mary. And though Magnus was infamous for his legendary exploits and skills, he was by no means a match for Decimus.

There was not a soul who could touch the man. The Church had given Decimus complete rein in tracking down heretics.

Many wondered if the Church Fathers themselves feared the man's power. He was relentless in his pursuit, and in his punishment and in the deliverance of those who did not abide by God's laws.

Michael turned at the crunch of twigs, knowing the soft footfalls belonged to Mary.

Her beauty startled him as it had the night before. Dirt and grime had disguised her loveliness in the daylight. He had given little thought to her features as they traveled through the woods toward safety, though he had caught a brief glimpse of her beauty when they stopped at the stream to drink. A quick handful of water to her face had removed some of the dirt and a twist of her blond hair pinned to her head had given him a slight indication that there was more to this woman then he had first noticed.

Now, however, seeing her in the bright sunshine was like seeing her for the first time. Her waist-length blond hair was scrubbed clean and it looked the color of rich golden honey. It was loosely tied near the end with a ribbon; the mass of curls laying over one shoulder. Her round face glowed and her full cheeks were rosy and bright like her full lips. Her blue eyes sparkled like a child eager to start the day.

But her body was all woman.

The village women had generously supplied her with clean garments, and Mary now wore a brown wool skirt and pale yellow linen blouse. The meager attire did not draw the eye, but the full rich curves of her body did. She had full breasts that gave way to a narrow waist that curved out to full hips. She was a woman of substantial form and beauty.

She waved to him and her smile grew.

If it were a different time, a different place, different circumstances perhaps, he could let himself care for her. But he could not and the thought was utter nonsense. It would not be safe for either of them.

He walked toward her, banishing all thoughts but her safety from his mind.

She pointed to the bright blue sky dusted with thick white clouds and a bright sun that was sure to help spring growth.

He commented on what she could not. "A beautiful day."

She nodded, her smile strong. She motioned with her fingers to demonstrate that she had not eaten yet and would he care to join her.

"You resisted Glenda's delicious cooking to wait for me? You must be insane." He attempted to tease, though his gruff tone made him sound surprised.

She nodded and held her hand out to him while she patted her stomach.

"You cannot wait another moment?"

Her expression turned serious and she shook her head, though there was a twinkle in her blue eyes.

"Then we must hurry and feed you."

She nodded, eagerly agreeing, and they walked toward Glenda's cottage.

After the morning meal Michael excused himself, letting Mary know that there were matters that needed his attention and he would return by early evening.

She knew those matters concerned her and she wished she could go with him, learn more about her fate. Was he meeting Magnus? Would they discuss her future? Were plans being made that she should be aware of? She disliked being left out of decisions that concerned her. Perhaps it was because she had no choice when she was younger, forced to leave the only home she had ever known.

"I have chores to see to," Glenda said, grabbing the handle of a basket brimming with dried herbs and covered crocks.

Mary pointed to herself then to Glenda, offering her help.

"Nay, you enjoy the sunny day. Rest in the sunshine and heal."

Mary shook her head and fumbled in her attempt to make Glenda understand that she felt strong and rested after last night's sleep. She had thought she would sleep much later than she had but woke with the dawn and felt remarkably refreshed. Her one insistent thought was to chase away the hellish memories of her capture, confinement, and escape and live a normal day. She wanted to smile and laugh and share her momentary joy with Michael. Where the desire had come from she did not know. She only knew that she felt it strongly and that was why she had gone in search of Michael to share the morning meal with him.

Glenda's full pink cheeks puffed as she chuckled and her worn features took on a youthful glow. "Want to live do you?"

Mary sighed with relief that she understood.

"Come on with me, then," Glenda said and Mary walked along beside her. "I understand how you feel, felt the same myself. Doing daily chores, baking bread, washing clothes, the feel of the sun on my face assured me, left not a doubt in my mind, that I was free. And with each chore I did I grew more and more thankful for my freedom. I have never taken a single day for granted since. I am grateful for every loaf of bread I bake and every garment I wash and the sun . . .

She paused a moment and turned her face up to the bright yellow circle in the sky. "I cherish the feel of it on my skin. It assures me that I am free."

They continued walking.

"Everyone is grateful to the Dark One, known to us as to you as Michael. His rescues have allowed us all a chance to live a near normal life."

Mary listened, wishing she could ask questions, but then silence usually proved useful in gathering information. She did wish to discover as many clues as possible. She hoped to piece them together and perhaps learn his true identity.

"We all understand the risks we take in helping him. And we have seen the results of what happens to someone believed to have helped the Dark One." Glenda shivered.

Mary glared at her anxiously, wishing to hear more.

"One night the Dark One had brought a man to the village." Glenda hesitated and shook her head. "It was terrible. We all knew the man would not survive the night. The only thing we could do for him was pray for a quick death to end his suffering. He had been accused of helping the Dark One and he suffered a horrible torture." Another shiver racked Glenda's body. "He had been a simple farmer, ignorant of the Dark One until the day Decimus's men arrived on his land. At least he died surrounded by people who cared."

The more Mary learned of Decimus the more fearful she grew.

"Michael offered us passage to safer land after that

night, but our blood is Irish and our home forever Ireland. We could not leave here or those in need. And if, or when, necessary we have no doubt that Michael will make certain we are moved to safer territory."

A tremendous burden for the Dark One, Mary thought, with so many depending on him for help. He forever lived in the darkness for others.

Glenda continued. "We do not know his true identity and that is fine with us. He keeps it that way for our own good, but if we did know there is not a one here who would betray him."

The Dark One was truly loved here in this tiny remote village, and Mary thought it would not be a bad place to remain and offer her help. But she knew in her heart that was not possible. Decimus hunted her and he would not stop until he caught her. If she remained, the village would be in danger. And neither she nor Michael could let that happen.

Glenda stopped at a small cottage. A well-tended patch of budding flowers and a bright yellow sun painted on the wooden door welcomed visitors.

Glenda lowered her voice as they approached the closed door. "This is Agnes's home. She has been here three months and continues to heal. She keeps much to herself and only allows me to visit and tend her since I was the one who cared for her when she was first brought here."

Mary nodded and motioned that perhaps she should wait outside.

Glenda knocked. "Nay, I think it fate that you and Agnes meet."

Mary wondered over her words as she followed behind Glenda and entered the cottage.

A small, thin woman with white hair, her back to them, stood by the fireplace warming her hands. "I want no visitors."

Her voice was clear and sharp and her stance straight, no curve or hunch to her shoulders to add to her advanced years.

"I think you are expecting this visitor," Glenda said to Mary's surprise.

The woman turned and Mary was stunned by her lovely face and shocked by her blindness. It was not torture that had caused her blindness but an affliction at birth, for her eyes were creamy white.

"It is you," Agnes said anxiously and hurried to Mary's side, reaching out and grasping her hand.

Mary stared at Agnes wondering how a blind woman moved as easily as one with sight.

"I see without seeing," Agnes answered as if hearing Mary's thoughts.

Mary understood instantly. The woman was a seer; she predicted forthcoming events good or bad. And while seers were often sought and respected, the Church had different ideas and branded them cohorts of Satan. She had heard they suffered the most when tortured, for it was believed they needed to be banished of their evil ways and suffering, and death was the only way to be certain they were cleansed.

Yet this woman looked as though torture had not touched her. Had Michael rescued her before any suffering befell her?

"Leave us, Glenda, I must speak with Mary alone."

"Mary cannot speak," Glenda said as she walked to the door.

"I know," Agnes said.

Mary nodded to let Glenda know she was fine.

"I will be at Brenda's cottage two doors down," Glenda said and closed the door behind her.

"Your mind is clear and aware of much, this is good." Agnes said. "You wonder about me, particularly about the sun painted on my front door. You assumed I painted it when you first saw it. But now you wonder, How does a blind woman paint a sun on her door?"

Mary squeezed her hand to let her know she was accurate in all she assumed.

"Good, you speak without speaking as I see without seeing, which is the way I painted the sun on my door."

Mary smiled, pleased and somewhat perplexed that conversation flowed so easily between a blind woman and a woman who could not speak.

"I feel your smile and it is as beautiful as you are, Mary. And it is long I have waited to meet you."

Mary shook her head as she gently squeezed Agnes's hand.

"I know how confusing this seems to you and how frustrating it must be to not be able to speak your mind, but trust me it is best for you at this moment. You are very special. You will succeed where others have failed, and in so doing you will save many lives."

Agnes grasped Mary's wrist tightly. "You must listen and remember. My imprisonment was brief, my freedom swift, all because I am to be here at this time, at this place to give you an important message."

A shiver raced over Mary that warned and frightened, or was this premonition?

"Decimus is close. He wants you and will have you."

Mary quaked at the insidious thought.

"You are his destiny, though he will bring you great sorrow." Agnes placed a trembling hand on Mary's shoulder. "But in the end it will be you who will be the demise of Decimus."

Chapter 6

There is knowledge in silence, Mary's father taught her. But presently she found silence to be a prison. After leaving Agnes's cottage she entered the edge of the woods, making certain to keep the village in view but needing privacy to consider the old woman's prediction.

You will be responsible for the demise of Decimus.

How could that be so?

Was the seer's prediction true? And what of her other words?

Decimus will bring you great sorrow.

He had already brought her great sorrow. He had been responsible for her parents' death. What greater sorrow could she experience than to lose those she loved dearly?

A chill moved through her and she hugged herself.

The sunny day had had her feeling optimistic. New starts. Fresh beginnings, she wished to believe them possible. But would destiny prove otherwise?

She looked to the village and watched as daily activities went on before her eyes. Children laughed. Women chatted. Men chopped wood. Gardens were tended. Life went on. She wanted to desperately be part of it all but she would not, not now and perhaps never.

Decimus would enter her life again. No matter how well Michael protected her, there would come a time that she faced Decimus; he was her fate.

She had hoped Agnes would tell her more, but the old woman offered her only an apology. Usually she could see far beyond, but her vision of Mary's future was limited and there was no more she could tell her. Her words worried Mary for if Agnes saw no more, then perhaps her own demise came with Decimus's.

She was too frightened of the answer to ask Agnes.

Mary ached to share this burden with another. Her bruised throat had yet to heal. Her thoughts were to remain unspoken.

She heard a shout and turned. Three lads were racing into the woods, shoving and jabbing as they each attempted to be the first to climb a large tree.

She had believed there would be a time when she would have a family of her own. She would be a good wife and mother, loving her children with a generous heart, tending to their needs, teaching them as her parents taught her.

She choked back tears, refusing to cry.

An arm draped in black gently took her waist and eased her back to rest against a hard chest. She went without protest, surrendering to Michael's solid embrace.

"You are troubled?"

She shook her head and thought how comforting it

was resting it on him, surrendering her momentary weakness to his strength. But he had done much for her already; she would not burden him more.

His arm hugged her waist tightly as he placed his face next to hers and whispered. "You wear no smile, your eyes wrinkle with concern, and you fight back tears. Do not tell me you are not troubled."

He was much too observant, and where had he come from? He appeared as if from nowhere. She had heard not a sound, not a footfall, not a breath.

"Tell me," he urged.

He held her with a protective confidence that made her feel safe and secure. No harm would come to her when he was near; she wanted to believe that with her heart and soul, but there was Decimus to consider.

"Mary."

She placed her hand on his arm and felt hard muscle beneath. He was a man of solid substance, not at all a shadow. She pointed to the lads who had managed to climb up into the tree and now pretended to sword fight with branches.

Then she brought her hand to her heart and shook her head, hoping he would understand her inadequate attempt to offer an explanation of her feelings.

"You wish for children of your own and fear you will have none."

She nodded slowly and a small bit of her disappointment faded, though she could not understand why. Perhaps it was the comfort of his strong arms and the knowledge that he protected her.

"Keep your wish strong in your heart, Mary, and it will see fruition."

She wanted to believe him but who would dare love

a woman who Decimus hunted tenaciously? This disturbing thought surfaced with a shiver and shake of her head.

"You will love."

She stepped out of his embrace and turned to face him, motioning anxiously with her hands to her ears, to him then to her head. Did he hear her thoughts? He knew too well her feelings, but how? Was he skilled in magic?

"I understand."

That was not enough for her. She motioned with her hands again, growing agitated as she demanded more.

Michael remained calm, his voice losing its harsh edge. "You say much without speaking."

She titled her head, her befuddled glance alerting him to her confusion.

He raised his hand slowly and placed a glove-covered finger to her brow. "Your brow wrinkles when you have a question." His finger drifted ever so lightly down around her eye. "You squint your eyes when you are confused." His finger lazily trailed down her cheek to delicately stroke her mouth. "Your smile . . ."

He paused and Mary waited with bated breath and a thumping heart.

"Your smile tells me you are well and your frown defines your concern. And," he said, reaching to take her hand, "you speak volumes with your hands."

She tried to respond by motioning with her hands but made little sense, even to her. Then he reached out and clasped her flailing hands in his. She thought that for a brief moment her heart stopped beating.

"I know that you are grateful that I understand you. You need not worry; I will always understand you."

He released her hands and moved his face closer to

her, or was it her imagination or the wishful thinking of a young lonely woman? She remained perfectly still, waiting.

A sudden scream and fit of laughter caused them to jump apart and their attention was drawn to the lads scurrying down out of the tree, tormenting each other as they returned to the village.

Mary turned to Michael but he was gone. He had stood to her side, directly behind her, a mere whisper away from her—and yet she had not sensed his departure.

He had entered her life when she needed him and he would leave her when his presence was no longer necessary. They would be brief acquaintances sharing a brief time together, offering comfort to one another—nothing more.

She shook her head and returned to the village to find Glenda. She needed to think on something other than Michael and her foolish thoughts.

Michael, behind a large oak tree, watched her walk away, annoyed that he hid from her. Or was he hiding from his own feelings? He had thought his emotions died with those he loved many years ago. Or had he buried them thinking them dead? Had Mary found a way to resurrect his feelings?

He turned away when Mary was no longer in sight, braced his back against the tree and slowly slid down to sit on the hard ground. He took his gloves off and rubbed his chin.

It was not only his heart he had buried; he had buried himself. The moment he slipped on the black shroud he had lost his identity. *He* was no more and it took a touch to his own skin to remind him that he was real.

Mary, however, had made him feel more than real; her simple touch also reminded him he was a man. *She* made him feel alive. *She* brought out feelings that he had thought dead and long buried.

He again rubbed his cheeks, then his neck before rubbing his hands together.

Mary was a woman of substance in many ways. Even though he sensed her full of fear, he saw she refused to surrender to it; she remained courageous and did what was necessary even when difficult. She was a remarkable woman who had withstood hardship and had grown in strength, character, and conviction.

And he found himself admiring her more each day.

He slipped his gloves on quickly and stood.

Admire.

He would do well to remember that he *admired* her and no more. He marched off into the woods muttering several oaths beneath his breath.

Michael did not return for supper, still Mary shared an enjoyable meal with Glenda, Terence, and Patricia. She listened as the three exchanged stories of their childhoods and talked of the future with a certainty that brought a smile to Mary's face.

It was a pleasant evening that reminded her of her own dreams of the future with family and friends, so that when the evening came to an end she felt a sudden sadness.

She climbed into bed alone and, though a fire heated the cottage, she felt chilled huddled under the covers warding off not only the cold but loneliness.

She had no one, her family was gone, the loving couple that had cared for her was lost to her forever, and Magnus would find somewhere safe for her but keep his distance as before, for her protection. Where did that leave her but alone? She shivered against her forced isolation.

Even sleep refused to befriend her, and she did not know how long she lay there. It seemed like an eternity, and whenever a shadow drifted into the room she thought Michael had returned. When she realized he had not, she felt disappointment. As the night went on she concluded that Michael would not join her. Was he busy tending to matters? Or had he simply chosen not to share the bed with her any longer? Both thoughts concerned her; after all, he was all she had at the moment and she missed him beside her.

She attempted to remind herself that self-pity did little good and perhaps it was better this way. She feared becoming dependent on him or perhaps she feared she might grow to care for him. It was so easy with him always around, making certain she was safe and secure. Perhaps she could get used to his presence, dark and ominous as he was, find a light inside him. She could, if they had more time together.

"Mary."

Michael startled her and she jumped, then she smiled.

He slipped in beside her, and they lay next to each other barely touching, but it did not matter. He was finally there with her and she felt at ease, and so very relieved. She convinced herself that her growing dependence on him was born out of uncertainty and fear and that once her fate was known she would release him into the shadows from where he had come.

She drifted off to sleep and her dream came fast and swift.

She was running on a long stretch of barren road,

her breathing labored as if she had run a long distance when suddenly her parents appeared on either side of her.

They looked healthy and strong as they did in life, though younger.

"Keep alert to your senses," her father said.

"Trust your heart." Her mother smiled.

"You must fight," her father said.

"You have the strength," her mother said.

"Love will be your only weapon," her father warned as he reached out and grabbed her hand.

Mary woke with a start; Michael had tight hold of her hand.

"I am sorry to wake you, but we must leave at once."

She shook away what little sleep remained and turned wide eyes on him.

He answered her silent query as he helped her out of bed.

"Decimus has found our trail; he is not far from the village."

Chapter 7

Mary did not know how long she slept but it mattered not, for she was startled fully awake by the terrifying news. A sack of food and her freshly washed garments were wrapped in a plaid cloth and fashioned into a sack that Michael flung over his shoulder.

With her eyes wet with unshed tears, Glenda draped a brown wool shawl around Mary's shoulders as she hugged and kissed her cheek and said, "Godspeed."

Mary nodded and placed her hand on her heart and then to Glenda's heart offering her appreciation for the woman's generosity. Then, within a blink of an eye, they were gone from the village, slinking away under the cover of darkness.

Mary feared that the village would suffer for harboring them and attempted to express her concern to Michael. She tugged firmly on his black shroud to get his attention since he refused to heed to a simple nudge.

He finally stopped. "We have no time to spare."

She frantically motioned her concern, pointing toward the village.

"They will be fine," Michael assured her. "They are experienced at this sort of thing. *But*"—his emphasis was meant to get her attention and it did—"if we do not make haste and place distance between us and the village, there will be trouble for all."

She understood, pointed her chin up, and waved him to follow her, as though he were the one delaying their escape. Before she even realized that she had no idea were they where or where they were going, Michael moved past her to take the lead again. His pace was swift and she kept up with him though visibility was difficult. The moon was new and its faint glow left their path mostly in darkness.

Michael walked the trail with confidence; Mary felt little of her own. The night shadows rushed along the ground, making it appear as if night demons scurried after them. She jumped more then once when large ominous shadows crossed her path.

They continued their journey, dawn near breaking on the horizon, when they came upon a mound of brush, which Michael moved aside to reveal a cave-like dwelling.

"No one will know we are here; we can rest. I doubt anyone has been following us."

Mary agreed, squatting to enter the small dwelling. No one on horseback could have followed their path, and to track them at night would be impossible. As Michael pulled back the brush to cover the entrance, cutting off the increasing light of dawn, she realized not a soul would know of their secluded nest. They were safe for now.

Michael opened the sack and offered Mary the bread and cheese that Glenda had packed for them. Mary gratefully took the generous pieces and ate, their long walk having fueled her appetite.

She was not surprised when he took a leather drinking pouch from the sack and offered it to her. The moment she tasted the sweet cider she blessed Glenda threefold for her thoughtfulness. But then Glenda had been where she now was, and she had known what it meant to be hungry and thirsty.

Sleep was ready to claim her as soon as she finished her food and drink. She looked at Michael—her heart suddenly ached for him.

She pointed to his mask. He had not removed it since they first met. Her hand signaled that he should remove it. She attempted to convey that his secret was safe with her.

"I cannot," he said, "for your safety and mine; I cannot."

She caught disappointment in his voice as though he wished to do as she suggested. Did he wish for her to know him as much as she wished to know him?

Or was she exhausted and not making an ounce of sense?

"Sleep," he ordered. "We still have much distance to travel."

With a raised hand she circled the air around her, tossed her hands in frustration, pointed to her feet, crinkled her face, and shook her head while waving her finger.

To her surprise he laughed, though it was a low rumble, restrained. "You are never going to walk long distances when this is over."

She nodded, confirming his understanding of her

fumbling attempts at sign language. Then with one hand covering her yawn, she tugged with her other hand at his shroud for him to lie down and rest as well.

With little space they had no choice but to snuggle against each other. In an instant Mary was fast asleep, her arms tucked in against his chest, her head to his shoulder, her body pressed firmly against his and his shroud used as a blanket to keep her warm.

Michael however found sleep difficult. His body was tired, but much too aroused to sleep. It had all been so innocent the first night he found her in his arms out of necessity. She needed warmth and he had provided it. But that need for heat from a chilled night was not necessary when they stayed at the cottage.

And still . . .

He sought her bed. Why? He could convince himself it was out of protection that he had remained by her side, though if he were honest he would admit it was his own need that made him seek a tiny bit of intimacy with her. It felt good to lie beside her, to hold her, to feel her warmth. Her tenacious nature, her smile, her endless attempts to speak with her hands, her willingness to trust him when he was nothing more than a shadow, made her a remarkable woman. And she had kissed him, if only with her fingers.

He grew annoyed with himself. She was grateful and dependent on him, nothing more. He had seen countless women to safety who had been just as grateful.

But how many women, fearing his darkness, had kept their distance no matter how grateful?

Mary had accepted his ominous presence from the beginning. She had not shied away in fright or feared being near him. And she appeared to have grown even more comfortable with him as the days continued.

She thought nothing of taking hold of his arm or expressing herself with a touch to his chest. And with each simple touch, he began to respond; it was a brief stirring of emotions at first, growing more evident with each contact until . . .

He took a deep breath and willed his mind to banish the crazy thoughts, but his emotions warred with him. His feelings had been locked away in a prison of his own making and somehow Mary had found a way to pry it open, if only an inch.

It had been too long since he had been touched with kindness and concern. He had forgotten what it felt like and the stirring of emotions it created. It was a brief spark at first, a faint flutter of recognition he could not quite grasp and it faded as swiftly as it had been born.

He had paid it no heed until the spark returned and finally ignited a response. He suddenly realized that he favored her hand on his arm, her head on his shoulder, her body snuggled next to his. He actually waited for her to move nearer to him, and found that his arms instinctively comforted her without thought or concern for his unusual actions.

Lonely.

He had been very lonely these many years, missing his family, remembering his mother's tender love and the joy and laughter he shared with his younger sister. Mary reminded him of his sister, young and courageous, an angelic smile. Their hearts were peaceful. Sometimes he would think of home and picture his mother and sister waiting eagerly for his return, but there was no home and he knew better than to think he could live a happy life once again. And love? He had no time to spare for love. He had been dedicated to his purpose, his intent to save the innocent. There was no time for love, family, children—and he had seen in Mary's eyes how she wished for children, wished for a fulfilling life.

He could give her none of that. He would only bring her heartache and sorrow. One day it would be necessary for him to walk away from her never to see her again. The thought stabbed like a knife in his stomach and he moved her closer to him.

He would cherish the brief time that was theirs. He would allow himself to feel and gather memories, but he would keep his distance for her sake as well as his own. When all was done between them, he wanted no heartache for her and no regrets for him.

He rested his cheek on the top of her head and closed his eyes to sleep.

They walked for three more days taking shelter during the day and continuing their journey from dusk till dawn. They kept a steady pace taking brief rests and forging ahead with determination.

On the sixth day, as dawn claimed the land, they came upon the ruins of an old castle. It was strange to look upon: the thick wooden front door, scarred with blows from a battle-ax, was shut solid as if to warn away visitors while the remainder of the castle lay crumbled around it.

A wooden stairway climbed to the sky and stopped suddenly; a few inner walls had remained strong while the outer walls had fallen. Vines, wildflowers, and nesting birds had claimed the decaying crumble as their home and given the sad edifice a small bit of dignity and hope.

It sat in a small valley surrounded by hills and woods with a stream running behind it. It was a difficult location to protect against attack, and Mary imagined that was why the small castle was now neglected and abandoned.

"We will be safe here for a while," Michael said. "This place has long been forgotten, proving too difficult to defend."

She nodded and walked over to the door, her fingers examining the deep scars the door had suffered.

"She stood against many blows and did not fall," Michael said and was about to step over the crumbled castle wall.

Mary shook her head and waved her hands frantically. She went to him, took his hand, and led him back to the front door. She knocked on the door, waited a moment, then opened the door and walked in with Michael in tow.

She released his hand, turned to face him and smiled, spreading out her arms.

He understood. "You feel that by using the front door, though the walls have crumbled and we could have easily entered, the castle appreciates our respect and welcomes us."

A sharp nod let him know he was right, then she turned and proceeded to investigate the rubble and decay.

A large fireplace remained solid in a partial wall with a good-sized cauldron hanging on the cooking hook. She looked forward to a hot meal but knew that would have to wait. They were both exhausted from the many days of endless walking and they needed a restful sleep.

Michael fashioned a sleeping pallet out of old brush and a worn tapestry he discovered beneath a few stones. He placed it beneath the stairway hidden from view just in case someone should happen by.

"Tomorrow we will see what we can do to make this place habitable for the time we are here."

Her soft blue eyes questioned and he answered.

"We may be here a week or several weeks; I am not certain just yet."

She hoped their stay would be for several weeks for she wished to regain her voice and have time to talk with him. She had not attempted to speak since last she tried a few days ago. Her throat had protested, her voice being weak, and her words much too strained. She feared if she forced herself that her voice might never return and the thought of being mute for the rest of her life filled her with dread.

Her sigh brought Michael to her side.

"All will go well for you, Mary. You will be moved to a safe haven where no one will ever find you."

She had thought that was where she had been these many years, tucked away in a safe haven. But not so, Decimus had discovered her whereabouts. What made Michael think she could be safe anywhere?

He sensed her doubt. "This time it will be different."

She attempted a smile to reassure him, or was the reassurance for her? The weak smile faded quickly and she pointed to the makeshift bed. Sleep would still her troubled thoughts. Michael seemed to agree. He moved like a shifting shadow in the night toward her, wrapped his dark embrace around her.

"It will take time, Mary, but I will make certain Decimus causes you no harm."

Decimus will cause you great sorrow.

The seer's words were clearly spoken in her head. Fear rippled through her—her distress palpable.

Michael's shroud enveloped her in a black cocoon.

She was safe, secure in this darkness in his arms. Nothing could penetrate, neither light nor . . .

The sudden thought startled her. The shroud protected his identity, but it was also *his* shield, *his* armor, through which no love could pass.

Chapter 8

Mary woke to the sun kissing her face. Fatigue nipped at her mind and body, but it had been too many days that she had gone without the sun's company or had seen the beautiful blue sky. She shifted her body on the sleeping pallet so the sun's rays warmed all of her. It felt glorious, and she was suddenly excited about starting the day. There would be no more endless walking in the black of night. She would once again know the beauty of the blue sky, the gentle wisps of clouds, the sweet smell of flowers, and plants fresh with morning dew.

With a lazy stretch to ease her sore muscles she sat up, relishing the thought that, for now, she did not have to rush away, hide, or run from Decimus. Today and tomorrow were hers, and hopefully a week or more.

Mary stood. She would not think on her present situation; she would remain focused on enjoying this day.

Glenda had generously tucked a bone comb in with Mary's clean garments. When she discovered this,

Mary felt she could have hugged the woman. The knots and tangles came undone and she braided her long hair, then secured it to the back of her head with the comb.

Michael was nowhere in sight but his absence did not alarm her. She knew she was safe and that he was not far. He would not leave her for any length of time without speaking with her first. She was certain he was nearby and would appear soon.

She foraged in the debris by the fireplace in hopes of finding a crock, pitcher, or bucket—anything that would hold water. No luck, though she found a few items that would be useful to them and she left them on the table.

Eager to give her face a wash, she headed for the stream. Michael was there, filling a bucket with water. Mary wished she could sing out what a glorious morning it was, but her throat was still healing, though now it did allow her to make sounds just above a bare whisper. She decided to wave her hands to express her excitement with the day.

"I thought you would sleep more. Our journey has been tedious and harsh."

He returned to filling the bucket as she kneeled down beside him.

She scooped up a handful of cool water and let it trickle through her fingers. Then she scooped another handful and splashed it over her face. She repeated the process over and over, enjoying the sensation of the cool water against her warm skin.

She felt refreshed, renewed, and giving her face another splash a thought struck her. How hot and miserable it must be for Michael in his dark garb, and on impulse she scooped up another handful of water and tossed it at his shroud-covered face.

He stared at her speechless and motionless, water dripping from his facial hood.

There was a hint of mischief in Mary's smile as she waited for him to respond and when he did not, she reached out to scoop up another handful of water.

"Do not dare," he warned in a strong, harsh tone.

Her blue eyes widened, her smile turned devilish, and when she threw the water at him he ducked and charged at her. She scrambled to get to her feet, laughter in soft ripples coming from her throat.

He had her about the waist, then up in his arms in seconds. He walked to the water's edge and when she realized his intentions, threw her arms around his neck to let him know that if she went in then so did he. She pressed her head to his chest and thought she heard the rumble of laughter deep inside him.

"Attacking when defenseless is unwise."

His breath was warm and scented with berries. She looked up at him, though she could see nothing but the black hood that concealed him. She ached to reach up under it to touch his face, if just for a moment. To know he was real and of flesh and blood.

She did not surrender to her foolish impulse, instead she smiled.

"I wish . . ."

His words were whispered but she heard them. What did he wish? She wanted to know, wanted to hear, wanted him to share his wish with her.

His hood brushed against her cheek and her eyes closed while her senses trembled. It was the closest she would come to feeling his cheek to hers.

He lowered her to her feet and stepped away from her as though he required distance between them.

This upset her. She did not wish him to move away, she wished him *closer*.

Foolish thoughts, she warned herself, but ones she could not ignore.

"I intend to hunt for food today. You will be all right?"

The brief moment of play had passed, leaving her to continue questioning her odd feelings for him. Was it simply gratitude or loneliness she felt, or had this shadow of a man touched her heart somehow?

She nodded letting him know she would be fine.

"What will you do?"

What should it matter to him? But then he probably wanted to make certain she would remain close to the castle grounds. She expressed herself by stretching out her arms to her sides, tilting her face up to the heavens, and turning in a circle.

"You will enjoy the day."

As strange as it seemed, she could feel the smile behind his words.

"I will not be long."

She patted her chest to let him know not to worry, that she would be fine. For some reason she felt safe here among the ruins of the castle. Perhaps she felt a kindred spirit with the place, or perhaps because it was her home for a brief time, she felt at peace.

"I left berries in a broken crock near the door and I will carry this bucket of water to the castle for you."

She pointed to her chest to let him know that she could handle the bucket.

"I will take care of it." He picked up the bucket.

"You should rest; you have been through much and unfortunately it is not over yet."

She attempted to motion that at the moment she was granted a reprieve and she intended to enjoy it.

"You are a courageous woman."

She shook her head and motioned that she had no choice.

He stopped by her side. "You chose to survive instead of surrendering and that is courageous."

She wished she could discuss his remark for she and her father had shared endless conversations on strength and survival, and she missed such stimulating conversation.

"I will not be long."

He seemed reluctant to leave her so she tried to convince him that she would be fine and that he should not worry.

"I will not be long," he repeated gruffly and then marched off.

He worried about her, she knew, but then he was her responsibility too. He put himself in danger because of her. Magnus had requested help of the Dark One, who granted him this favor.

She wondered if Magnus knew Michael's true identity. On second thought, she doubted if any knew the Dark One's identity. Michael would not allow that. It would increase the terrible danger of the people he rescued.

She returned to the castle, entering through the door and closing it behind her as though she could lock out the world. She busied herself with cleaning the large table in front of the fireplace and clearing away as much debris as she could. She then took the cauldron off the hook in the fireplace with plans for Michael to carry it to the stream for her to scrub.

She was about to clean the area around their sleeping pallet when she suddenly dropped down to sit on the broken bench at the table. The bench was missing one leg but if she balanced herself carefully the bench remained sturdy.

Was she attempting to find balance and a sense of sanity by treating this ruined castle as her home? This place was as battered as she, and perhaps in repairing a few things she was repairing herself.

She stood and the broken bench toppled over.

She could topple that easily if she did not remain balanced in strength, thought and conviction, as her father had often cautioned.

Mary walked out the front door, looked around at the beauty of the lonely valley, and walked to the stream where she stood, hugging herself.

She wanted to cry out of frustration, out of despair, out of fear for all that had happened to her, but she did not. She just held it all back.

She was not aware of much, looking out over the water, until the first tear rolled down her face, followed by a flood of tears. Michael came up behind her, turned her around, and hugged her tightly in his strong arms. Then she was aware only of the comfort he gave.

Her tears continued, wetting his black robe but he did not let go of her; he held her firmly. And when her soft tears turned to sobs, his hand stroked her back.

"Cry, Mary," he encouraged. "You have the right."

She pressed her face to his chest and wept in the safety of his arms.

Chapter 9

When Mary's tears finally subsided the Dark One wiped her face dry with the sleeve of his black robe.

"I had expected many tearful episodes before this. With all you have been through, shedding tears is natural."

She did not agree and expressed herself by shaking her head vehemently.

"Sit," he said, releasing her hands. "We will talk."

She shook her head again, reminding him that was not possible.

"Have faith, Mary."

He sounded like her father who had repeatedly cautioned her to have faith. In what should she have faith? She had been robbed of her family, of her life not once but twice now. With no one finding her after ten years she had thought her nightmare had finally ended, but perhaps she had finally woken up. So what about faith? Where was it? She stared at Michael, draped in darkness, and then slowly reached her hand out to him.

At this moment he was the only thing she had faith in.

He grasped hold of her hand and gave a reassuring squeeze before helping her to sit near the water's edge. He looked around and grabbed hold of a good-sized stick before sitting down beside her.

He broke the stick in half and handed her a piece. "Your voice."

She smiled, taking the stick from him, and cleared the ground in front of her with the brush of her hand. And wrote, *grateful gift.*

"Tell me what you would like to discuss."

Many things, she wrote quickly.

"Something tells me that when you reclaim your voice you will never stop talking."

She heard the teasing in his voice and Mary suspected it was closer to his own true tongue than the harshness she often heard.

Love to talk and sing.

"I heard you have a lovely voice."

Who told you that?

He hesitated then quickly said, "Magnus." Then even more quickly added, "I hope to hear you sing."

Will there be time?

"I do not know."

Decimus is relentless.

"That he is. He lets nothing stop him from finding and persecuting those who believe differently, and the Church has given him the power to do whatever is necessary to bring heretics to justice."

Her hand touched his arm and he turned his head.

Decimus hates.

"In more ways than anyone understands," he said.

Even Decimus himself?

He pondered her question.

Decimus hates for he cannot love.

"Why say you that?"

Hate and love, a fine balance. She shook her head and wrote. *A balance he has not found.*

Michael made no comment.

I pity him.

"You pity the man who hunts you?"

She nodded. *Prisoner of his own hate*, she wrote. *How very sad to torture yourself.*

Michael remained silent.

I am free. He never will be.

"You are free?" he asked, confused.

She tapped her head and wrote. *Free in thought, he will never imprison my mind.*

She tossed the stick aside, ending their discussion, tapped her chest, patted her stomach, then pointed to Michael.

"Aye, I am hungry too, which is why I snared two rabbits."

Her smile was broad and she scrambled to stand. Once on her feet she motioned for him to clean the animals. She reached down and grabbed the stick she had tossed aside, then wrote on the ground in front of them *hunt onions.*

"Do not go far into the woods," he cautioned.

She nodded and wrote in the dirt. *Edge of woods.*

"Good, I can see you while I clean the rabbits."

She tossed the stick aside and hurried off, eager to find wild onions and hopefully an herb or two to flavor the rabbit stew.

Michael watched her go as he walked slowly to the castle. She was graceful in her haste, her body swaying as if in rhythm with a melody, a soft, subtle melody. He watched her dip down and swing up, a smile of delight on her face and a plucked onion in her hand. She repeated the movement several times and he could not take his eyes from her.

She mystified him, this woman of strength and tears, of pity for the least deserving, of injured voice yet eloquent words.

Mary waved to him with a handful of onions, he smiled and waved back.

He had forgotten the simple pleasures of life.

A woman's smile. A woman's wave. A woman's *love*.

"Damn," he swore beneath his breath.

He thought all feeling had died. Died along with those he loved.

But damned, if she had not sparked life in his cold heart.

He stomped off to clean the rabbits when suddenly he sensed something. He froze, barely breathing so that he could hear, sense, feel another's presence.

In a second he felt it, a presence, strong and powerful and knew it to be a wild boar.

His glance shot to Mary. She was bent down, her interest caught by something on the ground. He tried to signal her but she did not take notice.

Suddenly he caught sight of the boar, in a dead run straight toward Mary. He took a deep breath and began to run.

Michael rushed at her, swept her up from around the waist and ran with her to hide behind a large tree.

Within seconds the boar passed, near to where she had been gathering onions.

He heard her sigh and she turned her face to his. His black mask brushed her cheek and she stilled.

"I wish . . ." he whispered.

Her eyes pleaded for him to tell her what he wished and he lowered his face, shifted his hood, and claimed her lips in a gentle kiss.

She seemed uncertain how to respond, and he wondered if this was her first kiss. The thought excited him. He slowly nudged her lips apart and, though at first hesitant, she became eager in her attempts to taste him.

They exchanged soft, tenuous nibbles as if sampling and savoring before tasting fully of each other. Michael did not hesitate to guide her and it was not long before their tongues were mating with the eagerness of newborn lovers.

The kiss was all too brief and Mary was disappointed when their lips parted and he moved away from her. She felt as though the earth shivered beneath her feet and her body flooded with a radiant warmth that tingled down to her toes. She wanted no distance between them; she wanted him as close to her as possible. His kiss had stirred her heart and now her heart ached for more.

He turned, his shoulders wide, his chest broad and his head high. "My apologies. That was wrong of me."

She shook her head frantically, letting him know he was not to blame and that she enjoyed the kiss, but he was adamant.

"I had no right. It can never be between you and me."

She watched him walk away and felt a sense of loss. It made no sense, but then it made much sense. She had hoped to love one day but was that truly possible? What could she offer a man? She was a hunted woman, hunted by a truly evil man.

And yet she wished, hoped; she closed her eyes against the pain in her heart.

If only.

She opened her eyes, now blurred with unshed tears, and searched the ground for the onions and herbs she had picked. They had flown from her hand when Michael had taken her around the waist into his strong arms, protecting her.

The strength of him, the power of his body, the taste of him; she shook her head. He was complete darkness and yet he shed light on her life. With him she knew safety, she knew protection and she knew . . .

She touched her lips. She knew her first kiss.

A tear fell and she was not certain if it was a tear of joy or sorrow or perhaps it was both. The joy of having known a kiss and the sorrow that perhaps she would never experience it again.

Her heart hurt and she did not know what to do. She understood his reluctance to love; theirs would be an impossible love. Her heart however did not understand and would not stop aching.

Mary wiped away her tear and finished gathering her onions and herbs. She was being foolish to think of love now. It would do her little good. She had no home. No safe place, *except with Michael.*

Stop, she warned herself. *You heard him tell you it cannot be.*

She refused to acknowledge the ache in her heart; it would go away if she paid it no heed, at least she hoped it would, after all they had been thrown together and had in a strange way become entangled with each other. It was nothing more than a bond of survival they shared.

Mary prepared the evening meal, Michael returned to the castle when the meal was just about ready to eat. He made no mention of where he had been, he simply offered her help, which she declined.

Michael and Mary shared the evening meal but little was said. Michael commented on the delicious stew and Mary's culinary talent. She responded with a weak smile and a nod, but offered no more.

A rumble of thunder was heard in the distance though the sky remained clear.

"Rain. We will need cover," Michael said as Mary saw to cleaning up after the meal.

Michael fashioned a cover from wood and brush over their sleeping pallet and then joined Mary where she sat on the broken stone that once was the sturdy front wall of the castle.

Dusk was setting and lightning flashed in the sky, a bolt striking the ground in the distance.

"The storm will be here soon."

She nodded and held her face up to feel the wind that had suddenly rushed down into the valley, swirling around the decayed castle. The air was cool and felt refreshing against her flushed cheeks.

The sky darkened fast, though night had yet to settle over the land. The wind caused macabre shadows to dance at the edge of the woods, an owl hooted eerily, and birds anxiously sought the protection of their nests.

The storm continued to brew, thunder rumbled, lightning struck, the wind blew, but no rain fell. It was as if the sky demonstrated its anger.

"Storms do not frighten you?"

Mary shook her head.

Michael leaned down and whispered. "What frightens you, Mary?"

That you may never kiss me again.

She shivered at the disheartening thought.

The sadness that suddenly appeared in her eyes was more powerful than any spoken word. In their blue depths he saw a potent mixture of love and sorrow and it upset him to know that nothing he did could change that. She would know sorrow if he loved her or if he did not love her.

Why then would it matter either way? If they shared a brief interlude, a moment in time loving each other, what difference would it make?

He tore his eyes away, looking past her and feeling the ache in his heart grow and spread across his chest, tightening, squeezing, reminding him of the tortuous pain of losing a loved one. He could not love Mary and let her walk out of his life forever, and he could not love her and let her remain in his life.

"You will know love one day, Mary," he said, averting his eyes from hers and fighting the pain in his heart.

She made no attempt to argue. She could not adequately express herself and would feel all the more the fool. And perhaps now was not the time nor was this decayed castle the place. She would do well to focus on her immediate situation. Or was she merely attempting to convince herself?

"You will be happy."

She slowly shook her head, stood, and waved her hands in front of her face. Happiness would forever elude her. Michael reached for her and lightning sparked in the black sky. She jumped away from him, shaking her head and stretching out her hands to keep him at a distance. She hurried off into the castle.

He ached to rush after her but it would do neither of them any good. He was there to protect her and to see to her safety. He would only place her in more danger if he surrendered to his desires.

Michael looked for Mary. He found her by the sleeping pallet unpinning her hair with trembling hands. He had not thought he would care for anyone ever again in his life. He had thought himself cut off from all emotions, and he had intended for it to forever remain so.

How, then, did this woman who could speak not a word penetrate his protective shield? How had she been able to touch his heart? Why was it that the simple thought of never seeing her again tore at his heart until he thought it had been ripped in two?

He watched from a distance as Mary lowered herself onto the pallet. He would soon join her there and keep her warm, just as he had done from the time that he rescued her. They had not slept apart since, and he favored snuggling with her at night, cuddling as lovers would. She felt so good wrapped within his embrace, warm and soft.

When she slept, it was deeply, from exhaustion. And she lightly snored. He enjoyed the sound, enjoyed feeling the beat of her heart against him, found joy in both her gentleness and strength.

She cannot be yours.

His own strong voice warned and he nodded, knowing there was no choice in this matter.

The first drop of rain fell and rolled off his shroud. How he wished to feel the rain against his skin and how he wish to feel Mary's warmth next to his.

Drop after raindrop pelted his shroud until he finally went directly to Mary. The pallet was thick and deep with brush and tree limbs, a blanket against the rain. He looked down to see her sleeping, curled on her side, her arms pressed firmly to her chest and her legs tucked up near to the end of her elbows.

Michael lay down behind her and pressed himself up

against her to let her know of his presence if she should need him. She made no move to respond and Michael made no move away from her.

They lay there quietly, with not a sound or movement except those of the other occupants of the castle, the small forest animals and the birds. Finally when night settled heavy over the land, Mary turned and Michael wrapped her in his arms and held her tightly to him.

And he wondered how he would ever let her go.

Chapter 10

Mary woke the next morning to the smell of roasting fish with wild onions and though the delicious scent tempted, she had little appetite. Her foolishness disturbed her. She was behaving like a young lass in love when she barely knew Michael. How ridiculous of her, or how needy?

Was it love? Or was it the need to be protected? She remembered her father telling her that love would come to her when she least expected it. It would find her, she would not be able to hide from it and she should not worry over it. But then he had been advising a young girl of ten who thought herself wildly in love with a local village boy.

She had not thought herself in love since, her life having been torn apart shortly afterward. With little experience to call on, she was not certain what to make of her feelings.

Perhaps she would just wait on love.

She brushed her hair and tied it in a ribbon before joining Michael at the table.

"I fished early and thought to surprise you with a good meal," he said.

Was he attempting to appease her for last night?

She nodded and picked sparingly at the fish. She simply had no appetite for food and could not force herself to eat no matter how delicious it tasted.

Michael said not another word until he was finished eating. "I need to make my rounds again to see that the surrounding area has remained free of intruders. It will take me most of the day."

She nodded and patted her chest, letting him know she would do fine that there was no need for concern, though she would have much preferred to spend time with him than away from him.

With a hint of annoyance he said, "You are brave to a fault."

Mary stared at him, confused by his statement.

He offered her no explanation, was only adamant in his demand that she remain close by the castle ruins.

She pointed in the direction of the stream, not far away but not noticeable from where they stood either.

He shook his head. "Nay, you will remain here while I am gone."

She sighed in agitation and with hands flying in all manner of movement, she attempted to tell him that a trip to the stream would not place her in danger.

His laughter is what halted her hand motions, so shocked was she to hear the clear distinct sound and how far from his annoyance only moments before.

"If you talk as much with your mouth as your hands there will be little quiet in these woods."

She punched him playfully in the arm.

His laughter stopped and he stepped closer to her. "You will need more strength than that to stop a man."

She shivered suddenly, recalling the strength of the man who had shoved her to the ground and choked her. Her hand went immediately to her throat.

"I did not mean to frighten you, Mary, though I do mean for you to be prepared."

She made a jabbing motion.

"Do you know how to use a knife?"

She nodded, but knew not how to explain with her hands how the metalsmith in her village had taught her to wield a knife with accuracy. After she had made a pest of herself in wanting to learn about swords and knives, he had finally surrendered and taught her much.

"Until I can be sure you know well how to handle a knife, you will remain near the castle."

She gave him an exasperated sigh and threw up her hands as though in surrender.

"Good, we agree. I will see you later near the evening meal, which I will have with me when I return."

She grabbed his arm as he walked passed her. How did she tell him to stay safe and return to her?

He appeared to understand. "I will be fine."

Her eyes questioned, *what if?*

"If I do not return—have faith, Mary—remain here. Someone will come for you and say the words you and Magnus agreed upon."

She nodded and could not help but place her hand to his chest, over his heart, for a brief moment before he left her side.

She thought she felt him tremble but it was too brief to be sure, for he quickly moved away from her. She watched as he disappeared into the woods.

She busied herself with cleaning off the table and

then explored areas of the castle she had yet to see. Much of the space was nothing but rubble, though on occasion she came across an exciting find. She found a tattered tapestry beneath stone and charred wood that would serve well as a blanket, Michael's shroud and the brush was not always sufficient against the chilled night. She was delighted when she found three pewter goblets and four plates. The find of several baskets delighted her. It would make gathering herbs, onions, and roots easier.

She smiled when she found a large brooch minus its jewels. It made her wonder about the lady of the castle. She could not imagine such a life of luxury. She was a peasant, though glad not to have worked in a castle. She had heard stories from those who had serviced a lord; many talked of cruelty and endless days of work.

Nay, she was glad to be free, a peasant but free of the cruelty of an oppressive lord. She continued to search the castle and was enthusiastic over several more finds. When she was done she deposited the items on the table in front of the hearth.

One look at her dirt-covered hands, and the feel of perspiration on her neck and back, and she knew that she needed to wash. But she was not to go to the stream and there was not enough water in the bucket.

She faced a dilemma. She had not actually given Michael her word on not going to the stream, and it was not far from the castle. It was a very warm day for spring and the cool water was enticing.

Should she take the chance or abide by Michael's dictate?

It would be hours before his return and she would not be long at the stream.

A trickle of sweat ran down her back, resolving her

debate. She hurried off to the stream to be done with it.

The cool water felt refreshing against her warm skin and before she realized it, Mary had shed her clothes and hurried into the stream for a quick wash. The strong, rapid flow of the water surprised her, and she lowered herself so that she could rinse her entire body of sweat and grime.

The water moved around swiftly and she sensed it was not wise for her to remain in the cold, forceful stream. She shivered as she made her way back to the water's edge. Return footing was a bit more treacherous and she slipped now and again.

She attempted to take each step more carefully, though try as she might her footing remained unsound and she fought to keep herself standing. Land finally was a few feet ahead and she sighed with relief when suddenly her foot slipped on a stone and she lost all balance and tumbled head first into the stream.

The water rushed in, swirling her up and around in circles. She was caught in a whirlpool making it impossible for her to grab onto anything. The water carried her, dipping her, swirling her, filling her with fright. She choked and sputtered each time her head surfaced and fought to gain control of her thrashing ride, finally reaching up to catch hold of anything solid. Her hand snatched a heavy branch hanging over the stream.

She dug her wet hands into the tree bark and looked around her. She could not tell how far she had traveled. The stream had widened and deepened as it had carried her off, but she had never gone farther than the castle, so she did not know if she was merely around a bend or a good distance away.

She felt foolish and fearful. She was naked and knew

not where she was, and she did not know what she would do. For the moment she thought it best to pull herself to the water's edge and sit in the shadows of the large tree that had rescued her.

When her mind calmed she gave her plight rational thought. If she followed the stream she was bound to return to where she had entered. Her clothes would mark the spot.

She would need to be very careful and extremely alert. She shivered at the thought of walking along the edge of the stream naked, but what choice did she have? She could not remain where she was.

She gathered all her courage and set a quick pace alongside the stream, keeping a keen eye and ear to her surroundings. Her pace was steady and she prayed that she was close to the castle.

She stopped suddenly, listening, sure she had heard something.

Voices and the snort of a horse.

She hurried reluctantly into the stream to hide in the water, her head concealed by the drooping branches of a large willow tree. She kept a firm hand on a thick branch so that the swift water would not carry her away. She heard the voices again. They drew closer and she shivered not from the cold water but from the sound of men.

Then one voice, far different from the others, spoke. He commanded like a man confident of being obeyed. His threats were subtle and meant to instill fear and he certainly succeeded, for the other men's voices quivered when they spoke. She imagined they cowered at his side like the dominions of the devil doing his bidding out of fear.

It could only be one man.

Decimus.

"You will travel where I order, do you understand?"

"Aye, sir." The voices responded in unison.

"I *will* snare my prey, no thanks to the likes of any one of you. You are a useless lot with not a brain among you."

Decimus continued to belittle his men and Mary closed her eyes and prayed they would not find her, though she opened them fast enough when a reference was made to her.

"You allow a mere woman to avoid capture. You were not even able to prevent her escape. She is more a warrior than any of you."

How odd to hear Decimus praise her.

"Find her or suffer the consequences," he said sharply. "Now, be on your way."

She remained perfectly still. They would be gone soon, very soon she told herself. Mary listened as rider after rider rode off. She waited patiently, taking extra care that all the men had left the area and just as she was about to pull herself out of the water, she heard a horse draw nearer to the stream.

"Idiots all of them."

Fear shot through Mary like an icy arrow. It was Decimus's voice and he was inching his horse closer to where she hid. She froze and urged her body not to tremble, but her fright was great and shivers raced through her.

She heard him dismount and walk to the water's edge. She bit her trembling lip and dug her fingers into the branch. She warned herself not to panic, to remain still and he would not find her.

The sight of his hand dipping into the stream suddenly made her angry. It was the hand of the man who robbed her of her family and her life. She took notice of his lean fingers and a sapphire ring he wore, and the urge to see more of her enemy tormented her. If she inched over just a bit she might be able to have a look at him.

He stood abruptly and she stilled.

Had he heard or spotted her? She waited for her fate to fall.

In seconds he mounted his horse and rode off and she remained in the cold water, shivering in relief. She would not dare leave its safety until she was sure Decimus was far away.

She waited and waited, then finally pulled herself out, her body trembling. She walked as softly and soundlessly as possible, hugging the water's edge. Every now and again she thought she heard voices and she quickly sought the protection of the stream or within the dense branches of a willow until she was certain no one was near.

Was Michael safe? Did he know Decimus was near? The thought haunted her, but she had no time to worry over him; she had to make her way back to the castle, and then she had to warn Michael that Decimus was nearby.

Relief sent a final shiver to rack her body as she spied her clothes on the ground by the tree. It was near to nightfall. She had stopped many times and waited endlessly to make certain no one was near. She hurried into her skirt and blouse and slipped into her boots.

She shivered, feeling cold to her bones from the constant dunking in the cold stream and her close brush with the devil himself, Decimus.

She was almost to the castle when Michael stepped out of the shadows and she jumped.

"Where have you been?" His voice was harsh and filled with concern.

Mary was so relieved that she had survived her ordeal and that Michael was safe that she wanted to throw herself into his strong arms, but she knew that it was imperative that he be made aware of Decimus.

"Your hair is wet." He grabbed hold of her hand. "Your skin wrinkled. You have been in the water."

She nodded, her eyes round with fright.

He grabbed her by both arms. "What happened?"

He did not wait for an answer. He hurried her along to the castle with a firm hold of her arm. He gently shoved her down to sit on the bench in front of the hearth.

She quickly sought the fire's heat, rubbing her hands together in front of the blazing flames. The warmth tickled her cold flesh and she shivered hard; it took several minutes before the flames' heat began to penetrate her cold flesh and set to warming her.

He handed her a branch. "Tell me."

Her hand shook as she wrote and he moved closer to her, wrapping his arm around her and pressing his body next to hers to share his heat.

Briefly she described her fall into the stream.

"You were naked in the water?"

She stared at him for she had purposely omitted that fact.

"Your garments are dry," he said, explaining how he knew.

Foolish, she wrote.

"Very."

His blunt, terse response told her he was angry.

"I told you to stay away from the stream."

Foolish, she wrote again.

"More than foolish."

She did not want to hear any more about that. It was imperative he know the rest.

Decimus. Men. Close by.

"You came across Decimus and his men?"

She nodded vigorously and explained as best she could what had happened.

"Decimus travels north, thinking we have gone to seek safety from Magnus."

Her eyes widen with fear for her friend.

"Do not worry for Magnus. He can well take care of himself. *Worry for you.*"

Her eyes rounded with the harshness of his words.

"Do you know what would have happened if he had found you?"

She did not want to think of the consequences of Decimus finding her. She had no strength left, but she wanted to let him know that she had been brave and courageous. It was important to her.

With few written words she tried as best she could to relate how she had hung by the branch as Decimus drank water just a mere few inches away from her. She let him know that she had caught a glimpse of Decimus's hand and his ring, and she had been close to seeing his face.

"You came that close to him?"

She nodded then raised her chin to demonstrate her pride and courage.

Michael growled low in his throat, sounding as though he was about to erupt. Mary's eyes grew wide with alarm.

The growl quieted, he shook his head and his glove-covered hand slowly stroked her face.

"You are braver than I."

She shook her head and quickly wrote, *No one brave as you.*

He took the stick from her hand, tossed it aside, and lowered his head.

"I should not do this, I have no right to kiss you, but I must."

He grabbed the edge of his face mask.

"Close your eyes, Mary, and give me your word as a brave warrior that you will keep them closed."

This was the second time she had been considered a brave warrior and it meant much more coming from Michael. She gave her word with a nod, accepting the distinguished honor of being a warrior in his eyes.

She closed her eyes and waited for his lips, but first his cheek touched hers, and she sighed with the pleasure of his warm flesh resting against hers. He was no longer a mere shadow. He was a man of flesh and blood.

Chapter 11

He could remain as he was, cheek against cheek, and not move, not kiss; just feel. It had been so long since he had allowed himself to feel, allowed himself emotions, allowed himself to care. He wanted to linger in the beauty of those long forgotten feelings, relish in their return and grasp them firmly if only for a brief time.

Mary rubbed her cheek against his and sighed softly.

"You feel so very good," he whispered.

She kept her eyes closed as she had promised and smiled, letting him know she felt the same of him.

Michael discarded his gloves and hesitated for a moment, reluctant and uncertain to touch her. He feared that once he did he would not want to stop. He took a deep breath and brought his hand to her neck; his fingertips gently grazed her silky skin.

She responded, tilting her head to the side, allowing him complete access to her neck.

She trusts me.

The thought sent a rush of emotions through him, heating his flesh and his loins. He wanted to protect her, love her, and worship her for she surrendered to him with the purest of hearts and emotions.

He slowly brought his lips to her neck and followed the path his fingertips had traveled. The taste of her was exquisite, soft, sweet and silky.

Her body surrendered with each kiss and he slipped his arm around her waist for support and to bring her closer to him; he wanted her as close as possible. He wanted to feel her body's response—a simple shiver, a tingle, a movement; he intended to feel all of her emotions.

He continued to enjoy the taste of her, feeling like a starving man who had gone much too long without sustenance. The more he tasted the more hungry he grew, and with a hasty grab of her chin but with reserve, he claimed her lips.

His kiss was filled with unbridled passion, and if he were not careful he would soon have her up in his arms and on the sleeping pallet. And that he could not do; he could not take from her that which should one day belong to her husband.

She was innocent and trusting and he had vowed to protect her, even if it meant protecting her from him.

He lingered in the kiss, knowing that was all they would share yet wanting to fill himself with the taste of her. He would at least have the memory of her on his lips to keep long after they parted.

He reluctantly brought their kiss to an end but she refused to let him go.

He wanted to rejoice, smile, laugh, and cry with the joy of knowing love once again, and he surrendered to her nervous and quick attempts to kiss him.

Michael eased his mouth from hers and whispered, "Easy and slow like this."

He taunted, teased, and tempted with his lingering kisses and when he was done, she smiled and patted her chest to let him know it was her turn.

She learned fast, much too fast, for in mere seconds her kisses had his blood racing and his loins swelling most uncomfortably. He eased away from her and pulled his black mask down over his face with much regret. If only . . .

If only he were free.

He pressed his glove-covered hand to her face. "Open your eyes."

They drifted open with a smile.

How could she be happy about kissing a faceless man? She had placed her trust in a stranger, in a shadow, in darkness where light never shined.

She motioned with her hands to let him know how much she enjoyed their kiss.

He pressed a finger to her lips. "I have never known such a beautiful kiss until yours."

She smiled wider and her shoulders sagged as she released a heavy sigh. She then hurried to tell him, her hand motions frantic, that he was her first; she had never been kissed before.

The knowledge reared a protective instinct in him that he knew would be hard to control. He was her first, the only man to ever claim her lips. The thought that someday another would kiss her lips filled him with anger.

He captured her waving hands in his. "I am honored to be the first to have kissed you. These lovely moments will live long with me." He turned her hand to kiss her palm and stopped when she winced.

He looked at the red welts crisscrossing her palm, then at her.

She attempted to free her hand so that she could demonstrate how she received her injury, but he would not let her go.

"I know how you came by these injuries. There are slivers of bark within the wounds that need removing."

She winced again.

"I will be gentle," he reassured her.

Michael placed a crock of water by the fire to warm and retrieved a knife from somewhere within the confines of his shroud. He held up his knife, the metal blade gleaming in the fire's light.

She frowned and skittishly presented her hand to him.

"I will be gentle, trust me."

She nodded, her eyes growing wide, letting him know that trust was not a question with him.

He kept a firm hold on her hand as he brought the tip of the knife to her wound. She squeezed shut her eyes and braced herself for the pain.

His hesitation made her wonder if he feared hurting her, and the thought touched her heart.

"Done," he said and trickled warm water over her wound, then patted it dry with the end of his robe.

Her eyes sprang open in disbelief. She stared at her hand to make certain he had removed the slivers, having felt not a prick or a pain. They were gone. She smiled and pressed her cheek to his.

They lingered against each other for a moment, then she moved to the table while keeping a hand on his arm. She pointed to the food.

"I set the bird to cooking when I returned," he said,

"and went in search of you, intending to admonish you for leaving the castle grounds. I found no sign of you, though I expected to find you at the stream."

After stripping a large piece of meat from the bird, Mary tried to explain that he had not seen her garments in his search because she hid them beside the large willow tree.

"You hid your garments?" he asked.

She shook her head.

"You hid them so I would not see them if I should return before you were done."

She shook her head again.

"Aye, you did," he said. "You knew I would glance past the tree line and if I did not spot you, I would go no farther. Your actions were born of intelligence and I commend you."

Her eyes rounded in surprise.

"Though I admonish you for disobeying my orders."

She sighed and nodded.

Foolish. She had been foolish.

Then she shook her head to let him know she would never disobey him again.

"Promise me, Mary. Promise me you will heed my orders for it may endanger your life as it did today."

She placed her hand to her heart and nodded.

"It is a warrior's honor that you give me?"

She stuck her chin up and then gave a firm nod.

"Good, then I will say no more about it."

They slept well that night wrapped in each other's arms, knowing time was their enemy. It would end and they would part, both understood the necessity of it, and both prayed for a miracle.

Early the next morning they sat on the bank of the stream fishing for their breakfast. Poles were made of thick willow branches and old frayed rope with rusty hooks fashioned from scrap metal. The fish seemed to ignore the hook, instead feeding on the tiny fish that swam near the surface.

"They taunt us," Michael said, humor edging his harsh tone.

Mary nodded and motioned that she was not that hungry. She reached for a stick and wrote in the dirt. *Speak with me.*

"Of what do you wish to speak?"

You when a lad.

That caused a pause and Mary hoped she had not stirred painful memories. Then she heard a soft rumble of laughter as though he had attempted to conceal it but failed.

Tell me, she urged, emphasizing her desire to hear about him with a deep underscore drawn beneath the words.

"Adventure," he said and she thought she could feel his smile; he sounded happy. "I was forever getting myself lost in the woods or stranded in a boat in the middle of a loch, or stuck in a tree that seemed far taller once I had climbed it. But no one or nothing could stop me from exploring and I was fortunate to have a family who encouraged my exploits." ·

Siblings?

A lengthy pause proceeded. "A sister."

She waited, the hesitancy in his voice making her wonder if he would speak no more about her.

Then as if he opened a door long closed and locked tightly, he began to talk.

"Cathleen was my little sister."

His voice swelled with emotion and Mary wondered if a tear touched his eye.

"She forever followed me around and I looked after her as an older brother should. I was there whenever she needed me. If she fell down, I picked her up and tended her wounds. If she cried I wiped her tears. It was my duty to see to her care, my father reminded me of that on his deathbed. I was to take care of my mother and sister, but it was no chore for me. I loved them both and would do anything for them."

It was not difficult to realize that something had happened to his family. Mary waited, hoping he would continue to share his past and his pain with her, hoping perhaps it would help heal him.

"Cathleen loved and trusted everyone. Her constant smile was born of a joyous and generous heart. And she was so very beautiful."

Was. What had happened to her? Mary wondered if somehow his sister was connected to the reason that he became the Dark One.

"She thirsted for knowledge."

Mary smiled and tapped her chest to let him know she felt the same.

He grabbed her hand so tightly that she winced, but he did not release it.

"Seeking knowledge can cause you harm."

She nodded and eased his fingers off her wrist before writing: *I know, but knowledge is power.*

"What power does it bring peasants? What good does knowledge do them?" He sounded angry.

Mary remained patient, aware that his anger came from a painful memory. *It frees us.*

"They continue to labor. How does that bring freedom?"

It frees the mind.

"And if peasants speak, they are persecuted."

No hope in silence. No hope. No life.

"It is dangerous to think that way. The peasant is taught to serve lord and master. That is his lot in life: service."

Who do you serve?

"Some say the devil."

She shook her head.

He held out his arms. "Darkness is born from the depths of hell."

Darkness is born of ignorance.

"Who taught you such dangerous knowledge?"

She stuck her chin up then wrote, *My father.*

His tone softened. "He must have been a brave man."

Sadness and sorrow filled her; she missed her father very much. *Very brave.*

"Then you truly are your father's daughter."

She smiled. *Thank you.*

"He would be proud of you."

She nodded, recalling how just before her father had been taken away, he had expressed his pride in her bravery. She was barely eleven years old yet was proud of her; it had shined in his eyes and smile whenever he had looked at her. Those memories kept her father alive in her mind.

"He was accused of heresy?" Michael asked reluctantly.

She nodded and asked her own question. *Your sister?*

"Her innocence caused her to suffer." His anger returned. "She trusted, she believed in good and gave no thought to evil. She would care for the ill, help the injured animals, and love those others would shun. She had an angelic heart and soul."

Precious woman.

"To me she was precious." He shook his head and turned to stare at the stream. "I was as precious to her as she was to me. She loved me, believed in me, and—"

With a vicious toss the fishing pole went flying into the stream. "She loved me, trusted me, and I failed her."

Mary placed her hand on his arm and he turned his head abruptly to see her shaking her head, denying his admission.

"She loved me and I failed her," he reiterated adamantly.

Mary shook her head just as adamantly.

"You know not of what you speak. She suffered and I did nothing." Anger and pain punctuated his words. "She loved me and I failed her. I will not see that happen again."

Mary understood now why he refused to love, but she refused to allow him his pity. She swallowed hard, recited a silent prayer, squeezed his arm and said aloud, "I love you."

Chapter 12

Michael was too stunned to speak. He had ached to hear her voice and had never expected these words to be the first to spill from her lips. They tore at his heart; his soul wept with sorrow—for upon hearing her words, her voice, his response was not what he had thought it would be. "You cannot love me."

She smiled and raised a defiant chin. "Aye, I can."

He reached out and stroked her neck. "It does not pain you?"

"Nay, I think I have finally healed."

The beauty of her voice was like a gentle lyric to his senses, and he smiled though she could not see it.

"I will hear your voice much now."

"Is that a plea I hear or regret?"

Peels of gentle laughter poured from her, and he favored the sound that seemed to rain down around him.

"I have yet to decide."

"I knew I detected humor in you," she said and coughed, clearing her throat of a sudden tickle.

He gently massaged her throat. "I know how much you must want to talk but be careful. Your voice probably still mends."

"Wise advice, which undoubtedly I will have difficulty following."

"There is nothing that important that needs immediate discussion."

She reached up to touch his face. "Aye, there is. I love you and I think you love me."

He stood abruptly and paced in front of her, the hem of his robe growing wet from the water's edge.

"Love is not possible for us."

"Why?"

A simple enough question requiring a much more complicated answer, of which he was uncertain. "You do not know who I am."

"Then show me," she challenged. "Though it will not matter."

He stopped pacing and with regret said, "I cannot."

"Are you ugly, scarred, reprehensible?"

"I think that would be for another to answer."

"Then let me answer."

He shook his head. "Nay, and that is the end of it."

Mary stood, then laughed softly. "You have much to learn about me, Michael. Lord, it feels good to say your name. *Michael. Michael. Michael.*" She whirled around, raising her hands to the sky. "I love *Michael.*"

He remained silent, secretly pleased with hearing her declaration sung to the heavens. He knew she should not love him or that he should not feel the same about her, but for now, for this moment, he would take pleasure in hearing of her love for him.

She stopped and stared at him.

"You wait for what?" he asked after several minutes passed in silence.

She walked up to him and tapped at his chest directly over his heart.

He understood. She waited to hear how he felt about her. Could he deny her? Could he deny himself?

Mary was patient, not moving, remaining silent, waiting: she would have an answer.

Michael finally surrendered; he had no choice, he simply could not deny his love for her. "Lord, help me. Mary, I love you with all my heart and soul."

She smiled, tilted her head, closed her eyes; she wanted a kiss.

But then so did he.

Their arms wrapped around each other simultaneously and together they surrendered to a breath-catching kiss. Lips touched, a hunger fed, a need filled, and love quenched. They nibbled at each other's lips unwilling to part, wanting to continue tasting and touching, never wanting to let go. When it was done, silence reigned, for neither of them could speak, but both worried about the day when they would kiss for the last time.

That evening after supper Mary went to the stream to wash their eating utensils. She felt content and at peace. She could speak again, but most importantly he did not deny his love for her. He admitted it freely; of course she asked, but how else was she to know? He intended not only to protect her from Decimus but also from his love, and she would not have that. She trusted him enough to know he would not lie to her; he would speak the truth.

Her smile was wide as she scrubbed the plates with sand from the bottom of the stream. And before long, without realizing it, as she had so often done when she was young, she began to hum a tune that turned quickly into a song.

Michael had followed her to the stream, though kept his distance giving her time alone, time to think and be sensible about their love. But then love was not sensible, as his mother had often warned him.

The soft tune she hummed delighted him, but when she broke into song he was astonished. He had never heard such a beautiful voice in all his years. It was like listening to an angel.

When she finished the song of finding first love he felt a sense of disappointment. He wished for her to continue singing; her voice soothed his soul.

He watched as she stretched her hands up to the heavens. "Thank you. Thank you for the return of my voice and thank you with all my heart for Michael's love."

He had thought she could not surprise him any more than she already had, but he was wrong. To hear her give thanks to the heavens for his love tugged at his heart and shivered his soul.

"One day you may regret loving me."

Startled, she turned—but she wore a smile. *"Never."*

He walked over to her. "You give your love to a stranger, that is not wise."

"You are not a stranger to me. You are my hero; you saved me and delivered me to freedom, and now you protect me." She walked to him and tapped his chest. "And *you* love *me*."

"You will not let me forget that."

"Never." She laughed. "I will remind you until your dying day and then beyond."

He reached out and slipped his arms around her waist. "I shall never be free of you."

"That is my plan." She drifted into his tender embrace and rested her head on his chest. She loved hearing the soft steady rhythm of his heart and feeling the strength of him wrap around her. And though her plan might be nothing more than a dream, she refused to allow her dream to die. She would keep it strong in her heart and mind and pray for a miracle.

A strike of lightning and clap of thunder moved them apart, though they clasped hands, then stared up at the night sky wondering where it had come from. There was no sign of a storm.

Was it an omen?

Mary shivered.

Michael tugged at her hand and led the way back to the castle. She scooped the plates up and hurried along with him. The dark sky suddenly grew darker and heavy clouds raced like avenging warriors across the starless sky.

The first drop of rain fell before they reached the safety of the castle. Once inside, Mary dropped the plates on the wooden table and they ducked beneath the partial roof covering their sleeping pallet.

The rain fell hard and fast; lightning struck, followed by a deafening thunderclap.

Mary rubbed the gooseflesh that ran down her arms.

Michael stepped behind her, wrapped his arms around her, his shroud completely encasing her, and rested his face next to hers.

She wished she could feel his warm flesh, but would that be wise? Once his skin touched hers she would want to feel more, touch more, and kiss endlessly.

The wind howled, screeching horribly.

"The banshees will ride this night," Mary said, her voice a mere whisper, and then she crossed herself in protection.

Michael laughed, a sound as chilling as the banshee's call. "You sleep with the Dark One. Do you believe the banshees would dare to disturb us?"

"You do not fear the night creatures?"

He pressed his lips near to her ear and whispered, "There is little I fear."

"Do you fear the light?"

"Perhaps the light fears me."

"Darkness and light, as one is born the other dies," she whispered.

"I am forever."

She turned in his arms and pressed her palm to his cheek, again wishing she felt his flesh and not the black shroud. "You cannot live in darkness forever."

"Darkness has been my companion for many years and has served me well. I warn you, Mary, do not ask of me what is better left unspoken. Do not look to see what is better left concealed. Do not attempt to save what has already been lost."

She pressed a finger to his lips. "And do not deny what we know to be the truth. The truth is always victorious."

He abruptly stepped away from her and she heard the anger in his voice. "The truth is never victorious. Truth causes pain, sorrow, suffering."

"Truth is an ally and is always there to help."

"Your father's teachings?" Michael asked more calmly.

"My father's belief and one that he lived by."

He shook his head. "And brought him sorrow."

Mary reached out to take his hand and tugged for him to join her as she lowered herself down to their sleeping pallet. Michael followed.

"Nay." Mary was quick to argue though her tone was

neutral. "My father was a happy man. He spoke the truth as he believed it and would have it no other way."

"And the truth earned him what?" Michael regretted his words. He did not wish to raise painful memories.

Mary did not take offense. The memories of her father had been good ones.

She smiled. "Truth earned him admiration, respect, honor, and a life that he cherished and loved."

Michael remained silent. He wanted to remind her that truth also earned him his death, but he did not wish to hurt her.

"You hold your tongue so as not to cause me pain." She placed a hand on his arm. "Truth did not kill my father, it was ignorance."

"An ignorance that spreads like wildfire destroying all in its path, including the truth."

She disagreed. "The truth cannot be destroyed. It may linger in silence for many years, but it eventually rises victorious as it will one day rise victorious over Decimus."

He laughed. "You think a man as vile as Decimus will one day be destroyed?"

She thought on his words and recalled the seer's words to her. *You will be the demise of Decimus.*

"His end will come," she said confidently.

He took her hand and squeezed gently. "I wish it to come soon, though I doubt my wish will be granted."

She smiled. "Wishes can only come true if you believe in them. They do little good if you do not hold your desire strong in your heart."

He brought her hand to rest at his heart. "I wish with all my heart that I would kiss you."

She giggled softly. "You better hold that wish tightly

and believe with all your heart or it will not come true."

"I believe," he said, his gruff tone making his plea sound like a strange litany. "I believe, I believe, I believe."

With each plea his face drew closer, and her eyes closed, and they kissed as they lay back on the sleeping pallet. His hands were at her waist, he did not dare move fearing that once he began he would not stop, and he sensed she would want the same.

Nothing mattered at that moment, not the storm, not their hunters, not Decimus, only the two of them and this moment in time.

They kissed and they hugged and settled deeper into each other's arms with sleep.

Chapter 13

"Will you be gone long?" Mary asked, concerned over the sudden news of Michael's departure the next morning.

"A week perhaps, but you will be in good hands."

They walked out the castle door, a beautiful spring morning having greeted them.

Michael took hold of her hand. "A good friend of mine will arrive shortly after I leave and will remain with you until I return. His name is Roarke. He is a large Scotsman and you can trust him. He will protect you with his life."

"You know him well?"

"We are true friends. I would have no other watch over you."

"And what of you?" she asked. "Where do you go, if I may inquire?"

"I go to speak with Magnus and make plans for your final destination."

"I should go with you."

"For your safety it is better you remain here," he said.

"But it is my future that Magnus and you are deciding. What of my choices?"

"Safety and freedom are your only choices," he reminded. "Your destination will be born of necessity."

"You will be careful?" She did not want to admit he was right and she did not want him to go. She wanted more time with him. Time to discover, time to love, time for a miracle.

He cupped her chin. "Worry not about me. I will be fine."

She smiled. "I love you." And her eyes drifted close, waiting for him to kiss her.

After a gentle kiss they parted and with a wave Mary watched him disappear into the woods. She sighed and sat on the castle's broken stone wall, already missing Michael.

He made such a difference in her life or perhaps it was love that made the difference. She had often wondered if she would ever find love, but then how could she not. Her parents had made certain to lavish her with love. At an early age she understood that love was unselfish, love was patient, love was security, and love was . . .

A tear trickled from the corner of her eye. And love was forever, even if that person was no longer with you.

Mary wiped at the tear with determination. She had lost her parents; she refused to lose Michael. Her life had been in the hands of others since her parents death, and it was time she took charge and made her own decisions.

Michael would be gone a week or more and his absence would give her time to ponder her options. But what were her options?

Run or face Decimus.

Neither was the answer she was looking for.

Could she find something in between?

A sharp crack of a branch caught her attention, and she immediately sought the safety of the castle. She hid behind a section of the crumbled wall and watched to see who approached.

A man stepped out of the woods, looked around, and then walked toward the castle. He was huge, tall as a tree, with the girth of a tree trunk and flaming red hair and a beard to match. His sword was strapped to his back and a sheathed dirk fastened to his belt. He wore a pale yellow linen shirt beneath his blue, red, and yellow plaid, and he carried himself with a confidence born of strength. And while he was not a handsome man, there was something about his features that appealed to the eye.

He stopped before reaching the castle door and looked about, then announced his arrival. "I am Roarke; Michael sent me."

Mary stepped into sight with a smile. "Welcome, Roarke, it is pleased that I am to have your company."

His grin was wide. "And pleased I am to be here, though tell me you can cook and I will be more pleased."

Mary laughed. "My food has been known to bring smiles."

"Then I am a happy man, Mary."

He stepped forward as Mary approached him and offered his hand. She took it, and the strength of his handshake caused her eyes to widen.

"You are an army of one."

"Aye, so you need not worry over your safety."

"I have been in good hands," she said. "And I remain so."

"Good, now tell me if there is anything you need of me before I hunt for our midday meal."

"Nothing at the moment, though the wood for the cook fire is growing low."

"I will see to that when I am done hunting." He turned, then paused and looked back at her. "Michael told me to remind you that you are not to go to the stream alone."

"He has told me that many times."

"Your near capture frightened him, and I have never known Michael to be frightened."

Mary watched the large man walk off and a soft smile slowly surfaced. She was part of Michael's heart and he a part of hers. Their hearts were one and must remain so. They could not survive without each other.

She looked to the heavens.

I need a miracle. Help me.

Mary made a fine stew from the rabbits Roarke snared. He did not stop praising her food, and promised to keep her well stocked with fresh game so that she could work her magic with food.

She, however, intended to work her magic on discovering what she could about Michael. She learned soon enough that Roarke liked to talk. The subject did not matter; he talked on anything and found interest in it.

"How long have you known Michael?" she asked.

"Some time."

"Did he rescue you?"

His grin prompted her to redefine her question.

"Did you rescue him?"

He shrugged, giving her no definitive response.

"He has a good heart."

Roarke nodded and his sudden silence warned her he would not be forthcoming. He protected Michael and she could not fault him for that, but she wanted to know about the man she loved and she was certain Roarke could provide insight.

Mary decided that being blunt might make a difference. "I love Michael."

Roarke misunderstood. "Everyone Michael helps loves him."

"I am sure they do, but *I love him*," she clarified.

Roarke was about to take a bite of a piece of meat but stopped to stare at her.

"I want to know about Michael," she insisted.

He dropped the piece of meat to his plate and shook his head. "I will not betray Michael's trust."

"I do not ask that of you." She pushed her plate aside, her food barely touched, and leaned her arms on the table. "I want to know the man behind the mask."

"You are serious."

"Yes."

"It cannot be." Roarke wiped his hands on a cloth. "You and Michael can never be."

"You repeat his words, but I pray that it can be."

"He speaks the truth and I am sorry to say you waste your time."

"Michael loves me," she said with confidence.

"Then I feel sorry for my friend for he knows the truth of the situation."

"Is he not allowed to love?" Mary heard her own frustration.

"I would want nothing more than to see Michael happy. But he chose a path to follow, a difficult path, and he knows the price of his decision."

"He can change his path."

Roarke sat back in his chair, crossing his arms over

his chest. "He would not do that. He made a vow and he is an honorable man."

Sadness gripped her heart. Was there not even a small chance for them?

"I wish I could explain, for I see it causes you pain, but it is not for me to tell you," Roarke said with sympathy. "It is Michael you must speak with."

"Can you tell me nothing?" She sounded as though she begged like an animal for a small scrap of food, for anything that would feed her need. Her weakness annoyed her but she understood it came from deep inside, where feelings nestled and grew.

Roarke took pity on her and leaned forward, bracing his arms on the table and looking ready to tell her a tale.

She waited with hope in her heart.

"Michael knows the ills of the suffering for he suffered greatly himself."

"He was tortured?"

"Ask me no questions, Mary. Listen and take what little I can offer you."

She quickly nodded, impatient for him to continue.

"His own suffering brought with it a vow of vengeance, a vow that would serve the greater good. He committed himself to that vow; it is his life."

"But what of love? Is he not entitled to love?"

"He surrendered his life when he took that vow."

"You are telling me that I cannot be selfish and expect him to forsake his vow for our love."

"Aye," he admitted. "I want you aware of the pain your love may cause the both of you."

"But—"

"Wait, let me finish. I have watched Michael endlessly give with no thought to himself. And I, as his friend, know that he cannot go on like this forever. It is a lonely, isolated existence . . ." He paused a moment and, almost in a whisper, as though he were not sure if he should voice his thoughts, said, "I sometimes think he punishes himself over and over—"

"For his sister's death."

"And his mother's."

"His mother?"

Roarke shook his head. "This is why it is better I say nothing. Once I start talking I do not stop."

"But he told me of his sister," she reminded him.

"If he had told you the whole story then he would have told you about his mother. They are the reason he became the Dark One."

"I want to love him, help him, free him."

"I wish that were possible," Roarke said sadly, "but Michael must free himself."

"Sometimes we need help."

"Trust me, Mary, there is nothing you can do to help him."

"I do not believe that."

"You do not want to believe that," Roarke said. "And I admire you for your courage, but it will do you little good against the strength of the Dark One."

"I have survived much suffering myself, and I would not have done so if it were not for my parents. They taught me courage and they taught me strength, and that both could not be gained without love."

"I know of your father and his beliefs. He was respected and admired by many, and his teachings continue to live on."

"I am glad to hear that," Mary said. "And I would not be my father's daughter if I did not fight for my own beliefs. And I believe that Michael and I will one day share a life and love."

"I would like to believe the same," Roarke said. "But believe me when I say you do not know the reality of what you face."

"Decimus?"

"Rest assured, he will stand in your way."

"Then I will have to move him out of my way."

"It is said he is pure evil," Roarke said as though warning her.

"Do you not believe that love can conquer evil?"

"I would like to think it were possible, but I have seen Decimus's wrath and what is left in its wake." He shook his head. "I do not know if love is strong enough to deal with such terror."

"Do you know much about Decimus?"

"Want to know your enemy?"

"How can a warrior enter battle and expect victory with no knowledge of his enemy? I have been protected since I was young and it has done me little good. I must know this man who chases after me if I am ever to be free."

"The Dark One will make certain you get to freedom."

"The Dark One," she repeated with a sad smile. "Not Michael?"

"You must leave Michael behind to do what he must."

She shook her head. "I cannot do that. I will not do that."

"There is nothing you can do for Michael."

"I believe there is. Will you tell me about Decimus?'

"I do not see what good it will do."

"Then you have nothing to lose by telling me what you know of the man."

"You are stubborn."

"Nay, I know what I must do to free not only myself but Michael."

"How will you, a woman with no battle skills, free Michael?"

Mary shook her head. "I do not know. I only know I must try."

Chapter 14

"Decimus approaches the village."

Magnus, earl of Dunhurnal crossed his arms over his broad chest. "Make certain the villagers see our force of strength so that they feel protected. I want every warrior's presence known."

The warrior gave a quick nod and left to do his lord's bidding.

"What does Decimus want with us?" Reena asked as she walked up to stand beside her husband on the keep's steps. Her constant companion, Horace, a large hound, followed behind her.

"Go in the castle. Your presence is not needed here."

She tilted her head to look up at the infamous Legend, a feared warrior whose exploits were well known throughout the Celtic lands. She sent him a smile to remind him that issuing orders did not work well with her. She would not run and hide while danger was about to descend on the village.

He shook his head. "I should know better." Magnus

took her chin between his fingers and rubbed at a smudge. "If you intend to make an impression, which you always do, it would be best not to make it with ink on your chin."

Reena waited patiently while he rid her of the mark and felt her heart swell with love. That he was the infamous Legend did not matter to her, that he was a handsome man whose features could steal women's hearts, that he was a strong and courageous warrior were all unimportant compared to the fact that he loved her, Reena, a simple mapmaker.

"I love you."

He kissed her. "And I love you more than you know."

She laughed. "I know how much you love me." She lowered her voice. "You show me every night."

He spoke in a whisper. "And if the devil were not at my gate, I would show you how much I love you right now."

She took hold of his arm, her smile fading. "What could Decimus want with us?"

He pushed a lose strand of her long black hair behind her ear and met her inquisitive blue eyes. "We will find out soon. Remember Decimus is a powerful man. He has the power of the Church and the king behind him and even they fear him. Tread lightly in his presence and hold your tongue."

She nodded. "I will do as you say."

Thomas approached, a giant of a man in height and width, a good friend to Magnus and husband to Reena's best friend, Brigid.

Villagers drifted up behind him, gathering in a crowd, seeking the strength and protection of their lord.

Thomas joined Magnus on the step below him. "They are frightened and there is gossip that even the

Legend may not be able to protect them from Decimus. Do you know why he comes here?"

"I have a thought and it concerns *me,* no other."

Reena was quick to object. "What concerns you concerns us all."

"She is right," Thomas agreed. "We stand together."

"This might be one time we have no choice but to stand apart."

Thomas and Reena had no chance to respond. The crowd had swelled to include nearly everyone in the village; her friend Brigid was sneaking up behind her husband and sending Reena a fearful look.

Reena understood her friend's apprehension. It was a day such as this when a new lord rode into their village and killed Brigid's first husband. The suffering was behind her now thanks to Thomas, but she imagined Brigid worried that sorrow would befall the village once again.

Whispers rushed like a sharp wind through the gathered crowd and turned to a sudden silence when Decimus and his men were spotted. They were in the distance, but fear that their words could reach his ears made everyone hold their tongues.

Horace growled, standing at full alert, and Reena ordered him to sit and be still. He sat, but a low growl continued deep in his throat.

Decimus approached on a fine black steed, the horse dressed in silk finery. A purple face mask and a gold blanket with two large purple crosses on either side were draped over the animal and pronounced the rider royalty of the Church.

Many villagers kneeled as the horse passed by them, not daring to gaze upon the man who rode him.

Decimus stopped in front of the steps of the keep,

dismounted, and tossed his reins to a man that rushed to his side. He remained where he was, glancing around at the crowd. His dark eyes settled on the group waiting on the steps.

Reena found herself unable to take her eyes off him. If the devil had climbed out of hell, he would surely look like this man. Black hair the color of a starless night sky was drawn tightly back away from his face. His eyes were just as dark and could very well resemble the recesses of hell itself. His skin looked weathered by the sun yet his face held not a line or wrinkle and no expression marred his darkly disturbing features. And yet once your gaze rested on him, it was hard to pull away. It was said that Decimus could see your soul, and if it were not pure you would suffer his wrath.

He was tall and slimmer than Magnus and looked fit in form. He was dressed in fine silks and linens of black and purple and he wore two rings, one a blood-red garnet and the other a dazzling blue sapphire.

He turned a slow gaze on the surrounding crowd and they bowed their heads, with some falling to their knees, their hands clasped in prayer. He nodded, pleased by their supplication, then advanced up the steps with a confident gait.

Decimus stopped in front of Magnus, ignoring those around him.

"We have matters to discuss."

"May I offer you food and drink first?" Magnus asked in an attempt to be civil to the devil.

"Have it served in your private solar; this matter is between you and I."

Decimus bumped Magnus's shoulder as he pushed past him and entered the keep.

Magnus looked to Thomas whose face grew red

with anger over the insult to his lord. "You heard him. It is between him and me. Keep the warriors alert and make certain Decimus's men are confined to one area."

Reena caught her husband's arm, preventing him from entering the keep. "Give him what he wants and send him on his way; he is evil."

"I will."

A servant directed Decimus to the solar, hastily left a platter of food on the table, then scurried out. Once outside the room, the young lass crossed herself and whispered a series of prayers as she hurried down the steps.

Magnus entered a few moments later, filled two goblets with wine, and handed one to Decimus. He then gestured for him to sit in one of the two chairs near the fireplace.

"This matter can be settled without difficulty or suffering; it is up to you."

"I have done nothing that should bring me difficulty or cause me suffering," Magnus said confidently.

"Are you certain of that?"

Magnus drank his wine, purposely delaying his reply to demonstrate to Decimus that he did not fear him. "Quite certain."

"What of Mary?"

"Mary?" Magnus inquired.

"Do not think me a fool, Magnus. You know of whom I speak. I have learned that you have protected her these many years, but no more. You will surrender Mary to me or you and that quick-witted wife of yours will suffer."

Magnus stared at him.

"You wonder how I know about your wife's sharp

wit. There is not much I do not know. I have eyes and ears everywhere."

"Yet you cannot find Mary."

The only indication that Magnus's remark angered Decimus was a slight flaring of his nostrils. "But I have found her. You have her and *you* will *give* her to me."

Magnus kept a tight rein on the anger that was slowly rising in him. He detested being backed into a corner, yet how could he honor his vow to Mary's parents to protect her and protect his wife at the same time?

"I will be generous and allow you a week to surrender Mary to me," Decimus informed him.

"And if I do not?"

Decimus shrugged as if it made no difference. "Then I will interrogate your wife. I hear she is adept at mapping and drawing." He stared at the wine in his goblet. "I wonder where her skills originated?" His dark eyes shifted to Magnus. "And what type of drawings does she do? There is much I can question her about, and if I don't like her answer—" Another shrug. "I will work with her until I receive an acceptable one."

Magnus remained silent, though his hand clenched at his side.

Decimus leaned forward in his chair. "You would love to kill me right now, would you not, Magnus?"

Magnus wanted to lunge at the man and choke him for threatening his wife's life.

Decimus leaned back in his chair, not a smile or snicker on his face, but with a subtle shift of his body that let Magnus know his word was law even in Magnus's own keep. And there was absolutely nothing Magnus could do about it.

"I almost had her, you know," Decimus said quite irritated. "She was safely locked away in one of my dungeons when suddenly she disappeared. Would you have any notion how she may have made her escape?"

It was Magnus's turn to shrug and he forced himself to take a swallow of wine, hoping the liquid would prevent his venomous thoughts from reaching his lips.

"Logic tells me that she could not have made an escape on her own. She had given my men quite a chase, and when the idiots finally caught her they mistakenly made her suffer. Of course they suffered for their stupidity. *I* and *I alone* pronounce judgment and punish wicked souls."

The man's arrogance astonished Magnus. He actually believed that he was a righteous man doing God's work.

Decimus leaned an elbow on the thick arm of the wooden chair and rubbed his chin. "How do you think Mary escaped?"

Magnus waited as if giving his question thought, then shook his head. "I do not know."

Decimus lowered his hand. "I think you do. I think *you* sent someone to rescue Mary."

Magnus refused to refute his accusation, after all it was true and they both knew it. He would not give him the satisfaction of denying it. His silence would speak for him.

"You were wise in sending someone rather than attempting the rescue yourself, but then I never thought you a foolish man. That is why I know you will not be foolish now. You will surrender Mary to me. You really have no choice. It is either her or your wife, then your friends until there is no one left but you."

Magnus took another sip of wine to prevent his rage from spewing forth.

Decimus stood suddenly. "I did not know that the

Dark One was an acquaintance of yours." He walked to the table and refilled his wine goblet.

Magnus had already surmised that Decimus knew who helped Mary escape. The man obviously enjoyed playing games with his captive, hoping he would make an error and provide him with further evidence of guilt.

"You choose silence, another wise move." Decimus returned to his chair. "Most people talk out of fear, hoping to convince me of their innocence until their foolish tongues help pronounce them guilty. But as I remarked before, you are not foolish, Magnus."

Magnus waited for Decimus to continue. He obviously had more to say or this conversation would have ended by now. What else did Decimus expect from him?

"The Dark One is a thorn in my side that I will one day extract with pleasure. He will suffer more than he ever thought possible."

Magnus had received word of Mary's successful rescue and her safety, and he knew that the Dark One would be in touch with him soon so that a decision could be made about her future. That decision had just turned more serious than Magnus ever imagined.

"He eludes me at every turn, which means he must possess powers far beyond the ordinary. And if that is so then you know what that means, do you not?"

Magnus shrugged.

"The man is obviously a cohort of the devil."

He certainly had that one scrambled. If anyone was a cohort of the devil it was Decimus, and the Dark One the avenging angel here to destroy him.

"The devil always shows himself, you know, and that is when it is easy to snare him. The Dark One will one day be mine and I will torture the devil out of him, purifying his soul and setting him free."

Magnus kept silent. He would never capture the Dark One, and if Decimus were not careful it would be the Dark One who sent his soul where it belonged— straight to hell.

"Enough of the Dark One," Decimus said. "It is Mary that matters at the moment." He stood. "One week, Magnus. You have one week to give her to me."

"I may need more time." He knew not where the Dark One had taken Mary, and, besides, he wanted time to see if there was another way to settle this problem.

"One week," Decimus said and walked to the door. "I know it is not much time for you to make a choice, but then you have no choice."

"What do you intend to do with her?"

Decimus stopped and turned. "I intend to save her soul and return her to God's good graces."

"By torture and death?" Magnus was disgusted with the thought of Mary suffering.

"Nay, by making her my wife."

Chapter 15

Magnus stared at the closed door. Surely Decimus was insane to think that he would surrender Mary to wed the evil likes of him. He could not condemn an innocent young woman to a life of such cruelty. But what choices did he have?

Magnus heard the creak of the door and watched as it opened slowly. He was relieved to see his wife peek her head in. He had no desire to speak with Decimus again so soon. The man sparked his temper with one arrogant glance.

Reena quickly shut the door and hurried to her husband's side. He opened his arms and greeted her with a hug.

"Something is wrong," she said and felt his reluctance to release her.

"Decimus wants Mary as his wife." He shook his head and dropped down into the chair near the fireplace.

Reena sat on the footstool beside him, her hand reaching for his.

He took tight hold of her hand. "I know not what to do. He insists I surrender Mary to him in a week's time. He will accept no excuses."

"Or he will inflict his evil upon us?"

Magnus could not bring himself to tell his wife who Decimus would start with. The mere thought set his blood on fire, and he gritted his teeth to keep from swearing.

Reena understood his distress. "He threatened my safety, did he not?"

"You are too perceptive for your own good."

"It is simple logic. Who else would he threaten that would stir you to such anger or force you to consider complying."

He moved his hand to cup her face. "I will let no harm come to you."

"I never doubted you would. But what of Mary? She cannot be condemned to suffer such a hideous fate."

"I agree, though at the moment I have no idea of how to prevent it. And I have no idea of Mary's where-abouts. The last message I received from the Dark One was that Mary was safe and in his care. I have no way of contacting him."

Reena attempted to ease his concern. "The Dark One seems to know when he is needed. I am sure he will contact you soon."

"I pray your words are true, for at the moment I can see no alternative to this problem."

"We will find a solution together. There must be something we can do."

"I would like to think there are possibilities," Magnus said, his fingers interlocking with hers. "But it seems rather simple. I surrender Mary or you suffer, and when he is done with you he will continue his sadistic tactics on others. I cannot allow that; I protect what is mine. My people expect no less of me, and *I* expect no less of me."

"And how will you deal with your honor, for I know it weighs heavy on your mind," Reena said. "You gave your word to her parents that you would keep Mary safe and you are a man of your word."

"I do not know."

A knock on the door interrupted them and Magnus bid the intruder to enter.

It was Thomas, his wife Brigid clinging tightly to his arm.

"Decimus has ordered his men to make camp at the edge of the village, and he has made certain to let all know that he will be here for a week or more," Thomas informed him.

"Everyone is frightened," Brigid said with a shiver. "They fear his wrath and punishment."

"Have you ordered all to stay clear of him and his men?" Magnus asked.

"Aye," Thomas said, "though I do not think it was necessary. There is not a soul who would dare go near him or even dare look his way."

"We need to talk, Thomas," Magnus said and glanced at his wife.

Reena stood, kissed his cheek, and walked to Brigid. "Come, we will see what needs attention."

"Evil cannot be trusted," Brigid said.

"I agree," Magnus said. "But rest assured that you have nothing to fear from Decimus."

Usually warriors filled the great hall for the evening meals but not this night. This night saw only a handful of the Legend's men gathering for the meal. All others stood guard over the village, their presence a show of force to Decimus's men and a show of strength to the villagers.

Decimus's men, of which there were few, ate hearty and thought little of strength and force. It was obvious they knew that their leader held more strength than all of Magnus's warriors. They were under Decimus's protection, and Decimus was protected by the king and the Church. There were no others more powerful.

"Tomorrow I wish to inspect your dungeons," Decimus said, reaching for his goblet of wine. "In case I have use for them."

Magnus knew he baited him, but he would not be hooked. "Do as you will, though my dungeons are not in use."

Decimus turned dark glaring eyes on Magnus. "I heard a different tale. I heard that you took the earl of Culberry's life in your dungeon." He looked past Magnus to Reena. "Culberry tortured you did he not?"

Reena sat straight and placed a hand over her husband's arm. "He tried but my husband rescued me."

"Really? I heard it was the dog who rescued you." Decimus threw Horace a scrap of meat.

Horace remained sitting beside Reena. He made no move to take the meat.

"A wise and obedient animal. I may have use for him."

"Horace is mine and will remain so," Reena said in a tone that had everyone at the table staring at her.

Decimus leaned his arms on the table and kept his dark eyes on her. "Foolish or brave; I cannot decide which one you are."

"I have been known to be both."

Decimus laughed and tension eased. "You speak with honesty."

"To a fault at times, so I have been told," Reena said.

"There is no fault in honesty." Decimus turned to Magnus. "Your husband can learn a lesson from you."

Reena was quick to defend. "My husband is a good, honest man."

"Not when he harbors a heretic."

Reena's skin prickled from the seething anger that filled Decimus's voice.

Magnus spoke up. "You have judged and condemned this woman without speaking with her."

"She was raised by heretics, what would you expect?"

"Fairness."

"Which I will offer her," Decimus said.

"Marriage is fairness?"

"I give her a chance to renounce her evil ways and live a good, clean, holy life. She has the opportunity to marry a man who will deliver her from sin and lead her on a righteous path." Decimus pounded the table with his fist. "You would be wise to pay heed to my words or I may think that *you* need a lesson in righteousness."

Magnus gripped the arm of his chair and held his tongue. He could not defend his own opinions without causing a threat to the safety of those he loved.

Decimus calmed though his warning remained strong. "It would do you well to think on how my generosity would benefit Mary."

"I will not see Mary harmed," Magnus affirmed.

"Good, then we want the same," Decimus said. "She will have a good life with me. I will teach her obedience and she will be a dutiful wife and serve me well."

Decimus stood abruptly and his men followed suit.

"I will meet you at sunrise to inspect your dungeons."

Without a word of gratitude for the meal or a kind good-night, Decimus pointed at his men. They turned and left the great hall, while he himself climbed the stairs to the bedchamber prepared for him.

"They obey like dogs to a master," Thomas said.

"Like dogs fearful of their master," Reena corrected, scratching Horace behind the ear.

"Decimus wields hefty power," Magnus reminded them. "There is good reason to fear him."

"It seems, then, that this woman has no chance of help," Brigid said, sadly. "Decimus has sealed her fate."

The two couples bid each other good night, Thomas and Brigid returning to their cottage and Magnus and Reena retiring to their bedchamber.

Reena sat on the edge of the bed. "I feel helpless just like I did when I thought there was no hope for my starving village."

Magnus sat beside her, taking her hand in his. "But you found a solution."

She smiled and rested her head on his shoulder. "I found you."

He kissed her hand. "And glad I am that you did."

Reena lifted her head to look at her husband; her blue eyes filled with sadness. "Mary has no chance of a rescue, does she?"

"Her rescue would mean the lives of many."

"I cannot bear to think she will suffer to save us."

"I have a week before she must be turned over to Decimus," Magnus said.

"You do not sound hopeful." Reena grasped his hand in her hands. "This must be so very difficult for you."

Magnus rested his forehead on hers and closed his eyes. "Her parents have been constantly in my thoughts since I have received this news. I did not want their suffering to be for naught. I gave my word to them that I would see their daughter kept safe, and they trusted my word; they trusted me."

Reena took his face in her hands and his eyes drifted open to look at her. "Good lord, Ree, I love you so much. I could not bear to see you suffer, and I would rather die than lose you."

"I would not want to live without you," Reena said and kissed him.

Magnus wrapped his arms around her and they fell back upon the bed; their kisses grew heated. But Reena pulled away, their breathing heavy, their hearts beating wildly.

"I feel guilty loving you, lying here in your arms, feeling your touch, your warmth. And I grow sad and angry to think Mary will never know such a love."

Magnus gripped her arm. "I know you well, Ree, do not be foolish and think you can outsmart Decimus. He is cunning, shrewd, and more powerful than the king himself."

"Then does Brigid's words ring true? Has Decimus sealed Mary's fate?"

"I have always entered a battle with one thought in mind—victory, that has not changed." He rubbed her arm where his fingers had dug into her flesh. "I do not know what I will do, though I do know you will not be harmed."

"We must put our heads together to solve this problem."

Magnus tapped her head. "You will keep your pretty head out of this."

"I fear I cannot give you my word on that."

With a swift roll Magnus was on top of her, pinning her arms to the bed. "You are a stubborn woman."

She laughed. "This is not something you just learned."

"Ree so help me—"

"That is exactly what I plan to do, help you."

He shook his head.

"I give you my word, I will be careful."

"You think to appease me."

"I do not want you to worry," she said. "And I wish to be truthful."

"Promise me you will not put yourself in harm's way," Magnus said, reluctant to capitulate.

"I am stubborn, not foolish."

"That could be debated. Now, promise me."

She wiggled beneath him. "If you release my arms I will promise you and seal it with a kiss."

"Are you trying to seduce me?"

"Am I succeeding?"

Magnus laughed, released her, and rolled over taking her with him so that she was now on top of him.

"I am all yours."

"I love it when you surrender to me." She kissed him quick.

"I did not surrender."

"You did." Her kiss turned slow.

"I never surrender."

"Then you would do well to prepare for defeat," she laughed.

Hours later Magnus left his sleeping wife with a smile on his face. He went to his solar so as not to disturb her. Sleep eluded him, his thoughts on Mary and his promise to her parents.

"What troubles you, my friend?"

Magnus jumped out of his chair and turned to see the Dark One walk out of the shadows.

"Your presence is a most welcome relief," Magnus said, catching himself before he reached out to greet him with a handshake. No one ever touched the Dark One.

"I imagined it would be when I saw who visited with you." He slipped back toward the shadows, movement the only indication that someone was present.

"I did not anticipate Decimus's arrival."

"No one ever does."

"Tell me of Mary," Magnus said, concerned for her safety more so now than ever before.

"She is safe and I intend to see that she remains so. *No one* will hurt her; I will not allow it."

Magnus detected a difference in his tone. He was adamant about seeing to Mary's safety as though he was personally responsible for her. In the short time he had come to know the Dark One, Magnus realized that he never displayed his emotions. He was like a true warrior who rode into battle with determination and indifference to all but victory. Now, however, he sounded as though Mary came before all. What had happened?

Had Mary penetrated this warrior's shield? She had a kind heart, a gentle manner, a soothing voice, and she took pleasure in life, enjoying every precious moment.

When Magnus had visited her on occasion he could not understand how she found such pleasure in all she did. No matter the task at hand, she approached it with a smile or a song and suffered no complaints. He wondered if her light heart had been made heavy with all she had gone through recently.

"I want the same for her," Magnus said.

"Good, then it is imperative that I remove her from the area at once. With Decimus close by I'm concerned that he will discover our whereabouts. I swear he has the nose of a bloodhound."

"He knows I sent you after her."

"I thought as much. What does he demand?"

"Mary's surrender," Magnus said.

"Obviously, but what is it he really demands?"

"He wants Mary as his wife," Magnus said, cringing at his own words.

"His wife?" the Dark One asked in disbelief. "He intends to wed a woman he claims is a heretic?"

"He intends to rid her of her evil ways and turn her into an obedient wife, showing all how righteousness can vanquish evil."

"He is mad."

"And a madman is not easy to deal with," Magnus reminded.

"He has threatened you?" the Dark One asked. "But of course he has. How else would he expect you to surrender Mary?"

"He has given me a week's time."

"Do I hear defeat in your voice?"

"Do I hear anger in yours?"

"Mary has suffered enough and asks for little. She bears her burden with strength, courage, and humility. She deserves to be free of *Decimus*, not wed him." The Dark One spit the name from his lips.

"I do not argue, but I do not know how to make this happen without my wife and my friends suffering."

"So Mary is to suffer for all?"

"I want no one to suffer," Magnus said forcefully.

"Decimus has placed us in a maze and expects us to

stumble about in confusion, unable to find our way out. But there is always a way out."

"Then I suggest we find it fast."

"I will be in touch," the Dark One said and then was swallowed by the shadows in the corner.

Chapter 16

The days sped by thanks to Roarke's company. He always had a tale to tell or an interest to share, and Mary, having finally regained her voice, was ready to converse about anything.

She did, however, miss Michael more than she had expected. It had been almost a week since he had taken his leave, and she had watched the edge of the woods every day, hoping to see the dark shadow emerge into the light.

"He should return any day now," Roarke said, busy cleaning his sword.

"I hope he does; I miss him."

"I have come to realize this past week how much you care for the Dark One."

"You doubted my love for him?" she asked with a smile and shook her head. "I have never doubted. My love for him is bold and strong and *forever*." She threw her arms to the heavens as if inviting their blessings.

"Bold and strong is what you will need to deal with what you will face."

"You have continued to warn me of my feelings for him. I think you know something that you do not share with me."

He shrugged. "I know the Dark One's life is difficult, and love, on its own, may not be strong enough to overcome the obstacles you will meet."

"I would like to believe that love is strong enough to perform miracles."

Roarke stopped his work on the sword. "I suggest then that you hold firm to your belief, for you will need it."

A chill raced through Mary and the old seer's words echoed in her mind.

You will be the demise of Decimus.

She walked off toward the woods, her mind burdened with thoughts. A shout from Roarke reminded her not to go far. She acknowledged him with a wave and kept to the edge of the woods.

She had thought on her problem while Michael had been gone and had realized there was no easy solution. She was a hunted woman and that would not change, but then Michael was also a hunted man. What kind of life would there be for them? But what kind of life would there be without him?

She also realized the importance of Michael's work. He would not simply walk away from so many tortured souls. He had made a vow and it seemed unfair to ask him to forsake it for her love.

With so many obstacles in their way, how then could she possibly believe they had a future together? How did she conquer evil so that she and Michael could be free?

Love will be your only weapon.

Her father's warning was just as clear now in her head as it had been in her dream. How love could be a formidable weapon she did not know, but she would remember and hopefully strike with it when the time was right.

Mary enjoyed a good meal and a good conversation with Roarke that evening. They discussed many things but for some reason shied away from any talk of the Dark One. Mary sensed something was on his mind concerning Michael, and though she wished to question him about it she decided he would tell her in good time.

He did.

Just when Mary bid him good night, Roarke spoke up.

"I will be gone when you wake in the morning."

"I will miss your company," she said with sincerity and a twinge of joy, for his departure surely heralded Michael's return.

"And I yours, but I know you miss Michael very much and will be happy with his return."

She grew excited. "Will he arrive with your departure?"

"Within a short time of my leaving he will arrive. He would not feel it safe for you to be alone for too long."

"How do you know of his return?"

"Do not ask me what I cannot answer," Roarke urged.

"Michael remains cloaked in darkness in more ways than one."

"You would do wise to remember that, Mary."

"I find ignorance a foolish mask," she said.

"Sometimes masks are necessary; they protect."

"Who?"

"The innocent."

* * *

Mary had difficulty sleeping. She would have thought anticipation of Michael's return would rob her of sleep, but it was Roarke's last remark about the innocent that had her thinking most of the night.

Who did he mean?

The innocent victims of Decimus's persecution or did he refer to Michael's innocence? And if so, what innocence did he speak of? She sensed there was more to Roarke's warning than she understood, a clue of sorts, possibly to his identity.

She turned and tossed, her mind refusing to let go of her chaotic thoughts, and it was near to sunrise when, finally exhausted, she drifted off to sleep.

Waking to the smell of freshly cooked fish, she yawned, stretched and, grinned wide.

Michael will be home today.

Home?

Home, Mary realized, was where Michael and she were together. It did not matter if a sound roof covered their heads or the land beneath their feet belonged to them. What mattered was that they were with each other, sharing their life, their love.

Mary stretched herself fully awake and after combing her hair and plaiting it, she hurried to join Roarke for breakfast. She stopped abruptly when she discovered she was alone. Roarke was nowhere to be found and she understood that this simple breakfast was his way of saying goodbye.

She was saddened by his departure. She had wished to thank him for all he had done for her. He had listened endlessly to her speak of her love for Michael and did not discourage her, though he urged caution. She hoped their paths would cross again.

She ate her breakfast, her glance constantly drifting to the woods, hoping to see him emerge. She ached for Michael's return; actually she ached for his arms, his touch, his kiss.

She was beginning to understand the ramifications of love. It consumed the senses and the mind. Nothing else seemed to matter; thoughts of the person lingered on the mind and the need to be with that person overwhelmed.

That was how she presently felt, *overwhelmed* with the need to see Michael again, to know he was well, safe, and that he missed her as much as she missed him.

Childish thoughts?

Selfish thoughts?

Or thoughts of love?

She laughed at her own musings and if he did not return soon, she would probably drive herself mad by day's end.

"What is it you find humorous?"

Mary jumped from her seat, startled by the familiar voice behind her. She turned with a brilliant smile.

"Michael!" She flung herself at the dark-robed figure, holding on to him as if she never intended to let him go ever again.

He clung to her just as tenaciously.

"I have missed you so very much," she said and laid her head on his chest, rubbing her cheek against the coarse material of his robe, wishing the shroud did not separate them.

"And I you, though I carried your sweet voice in my mind and whenever I missed you I heard you in my head and felt you close to me."

"Pleased I am to be there for you." She placed a hand to his heart. "I will always be there for you, Michael."

Holding her, he said, "I too, Mary, I will always be there for you. You must remember that."

She closed her eyes, smiled wide, and raised her head, offering her lips to him.

He took them, eager to taste her once again. He had missed her so very much. There had not been a time he had not thought about her; she had been forever on his mind and he liked the way she lingered there. He did not feel alone; he felt part of her and it felt good.

He kissed her slowly and with purpose, the purpose being to love her with all his heart. He took his time, wanting their kiss to go on and on, wanting this close, intimate connection with her, wanting her with him forever.

The thought jolted his senses and he remembered the news he was to deliver—but not just yet. He did not want to wipe the smile from her face, or the joy from her eyes.

He stepped away, though he took hold of her hand. "You look well and happy."

"I am happy now that you have returned."

"Roarke was good company?" he asked.

"Aye, that he was. He entertained me with many good stories and he loved to eat, supplying us with more than ample food." She patted her stomach. "I think I have added to my weight considerably."

Michael held out her arm and pretended to inspect her. "You look the same. Nay," he said with a shake of his head. "You look more beautiful than I remember."

She did. She seemed somehow to have blossomed in his absence. Her face was full and touched by the sun. No worry lines marred her brow or crinkled at the corners of her eyes. Her lips were rosy, her blue eyes brimming with joy, and her long blond hair was neatly plaited and shined like a summer's sun.

"It is love that gives me such beauty."

He wanted to warn her not to love him, that it was a mistake she would surely regret, and yet his heart and soul screamed for her to love him and not give up on them.

"Your love," she said and tapped his chest. "It is strong in my heart. No one can touch it, no one can harm it, no one can take it away from me."

With her back to his chest and his masked face next to her cheek, he swung her around in his arms. "Promise me that. Promise me that my love will forever remain in your safekeeping."

"I promise," she said without hesitation.

He hugged her tightly to him. "Your promise means much to me."

"And will you promise me the same? Will you keep my love safe in your heart?"

"Forever and beyond time your love will rest safely in my heart, my mind, and my soul."

"I expected nothing less from you." She wiggled out of his arms and turned, holding on to his hands. "Tell me what you have learned from Magnus. I am eager to know where we go from here."

Her reference to *we* did not escape his attention. She expected them to continue on from here, and he had wished the same, though he knew it was nothing more than a futile dream.

"I will not lose you," she said, taking his prolonged silence as ominous.

"Mary," he said slowly and softly. He attempted to pull her to him but she yanked her hands free and stepped away from him.

"You do not have good news for me."

"I have news that I thought not to deliver."

"It is not what you wish?" she asked cautiously.

He heard hope in her voice and it tore at his heart. "It is not what I wish, and I will do all I can to see that it never comes to pass."

A shiver ran through her, leaving her with a sense of dread. "Tell me and be done with it."

He clasped his hands in front of him, holding back his anger over what he must tell her.

She waited anxiously, her own hands grasping at the sides of her skirt as though grasping for sanity itself. She sensed she would not at all like what she was about to hear.

"Magnus had news from Decimus."

She nodded, her stomach tightening and her heart pounding.

"Decimus demands you wed him."

Chapter 17

Mary stumbled backward as though Michael had struck her. He reached out to steady her but she shook her head and righted herself.

"Wed me?" She repeated his words to make certain she had heard him correctly.

"Aye."

"But why?" It made no sense to her.

"He wishes to wed you to show how a sinner can be made righteous. He intends to make you into a dutiful wife who obeys without question."

"Who does he threaten to guarantee my surrender?"

"Magnus's wife Reena to start with."

"He knows I would not let another suffer." Mary sighed. "My father taught me that for every action there is a cause that sets things into motion and creates consequences, good or bad." She looked to Michael. "There is more to this plan than he tells."

"Magnus and I also considered this to be a trick to force you to surrender—"

"And you reached the conclusion that Decimus is truthful in his evil," she finished with a sad smile. "By becoming his obedient wife I surrender everything, my freedom, my will, my very life. My complete surrender demonstrates his complete power."

She wondered . . . complete power over whom?— for she herself was insignificant in his quest.

"We must leave by tomorrow if we are to arrive at the prescribed time," Michael said.

"Or Decimus will begin his torture of the innocent. And knowing Magnus he would never allow those he loved to suffer. And to kill Decimus would bring on the wrath of the king and the Church. Decimus has planned well."

"You need not make a choice at this very moment."

Her sad smile turned sadder. "The choice was made when Decimus delivered his ultimatum."

"I swore to protect you."

"And you have."

Michael, standing near the hearth, pounded the mantel; the sound of worn wood cracking filled the momentary silence. "This is a life sentence for you. He will be your husband with all husbandly right. You will submit to his every need, his every whim. You will *never* be able to leave him."

"Complete surrender is what he is looking for."

"There must be something that can be done."

Desperation edged his harsh voice and filled Mary with sadness. Decimus had complete control of the situation. There was nothing they could do but submit to his demands. She sighed heavily with the knowledge that for now Decimus had won.

Michael cursed beneath his breath as he walked over

to Mary's side and took her gently in his arms. He brought her to him.

Mary clung to him in hopes of never letting go, in hopes of discovering this was all a bad dream that she would suddenly awake from and life would be good.

She laid her head on Michael's shoulder.

"I will always be there for you, Mary. *Always.*"

"I have no doubt of that," she said and moved slowly out of his arms.

He released her reluctantly. There was no more that could be said between them. The truth presented itself like a blazing message in the sky, scribed by the finger of God.

"I need time to consider all this," she said, backing away from him.

Michael urged her not to go far and she promised him she would only go to the stream. The flowing water helped soothe her mind, calm her worries, and bring her peace though she feared that never again would she know peace.

She walked with worried steps to the stream and sat beneath a large willow tree, its branches weeping around her.

She had not expected such dire news. She thought they would have more time together. Their love would only grow stronger with time. She hoped the strength of their love would allow him to trust her enough to reveal his identity, sealing their future together.

Sadness settled heavily in her heart. How could she wed Decimus when she loved Michael? How could she live out her days with a stranger? A man she cared nothing for. A man she had feared for the last ten years.

A man who tortured and killed the innocent. A man more evil than the devil himself.

The idea that he would hold dominion over her angered her. Choices, however, were not open to her. It was either accept and deal with the consequences of her decision or go insane from constant sorrow and regret.

She struggled with her thoughts and feared losing what sanity she had managed to retain. Her heart ached at the thought of never seeing Michael again, of him never holding her, kissing her, loving her.

Loving.

She would know no intimacy with Michael and the thought saddened her heart even more. It would be Decimus's hands she would feel on her flesh and Decimus's body joining with hers.

Her skin crawled with gooseflesh and she shivered.

"What shivers your skin?" Michael asked and pushed the weeping branches aside to join her beneath the tree. "You were gone too long."

"It has been mere minutes."

"Too long," he whispered and stroked her lips with his glove-covered finger.

She was glad he had followed her. Precious little time remained for them and she wanted ever second spent beside him.

"The shivers?" he reminded.

She did not wish to burden him with her thoughts. The time they had left was for happy memories. "Concerns that I refuse to fret over right now."

He took her hand and with one finger traced circles in her palm.

"I like those shivers," she said, smiling as gooseflesh scurried along her arm.

He stopped suddenly. "I cannot allow you to surrender to Decimus."

His words tore at her heart. She wanted so badly for him to rescue her just as he had done from her prison cell. But this time the Dark One could not. Her fate had been sealed.

"You cannot prevent it," she said with regret.

"I cannot let you go."

"Then do not," she said. "You promised me you would always be there for me."

"Aye, you have my word."

"Then you mean that I will see you from time to time?" she asked though hurried to add: "Only if it does not present a danger to you?"

"I am not done with Decimus."

She suddenly grew fearful, remembering the Dark One's mission and realizing now he had even more reason to hate Decimus.

"I do not want any harm to come to you."

"No harm will befall me or you. I will make certain of it."

She realized then that he would always be nearby, rescuing, helping, plotting against her future husband and forever placing his life in danger.

And *one day*, possibly, rescuing her.

"You will keep yourself safe, promise me this."

"I promise I will keep both of us safe."

She rested back against his chest, her head on his shoulder. "We have this day to enjoy. I want to think of nothing else but the two of us and this time we have together."

"You wish to shut out the world."

She took his gloved hand in hers. "Aye, only you and I exist, nothing else."

"And what is it you wish to do?"

"Be happy," she said with a joy that sprang from deep within her. She jumped to her feet and spun around beneath the willow tree. "We shall eat, laugh, be merry—"

She stopped suddenly and dropped to her knees in front of the cloaked man she loved with her whole heart, her whole being.

"Love," she said on a whisper. "I want you to love me."

"I do love you. I will always love you," he said, reaching out to cup her face.

She rubbed her cheek against his leather glove. "Nay, I want you to *make love* to me."

The thought had been a faint echo in her mind, and she had paid it no heed when suddenly it had risen in a fury to overwhelm her.

"You do not know what you ask."

"Aye, but I do," she said with a soft conviction. "I do not want to completely surrender to Decimus, but I do wish to completely surrender to you."

He took her face in his hands, holding it gently, lovingly. "I do not want your surrender."

"Then take my love, for I give it to you freely, willingly, and from the depths of my soul."

He rested his forehead on hers. "Do you know what you say?"

"Aye, I free myself of Decimus by loving you. He then can have no complete surrender from me and I can have what I ache for—you—if only for tonight."

"My identity must remain concealed, for your safety as well as mine."

"I understand," she said with excitement. "We can wait until dark, or I will keep my eyes closed, or you can blindfold me and then we can love throughout the day."

He laughed at her joyous enthusiasm. "And when do we rest?"

"We will not need to rest. Time does not exist; it is irrelevant, therefore it will not affect us."

"If only that were true," he said, running his finger over her lips and growing hard as he watched her eyes flutter closed and her mouth open to nip playfully at his fingers.

"I want my first time to be with you. I want to know your touch, taste your kiss and feel your body." She moaned. "Oh, Michael, you have no idea how much I wish to touch you, feel your flesh, and kiss it. I need to know you are real, flesh and blood and not a mere shadow of a man. I want those memories to keep with me forever."

"What of Decimus?"

"I do not care."

"You will not go to his bed a virgin."

"He did not ask for a virgin."

"He expects one," Michael said.

"That is his problem."

"It could very well be yours. I do not wish to put you in harm's way."

"At this moment, Michael, I have free will. I can make a choice—"

"That will have consequences."

"Leaving me to choose, fully aware of those consequences."

"I should say nay," Michael said.

"Why deny ourselves the love?"

"You will face the consequences of *our* actions, not I."

"Which I am willing to do." She pressed a finger to his lips to stop his protests. "The answer is simple, nay or yea, which shall it be?"

A second of silence followed and it felt like an eternity to Mary before she heard him whisper.

"I shall make love to you."

Chapter 18

"**T**onight after it grows dark—"

"Now," Mary insisted. "I want you to make love to me now."

Michael had no chance to respond.

"I want every moment I can with you so that when our time together is done, I will have memories to keep safe in my heart."

Michael reached out and grabbed her wrists. "Do you realize what you ask? How do I make love to you and then watch you surrender to a madman?"

"We cannot think of that now. Nothing else exists except you and me."

She didn't plead or beg him, she simply stated her desire with a soft and gentle urging that Michael found weaved its way inside him to stir his senses. He felt more alive than he had in a very long time, and it was a passion born of love.

He had thought love lost to him and here Mary was offering it to him freely, willingly, and unselfishly. He had denied himself much these many years, but how could he deny her?

She slipped her hands beneath the dark shroud to press her palms to his cheeks.

"You will not be able to look upon me; you must promise me that."

She smiled. "But I will be able to touch you." She stroked his face, a fine bristle of whispers tickling her fingers.

"All you want."

He pulled her hands from beneath his mask and lifted her up into his arms. He carried her to the keep, stepping over the crumbled stone wall, and walked straight to the bed they had shared since their arrival.

He laid her down, stretching out beside her. He skimmed her lips with his leather-clad finger. "I cannot take the chance of you looking upon me. I wish it could be different, but . . ."

"Cover my eyes, I trust you."

"You do not know me," he said sadly.

"Just because I have not laid eyes upon you, does not mean I do not know you." She placed her hand to his chest. "I know you well enough and I know that you would never hurt me."

"How I wish this could be different."

"But it is not, and I want this time with you."

She reached for an old strip of silk cloth she had found and had torn to make ribbons for her hair. She handed it to him.

"When our time together is done, I will know you well, for I will have touched all of you and no longer will you be a mere shadow to me."

He took the cloth and leaned down close to her face.

His voice was a coarse whisper. "Someday I will love you in the light."

Her heart fluttered with joy. Someday, somehow he would once again rescue her, and knowing that gave her hope and lifted her spirits.

"I look forward to it."

He placed the blue silk over her eyes, tying it in a knot behind her head.

"I can see nothing," she said and a chill rushed through her at the sudden thought of being in complete darkness, like the prison cell that had once held her captive.

"That was the question I was about to ask you, you read my mind," he said and brushed his bare cheek next to hers when he felt her slight tremble. "Know that I intend to love you with all my heart"—he kissed along her cheek to her lips and nibbled lightly—"*and soul.*"

She shivered away her misgivings, replacing them with delicious anticipation. "You will not keep me waiting?"

He nibbled at her lips again. "I am in no hurry."

She smiled. "We do have the whole day."

"I may need to rest from time to time."

"We can nap."

"Then wake and love again?"

"Aye," she said and jumped when his hand gently squeezed her breast.

"I have longed to know the feel of you."

"I feel the same of you."

"Then I will not deprive us both any longer."

Mary was glad he divested himself of his shroud before undressing her. He left himself vulnerable to her first, and she enjoyed the thought, and she did not wait to reach out and touch him.

His arm was thick, hard, and warm and she squeezed at his flesh. It felt so wonderful to finally touch him. She never wanted to stop.

He took her arm and placed it round his neck. "Hold on while I remove your blouse."

She held onto him as he raised her up to slip her blouse off. The cool air brushed her naked skin, but she was so intent on acquainting herself with the feel of him that she did not realize she lay completely naked until his hand began to wander over her breast, his lips following. He nibbled, sucked, and teased her nipples into submission.

"Oh my, that does feel so good."

"That is only the beginning," he whispered and nibbled his way up to her neck, sending gooseflesh racing over her.

While he tempted her with kisses, she became familiar with his body running her hands up and down his arms, over his broad shoulders, down his chest, and up his back in long, broad strokes. Her touch helped produce images of him in her mind, and the sensation of his warm, hard flesh against her fingers inflamed her passion.

They soon became lost in touching and tasting each other. Mary nipped at his lips and tasted his neck, salty and warm and oh, so satisfying.

Michael eased himself away from her lips, to Mary's chagrin.

His fingertips went to work on her naked flesh, touching her ever so lightly and heightening her desire to raging proportions.

"You are so very beautiful," he whispered in her ear. "Every inch of you."

His fingers stroked the inside of her legs, spreading them apart, and ever so gently he touched her with the faintest intimate touch causing her to lose all rationality, to moan with desire.

She almost sprang off the bed when Michael began to kiss the inside of her legs and moved upward.

"What are you doing?"

"Loving you," he said and kissed her in the most intimate of places she never imagined his lips would touch, but was so very glad he did.

She moaned.

There was not a part of her body he did not touch, kiss, or nibble. He brought her to a fever pitch and watched as she arched her back and cried out with the pleasure of her first orgasm.

When she regained her breath, she reached out to touch him. He let her have her way, understanding she needed to know him as well.

His chest was firm, his belly flat, and his manhood hard, solid, and a size that startled her. "You are so very large."

His hand covered hers. "There is nothing to fear from me."

She stroked him and his hand drifted off her. She smiled when she heard him groan. "I like the feel of you."

"Touch all you wish."

She did, enjoying the intimacy until he said, "No more or I will be spent before we finish."

"I do not want that," Mary said. "I want you inside me."

He moved over her, kissing Mary like a starving man, and she returned his kisses like a woman eager to feed him. Her arms wrapped around him and he held her as he settled slowly into her inch by inch, her moans growing as he entered her more deeply.

"Shhh," he warned, "Or the whole forest will hear you."

"I cannot help it, you feel so very good and I love you so very much."

He tickled her ear with his tongue. "And I love you. Now hold on to me tight for this moment we share is precious, and I will forever hold it in my heart."

He claimed her mouth, so that her moans of pleasure emptied into him as he entered her completely and demanded a rhythm of her that she matched with equal enthusiasm.

Mary lost all sense of time and place; her only thought was that of the wickedly delicious sensation she felt with him buried deep inside her. His precise strokes tingled, excited, and drove her near mad as they built in her a crescendo of passion that consumed her. She held onto him, knowing he rode her toward a crest that once reached would devour them both.

They soared and spun and crested until a shocking explosion racked their bodies, and together they grasped and moaned their release, sighed with pleasure, and slowly returned to reality.

Her body tingled and when he rolled off her, she turned and rested against him, his arm wrapping around her.

"I never imagined it to be so beautiful," she said when her breathing calmed.

"Love makes it beautiful."

"Then I am glad that I could know this moment with you."

Michael held her tightly and she clung to him as though she feared to let go.

"I will keep you safe," he said, knowing he reminded her much too often, but needing more so to remind himself, to believe and keep that belief firm in his heart.

"I know." She fought not to shed the tears that threatened. It was hard holding them back when she hurt so badly. And she should not hurt now, not while she continued to bask in the pleasure of their lovemaking. But she could not help but wonder how she would share such intimacy with a man she hated. Could there be a worse torture?

"Are you all right?" he asked, having felt her tremble.

She would not let him know her thoughts for it would make their time together more difficult for them both.

"I am more than all right; I am wonderfully happy and deliciously content."

He laughed and kissed the top of her head. "The feeling is mutual."

"Good, then we shall rest so that we can feel this way again and again and again."

"I could love you forever, Mary, and never tire of it."

She sighed. "You say the most beautiful things to me."

"When love fills one's heart there can be only words of beauty."

"Where did you learn of love?" she asked as she felt him drape his shroud over them and she snuggled more comfortably into his embrace.

He hesitated a moment. "My mother was a remarkable woman. She taught me much about the beauty and unselfishness of love."

"My mother did the same," she said. "How lucky we are to have had such loving mothers. And have you loved any women before me?"

"Nay," he answered quickly. "And I shall love no other but you."

She touched his cheek. "And I shall love you and you alone."

"Mary—"

She pressed a finger to his lips sensing he would say something that would rob them of this special moment. "Please say nothing more. Let us have this time."

He remained silent and Mary closed her eyes to dream, falling quickly asleep while clinging tightly to him.

Late afternoon found them sitting by the stream eating blackberries. Michael wore his black robe and she her blouse and skirt, her feet were bare.

They had avoided speaking of tomorrow, clinging tenaciously to today and the little time afforded them.

A thought had been stirring in Mary since he had planted the idea in her mind that perhaps one day he would be able to free her of Decimus. Until then he would be freeing others and she could help him.

"I have an idea," she said.

"Will this idea find favor with me?"

"I think it is a good idea."

"That does not answer my question, which is," he said, "a sure indication the idea is not acceptable. Do you know that your voice sounds like a melody carried on a gentle breeze? It is very soothing to listen to."

"You attempt to avoid my idea, though I do appreciate the compliment."

He was firm in his protest. "I do not wish to argue, and your idea will cause an argument."

She hurriedly told him what she thought before he could stop her. "I will help you in your quest to free those imprisoned by Decimus."

"You will not." He sounded as if he held his temper.

She looked at him, his dark mask in place but no longer hiding him from her, not since her freshly acquired memories reminded her of the flesh and blood man that lay beneath.

"Just think of the important information I could supply you with, making it less difficult for you and the prisoners."

"And how long do you think it would be before Decimus caught you?"

"If I played the dutiful wife he would never suspect me," she said with excitement. "This could work well for us both."

"It would not," he insisted. "It would place you in harm's way and I will not see that happen."

"I am intelligent and could well handle the masquerade. Decimus would suspect nothing. He would be too pleased with gaining me as his wife and will pay me no heed."

"He is not an ignorant man."

"He most certainly is," she said. "Any man who treats the lives of others so carelessly is an idiot."

"Do not make the mistake of misjudging his worth. He is sharp of eye and keen of hearing and there is little he does not know."

She tapped her chin with her finger, wrinkled her brow, and looked to the sky.

"No more ideas, Mary," he warned.

"It is not an idea I contemplate. If you tell me that Decimus sees, hears, and knows all, why was he unable to find me these many years?"

"Magnus did a splendid job of hiding you."

"Then suddenly he discovered my whereabouts after eleven long years?" She shook her head. "It does not make sense."

"He has men who he sends out in search of people."

"No one knew of my real identity except Magnus. The man and woman he left me with were told that I was orphaned and needed a home. Magnus offered them money to take me in and they gladly did. My presence made their life easier. Coins would cease if I was gone."

"Or perhaps they were more richly compensated for providing Decimus with information."

Mary shook her head again. "They grew to care for me. They would never want to see me harmed."

"Coins can loosen the tongue."

"I do not think that Decimus would pay for information. Torture is more his way, gaining him whatever information he seeks. His discovery of me does not make sense."

Michael reached out to lay his glove-covered hand on her arm. "Do not hunt for things that could be harmful to you."

"Do you actually expect me to wed him and do nothing but submit?"

"For your safety? Aye, I do."

"My fate is sealed once I exchange vows with him. I will not spend my life in fear, nor be imprisoned by his ignorance. I will do what I must to survive and to find a way to make my time with him productive."

"Productive?"

"I wish to help you—"

He attempted to protest but she silenced him with a quick raising of her hand.

"Do not waste your breath on me. I will do what I can to help those I can."

"And find yourself suffering," he said exasperated.

"I cannot completely surrender my will. I would rather die."

"You would place yourself in danger helping the innocent?"

"I am in danger now."

"Free yourself of that danger," he said. "When you wed Decimus obey him until another way can be found to free you."

She shook her head adamantly. "And how long do I obey? Weeks? Months? Years? Until I lose myself completely to him? I cannot."

"You are stubborn."

"A trait we share." She laughed.

He grabbed her chin. "How can you find humor in all this?"

"That is easy," she said softly. "I find humor in it all because you loved me. I shared true love with you and because of you I know its joys and pleasures, and no one, not even Decimus with all his power, can take that from me."

Michael knew not how to respond.

She reached beneath his mask to touch his face. "Do you know when I touch you that I ache for us to make love?"

"Mary, listen to me—"

"Only if you tell me you will make love to me."

"You are willful—"

"Aye, which does not make me a docile wife, though I can convince Decimus otherwise."

He released her chin and pointed a finger at her. "You will—"

Love me," she said and nipped at his finger.

"Mary it is important that we—"

"Make love," she finished, and laughing, jumped at him toppling him to the ground.

He grabbed hold of her. "We will talk."

"Later," she said and wiggled her body against his.

"You are—"

"Hungry for your kisses."

Before Mary knew what happened he had her off the ground, in his arms, and was walking to the willow tree. He spread the thick weeping branches with his shoulder, and without removing one stitch of clothing, he made love to her beneath the willow tree.

Chapter 19

I t seemed as if the heavens obliged them that night. A cloud drifted over the half moon, blocking out what light there was and leaving their sleeping nook in total darkness. They were like shadows in the night, barely visible to the eye.

Time was closing in on them, the hours slipping by until it would be morning and their time together done. They had made love often and Mary burned every second of it into memory.

Now snuggled in his arms, her leg over his, her hand on his chest, she felt content. In a few short hours that would change, and how she would say goodbye to him she did not know. She did not want to think about it, for it caused her heart to ache and her stomach to churn.

"I love you more than I ever thought possible, Mary."

His soft declaration brought a tear to her eye. "Something we have in common, for I never thought I would love someone as strongly as I love you, Michael."

"How do I let you go?"

"I thought the same of you, but we have no choice." Her tear dropped on his chest.

"Damn," he whispered, then eased her off him, leaned over and kissed her tears away. "I will find a way for us, Mary, I promise." He kissed another falling tear.

"I know, Michael, I know, but for now just love me."

They loved slowly and gently, savoring every touch and kiss, lingering as if they wished the moment would last forever. When it was done, their bodies misted with their lovemaking, they wrapped around each other tightly and slept.

A rumble of thunder woke Mary in the morning, and she was not surprised to see that Michael was not there.

She had expected his absence in the morning, his last words to her indicating his early departure.

"I will always be near."

Mary fought back tears as she dressed and gathered her belongings. She had to remain strong. She would face much adversity in the days ahead and she could not resort to tears whenever she was upset. But the persistent tears threatened again when she saw that he had left her berries and roots for breakfast. She could not, however, hold her tears in any longer when she went to the stream. There near the water's edge, written deeply in the dirt was *I love you*.

She cried, aching for his arms to wrap around her, aching for this to be a nightmare that she would wake up from, aching for his love.

She forced her sobbing to stop. Strength would be her shield and love her weapon to use to defend herself against Decimus. She would be victorious, for life without Michael would be much too empty. And if her suspicions were right Roarke would soon arrive to take her to Magnus, and she would not greet him with tears. Michael would never leave her on her own. He would always make certain she was protected.

I will always be near.

She dried her face with the edge of her skirt, looked around and called out, "I love you, be safe."

She returned to the keep, packed the last of her few meager belongings, and walked to the door. Before she closed the door behind her she took one last look around and smiled. This crumbled-down keep would always hold a special spot in her heart. She shut the door and sat on the stone wall to wait for Roarke.

It was not long before she heard his approach. She knew his footfalls were purposely heavy, making her aware of his arrival. She liked Roarke, he was easy to talk with, kind, and trustworthy. She could understand Michael and he being friends.

Mary stood when Roarke emerged from the woods, a broad smile on his face. He would try to cheer her, he was like that, always being in good spirits and wanting to share his mirth with others.

"It is proud I am to accompany a brave warrior into battle," he said once he stood in front of her.

She forced a smile, not feeling brave, though knowing this was her destiny. The seer's words helped.

You will be the demise of Decimus.

If she was right then there was hope for her and Michael.

The day's journey was slow, rain forcing them to seek shelter. Mary was too preoccupied to hold a conversation and Roarke seemed to understand and remained quiet. They camped early that evening due to the uncooperative weather, and after a quick meal they both slept.

Mary woke early upset by a dream. She had dreamed that Michael lay beside her, his arm wrapped around her. She could almost feel him, hear his breathing and the steady beat of his heart. She allowed herself only a moment of sorrow.

Her own pity would do her no good. Soon she would come face-to-face with the man who had robbed her of her parents and her life. She would need all her strength and intelligence to deal with him.

"Do you know of Decimus?" she asked Roarke once they began walking.

"Unfortunately I do."

"I would like to know all I could about him."

"It is always wise to know one's enemy when entering into battle," Roarke said.

"And this marriage will be a battle."

"A silent one would be more beneficial."

"I thought the same myself," she said. "The more I listen, the more I learn, the more I gain."

"Your freedom?" he asked with a smile.

She laughed. "Freedom is intoxicating." Her laughter faded. "And it is our God-given right."

"Aye, that it is."

"So tell me what you know of Decimus."

"His temper is what you will need to be most careful of."

"It is unpredictable?" she asked eager to learn all she could.

"Extremely, no one knows what will ignite him and send him into a rage. I have heard people quake at his feet and beg for mercy without him having raised a hand. I wonder if he is feared more than the devil."

"How does he treat women?"

"He treats the accused no differently, be they man,

woman, or child. They repent or suffer the consequences. He believes himself on a mission for God. He will let nothing stand in his way."

"I stand in his way."

"More than you know."

She shook her head, confused. "I do not understand his obsession with me. I am no threat to him."

"Know that you are and tread lightly or you will suffer more than you thought possible."

"You need not worry, I will be careful."

"Be more than careful," he advised. "Be aware, very aware."

Sleep eluded Mary that night. She tossed and turned until the sun began to rise. She rose quietly, not wanting to disturb Roarke who was snoring softly, and walked to a clearing where she could watch the sunrise.

It was a beautiful sight, the bright orange ball looked as though it rose from the depths of the earth. It heralded the birth of a new day. Her heart quickened and she smiled. She would face today with courage and determination.

"I love you, Michael, wherever you are, know that I love you, and keep safe."

Mary stood on the crest of a small hill overlooking Magnus's keep, silently watching everyday life go by for the villagers.

"They are good people and have been through much," Roarke said beside her.

"Tell me."

"They were serving a selfish and cruel lord when Reena boldly entered the Legend's land to seek his help." Roarke smiled. "And she got it, and Magnus got a wife in return. They suit each other well."

"I look forward to meeting her."

"Are you ready?"

She took a deep breath, raised her chin, and said, "I am ready."

As soon as they approached the village Mary could tell she was expected. There were whispers scurrying about and sorrow-filled faces at her arrival. A few women whispered *bless you* while others shed tears.

An older woman approached her and handed her a sprig of lavender. "You will not be sorry," she said, her aging eyes filled with unshed tears.

Her own steps faltered when she caught sight of Decimus's men. She recognized two that had chased her and one who had tormented her when she was a prisoner. Roarke was quick to grab her arm and keep her walking steady.

"When you entered the village you belonged to Decimus. His men know this and will not harm you."

But what of Decimus? What could she expect from him?

She spotted Magnus on the top step of the keep and she hurried forward.

"Magnus," she cried and dropped her bundle on the steps before throwing herself into his outstretched arms.

He gave her a hug, knowing she regarded him as a father figure, someone who had saved her and protected her these many years.

"I am so happy to see you," she said, fighting to keep her voice from quivering.

"I wish the circumstances were different, Mary."

"It is all right, I understand."

Her words did not console him; they made him feel

far worse than he already did. He had given his word to her parents to protect her and now he was breaking it. It did not sit well with him.

"This is Thomas," he said, indicating to the large man beside him. "He is my second-in-command."

"It is pleased I am to meet you, Mary," Thomas said, and then tugged a beautiful blond woman from behind him. "This is my wife Brigid."

The woman looked on the verge of tears. "You are so very brave."

Then a small woman, her long dark hair in disarray and an ink smudge on her cheek, appeared out of nowhere, stepping between Mary and Brigid.

"I am Reena, Magnus's wife." She held out her hand.

Mary took it. "I am delighted to meet you."

Reena lowered her voice, intending her words to be for the two of them alone. "Do not worry. We will talk and plan."

"Reena," Magnus said firmly.

She turned to her husband while wrapping her arm around Mary's. "The poor lass is starving. She requires a decent meal immediately."

Magnus stepped forward, taking them both by the arms and walking into the great hall of the keep. Once inside, and out of hearing range from everyone, Magnus spoke his piece.

"I do not wish to sacrifice one of you for the other, and it is for me to see what can be done. I will not have either of you jeopardizing your safety or your lives. You both will leave this matter to me."

Mary spoke before Reena could. "You have protected me since I was young. It is time for me to defend myself. I freely made the choice to wed Decimus. It would seem he is my destiny, and you cannot take my destiny from me, Magnus."

Reena smiled and poked her husband in his arm. "I like her."

"Your parents would be proud," he said, "but I gave my word to them and—"

"That promise is no longer valid. I am grown and capable of taking care of myself. My parents did not expect you to watch over me for the remainder of my life, only until I had grown and could look after myself."

"You do not know that," Magnus argued.

Mary grinned. "You were my father's student and understood his ways. Tell me, then, do I not speak the truth?"

Magnus looked about to disagree when he stopped and shook his head. "You are truly your father's daughter."

Mary stepped up beside him and kissed his cheek. "Your words mean much to me."

Reena reached for her hand. "You need a good, solid meal before you meet Decimus."

"You intend to scheme with Mary," Magnus accused his wife and sent her a warning look that would make most men tremble. Not so with Reena.

"I want to get to know Mary better, and I am certain she would be interested in my mapmaking skills."

"You are a mapmaker?" Mary asked with excitement.

"See, husband. She is interested."

"And what maps have you already drawn for her, wife?"

"None yet."

"I knew it," Magnus said with an accusatory shake of his finger.

"Mary needs to be prepared."

"To get herself killed?" Magnus asked, keeping his voice low though firm. "I warned you about interfering, Reena."

"This is true, but you said nothing of helping her."

Mary laughed.

"Do not encourage her," Magnus snapped.

"I do not think she needs encouragement," Mary said.

"Nay, she is stubborn enough not to need it," Magnus said.

"It is understandable that he worries over your safety," Mary said in defense of Magnus.

"He will always protect me, so I have no need to worry."

"Did you not suffer in my own dungeon?" he asked, wiping the smudge from her cheek.

"You rescued me," she said with pride. "And"—she held up a finger to make an important point—"you forever wipe smudges off my face."

Mary laughed softly and was about to comment on how perfectly suited they were for each other when her eyes caught sight of a man at the far end of the great hall. He leaned against the table on the dais, crossed his arms over his chest, and stared.

"Decimus," she whispered.

Chapter 20

Magnus's protective instincts had him moving to step in front of Mary, but his wife's hand held him firm.

"She will face him with courage," Reena whispered to her husband, and they both moved aside.

Mary approached Decimus with her head held high, though her legs trembled. He intimidated even with the distance that separated them. He was taller than she had thought him to be and his features were dark, his black hair lustrous. His garments were rich in texture and in colors that befitted royalty, gold and red. He looked fit, in fine shape for a man who did nothing but condemn and torture.

He remained braced against the edge of the table in an arrogant stance, as though annoyed that he had to wait for her approach. The closer she got the more she realized that it was his eyes that held the most power; dark and menacing, cold and calculating, a heartless man devoid of a soul.

"Do you intend to keep me waiting all day?"

His voice was strong, filling the great hall with a thunderous rumble.

Mary did not hasten her step, she could not, her legs trembled far too much; she felt lucky she was able to remain upright. To others she appeared confident and proud, and she intended to keep it that way. No one knew of her trepidation.

She stopped a few feet in front of him. "I am Mary, you requested my presence."

Decimus assessed her with a cold stare, rubbed his chin, then shook his head as if he found her lacking in some way.

Mary chose silence, knowing her tongue would only get her into trouble.

He straightened. "I thought you might find my proposal acceptable."

"You gave me little choice."

"I was generous in my offer," he said.

Mary shrugged. "That is a matter of opinion."

He lunged at her, causing her to jump back. He halted only inches in front of her. "I will teach you obedience, and you will learn."

"As you say," she said with a curt bow of her head.

"Docile so soon." He frowned and circled her. "You think me a fool?"

"I do not know you, sir, therefore I cannot say for certain."

He leaned in close to her. "Watch your tongue, Mary, I can easily have it removed."

He summoned Magnus with a snap of his hand. "Have her cleaned up and brought to my bedchamber. She looks a sight covered with dirt and grime."

"I cannot send Mary to your bedchamber," Magnus said adamantly. "It is not proper.

"You challenge my authority?"

"Your intentions," Magnus said.

Decimus looked ready to spew forth his anger.

Reena sought to quell tempers. "Perhaps the solar would do."

Decimus gave a quick nod, then turned to Mary. "When you are made more presentable, we will talk."

He strode off, sniffing the air with disgust as he passed Mary.

Reena walked up behind her husband and waited until Decimus left the hall to say, "That is one way to keep him away from you, remain disheveled."

"A good thought," Mary said. "Though I expected him to demand more from me."

"Give him time," Magnus warned. "He does nothing without purpose."

"Come with me," Reena said. "I will see to a bath and clean garments for you."

Mary looked to Magnus before following Reena. "Has Decimus made mention of when he intends for the wedding to take place?"

He shook his head. "I am sure he will speak to you of it soon." He squeezed her arm gently. "Go eat and wash up and do not rush. Decimus will wait."

"Will he?" Mary asked in a way that had them all wondering.

A tray of food and a full tub awaited her in her bedchamber. Mary wasted not a moment. She shed her garments and climbed in, a grateful sigh spilling from her lips as she sank into the hot water.

The heat soaked into her bones; she relaxed and her

mind drifted. It would be difficult keeping her feelings for the Dark One hidden. Magnus was an astute judge of character, and Reena seemed curious and not averse to asking questions. She would need to be careful.

After eating far too much food, Mary found herself sleepy. She lay on the bed for a brief rest. She no soon as closed her eyes than she thought she heard someone whisper her name.

It was a harsh, familiar whisper, and then she felt the familiar feel of a leather-clad hand touch her face.

Michael.

She instantly became concerned that he should be there. It was too dangerous, yet he stroked her warm cheek with his cool leathered touch, and it felt so very good and so very right.

He ran his hand slowly down her body. *I miss you.*

She wanted to reach out and touch him, know he was real, not a dream, but he denied her.

Lie still, I cannot stay.

She wanted to cry out not to leave her that he should take her with him, but even in her dream her choice remained the same.

"Come back," she whispered.

I am not far.

She reached out and took hold of his hand. He was solid, real, not a shadow. But then he was no longer a shadow to her, not since they had made love. Though faceless he was a man of flesh and blood.

What did he look like?

She wanted to see him, know him for who he was; it seemed imperative.

She tried to turn.

Nay!

He denied her. Why did he deny her? Her own

safety? It seemed not to matter to her. What mattered most was that she saw him for who he was.

"Please, Michael."

Do as I say, and you will be safe.

She tried to turn and felt as if someone held her down.

"Let me see you." She struggled with the weight that held her.

You fight yourself. You fight the truth.

Mary grew agitated not understanding what he meant. The more she struggled, the heavier her burden felt.

She thought she heard him drift away and still she could not move.

"Michael?"

No answer, she panicked and fought against the weight that imprisoned her. She wanted to see him, know he was there, not a dream, lord she did not want it to be a dream. She wanted him there beside her.

She woke shouting, "Do not go!" with the light wool blanket twisted around her and her hair tangled and half-covering her face. A sense of emptiness filled her. Sitting up, she tried to free herself of the blanket and gasped when she spotted a shadow near the window.

Chapter 21

"**M**issing someone?" Decimus stepped out of the shadows.

Mary glared at him. "My parents."

"Your tongue is quick."

She amended his accusation. "My tongue is truthful."

He stepped closer, his dark eyes narrowing, his nostrils flaring. "You have much to learn."

"We all do."

He walked over to her, his hands grabbing her by the shoulders. "You will learn the truth once you wed me."

"The truth defines itself."

"As you will learn." He shoved her away from him. "You have kept me waiting."

"I was more tired than I thought and meant to rest only a moment. I am sorry for delaying our discussion."

He seemed appeased by her apology, though she never actually apologized to him. She regretted wasting precious time on sleep more than she regretted speaking with him and discovering anything she could that might help free her of him.

"We will talk here," he said and turned his back to her. "Finish dressing."

She made haste to don the dark green tunic Reena left lying across the foot of the bed and snatched the soft tan leather boots from the floor to slip on. She ran her fingers through her damp hair, knowing there was not much that could be done with it, and finished by knotting a thin leather belt around her waist.

"May I offer you a drink or food?" she asked, letting him know she was now presentable.

"Wine," he said and took a seat by the fireplace.

She handed him a goblet of wine.

He took it, stared at the red liquid, sipped, then sipped again before he said, "You may sit."

Mary knew patience would be her strongest ally when dealing with Decimus. And she would need to remind herself daily of it. She chose the small stool nearer the hearth, feeling chilled.

Was it her own mixed emotions that caused the shivers? Or was it Decimus?

"It is good you know your place."

"Perhaps you should define my place," she said, hasty to add, "so that I know for certain what is expected of me."

"Obedience in all things."

His dark eyes heated with pleasure at the thought, and she noticed then how richly defined his features were, with high cheekbones that appeared sculpted, a narrow face that defined a rounded chin and narrow lips that showed not a sign of a smile. If he were not so loathsome a creature, he would be a handsome man.

"It is good that you are attentive," he said, mistaking

her introspection for attentiveness. "It is one less thing you need to be taught."

"Why wed me if I burden you?"

He leaned forward, his face close to hers. "Did I give you permission to ask questions?"

He spoke with a cold harshness that chilled and unnerved. Her shivers increased and she dropped her hands to her sides to grasp the edge of the stool. She hoped the fire's warmth would at least toast her trembling hands and send warmth through the rest of her body, easing her shivers.

When she dutifully remained silent, he leaned back in his seat. "You are nothing compared to the burdens I carry."

"Why then?" She bit her tongue after the query slipped from her lips, and hoped her mistake would not cost her.

His dark eyes glazed with a fiery pleasure. "To cleanse your soul and prove to all that sinners can be made righteous."

She did not need to ask why, she understood. If he wed a sinner and changed her into a dutiful wife, his power would know no bounds and he would be untouchable. Neither he nor his work would ever be doubted.

You will be the demise of Decimus.

She hoped the seer's words proved true for she could not be responsible for Decimus growing in power and in position. It would mean more innocent people would die.

Again he took her silence as submission.

"I have made arrangements for our wedding. Two weeks from tomorrow we will wed here at Magnus's keep."

"You have discussed this with him?"

He glared at her as if she were daft. "I have no need to discuss it with him. I will tell him of my decision. Besides, I thought he would like to be present at your wedding, after all he was *your protector*."

Mary bit her tongue. He would have the wedding at Magnus's keep to prove that he had been victorious over the mighty Legend.

"The wedding will be a dignified affair followed by a festive celebration. All will participate in this joyous occasion. There will be an extended church service and you will kneel beside me in prayer."

Mary wanted to remind him that she did not believe as he believed, but it would not be wise of her. Silence was her ally, she reminded herself over and over.

"Make certain an appropriate wedding dress is sewn for you, a gown that signifies my status in the Church. I will not have you appear a dowdy bride. Remember we are exchanging vows and you are committing yourself to me forever."

"Forever?" she asked, the awful thought setting her legs to trembling.

"Of course," he said as if she seemed ignorant. "We wed before God and man. We become man and wife for eternity."

Man and wife, not husband and wife. He would rule her as he saw fit, but Michael would not. He would be a true husband to his wife. She missed him terribly, and more so since she had dreamed of him. It was as if he had been there with her, touching her, holding her and loving her.

She chased Michael from her thoughts for fear of bringing tears to her eyes.

"Your silence is good. I will not abide a wife who

speaks when she pleases. You will speak when spoken to."

That was definitely going to be a problem. She could chatter a day away without difficulty. Michael liked her chatter.

Stop.

She grabbed the edge of the stool tightly, her silent warning echoing in her mind.

Decimus handed his empty goblet to her. "Get me more wine."

Mary feared her hand would tremble when she reached for it, but she was quick and snatched the goblet away from him. She walked to the table to pour him another.

"Now that we are finished with the wedding plans, there is something else I want to discuss with you."

She walked toward him with the filled goblet.

"Tell me of the Dark One."

The silver goblet dropped out of her hand and fell to the floor.

"How clumsy of you, Mary."

Much too clumsy, she thought. He had tricked her and she had fallen for his trickery. He now knew that it was the Dark One who had rescued her, and he intended for her to supply him with information.

"Clean it up," he ordered.

She did as he commanded, reminding herself that she had to be more aware of his devious tactics or she would chance getting Michael caught.

She finished the chore and returned to her stool, handing him the refilled goblet.

He once again purposely took his time sipping the wine before speaking.

Her hands no longer trembled. It was imperative she remain aware and alert so she did not accidentally give Decimus information that would lead him to capturing Michael.

"I will capture the Dark One. Like your capture, his is only a matter of time."

Her capture. This was what she wanted to hear about. She remained silent, hoping it would encourage him to talk.

"Magnus is a worthy opponent, but I knew I would find you if I were patient. He could not hide you forever. And there is always someone who will, for a coin, or if forced to, divulge information I seek."

Someone betrayed her?

"I will be patient and wait. *Someone* will give me the Dark One."

He had to be a fool to think she would betray the man she loved, but then he did not know she loved the Dark One, and he must never learn of it. He would use her to force Michael to surrender. She had to be careful, very careful, or she would be the demise of the Dark One, not Decimus.

"What do you think of the Dark One?"

She shrugged. "I know nothing of him."

"I am not a fool, Mary. The Dark One freed you from my prison cell, and I believe he killed one of my men, since he never returned after tracking you. And his body has never been found."

"Perhaps the man chose his own freedom."

"Watch your tongue with me, woman," he warned sternly. "I will not tolerate caustic remarks from you."

She bowed her head as though demonstrating obedience when she actually bowed so he would not see her squeeze her lips shut to keep from lashing out at him.

"I only ask a question once, and yet I find I have asked a question twice of you. If an answer is not forthcoming immediately, you will feel a heavy hand."

It would be foolish to continue to deny any knowledge of the Dark One. It was what knowledge she divulged that was important. "I never saw him."

"That was not what I asked. I asked what you thought of him."

He is brave, unselfish, and I love him. The words remained silent on her tongue, instead she said, "He is a man intent on his mission."

"Rescuing people God has judged to be sinners? Does this seem like a noble cause to you?" he asked annoyed.

"I believe the Dark One a noble man. He fights for his beliefs."

"You sound as if you admire him."

"It takes courage to be different," she said softly.

"And the Dark One certainly is different, hiding in darkness like a demon fearful of the light. He serves an evil lord and you should go down on your knees and give thanks I rescued you."

"I am thankful," she said. *For Michael's love, for no longer having to hide, for a chance to one day truly be free.*

"Good, now you are on the path of righteousness," he said with satisfaction. "Now, what of this man Roarke who brought you here?"

She had not thought of Roarke, and how it would appear with him escorting her here. But he did not know that, or did he? And where was Roarke? She had been so caught up in seeing Magnus again she had not given Roarke any thought, not that he could not take care of himself, but she wished to know he was safe.

"I know nothing of the man Roarke. I met him along the way."

"You lie."

"Nay, I do not," she insisted.

"You expect me to believe this man Roarke just happen to be going your way?"

"Farther than my destination, but I told him that Magnus was generous to travelers and would feed him a decent meal."

"And he will attest to this, if asked?"

Could she get to Roarke before Decimus? She had not thought of the consequences of Roarke helping her. And why had she not considered his safety? She continued her bluff followed by a silent prayer.

"It is the truth," she said.

He stood and went to the door.

Mary was surprised to see one of his men standing outside the door.

"Bring me the man Roarke," he ordered and shut the door.

What had she done? She had placed Roarke in jeopardy. Now what?

Decimus returned to his seat. "You never once saw the Dark One's face?"

She shook her head and clasped her hands together to keep them from trembling. She should have given more consideration to her response. She had warned herself to be careful, and she had not been careful. If he discovered that Roarke was a friend to the Dark One, he could use him against Michael.

"I have not found a soul who knows the Dark One's identity, though perhaps Roarke will know something."

She had never considered that Roarke actually might

know the Dark One's true identity. Was it possible? Could Michael have confided in Roarke? Was he more a friend to him than she knew?

Her heart pounded in her chest and her trembling hands grew icy cold. What had she done? Had she carelessly betrayed both men?

"I warn you, Mary, to be truthful with me, for you will suffer at my hand." He glared at her accusingly.

She placed her cold hands between her knees for warmth and to stop them from trembling. She raised her chin feigning confidence, though she felt none.

"The Dark One confided nothing in me."

His fist pounded the arm of the chair. "What of help? No one helped him?"

Mary recalled the people in the small village who were so generous. She would never betray them even if it meant her suffering. She attempted to appease him.

"I saw no one, though there were times he left me alone."

Decimus leaned forward interested in the bit of useless information. "Where did he leave you alone and for how long?"

"We traveled mostly at night so I could not say where it was exactly he left me, or how long he was gone. During his absence I slept heavily, exhausted from our walking."

"He must have people who help him, and I intend to find them and make them pay for aiding a sinner." Decimus leaned back in his chair as though worn out from battle. He folded his hands and rested them near his mouth, his eyes focused on the flames in the hearth.

Mary was glad his interrogation of her was done. She had erred enough with Roarke. She did not wish to cause further problems for anyone. And what of Roarke? Good lord, she prayed she would not be the cause of him suffering.

A knock sounded at the door.

She remained where she was, her heart beating madly and her stomach churning.

Decimus looked at her as if to let her know her time had come.

He stood and called out, "Enter."

The door opened and the man who had stood guard entered alone.

Mary wanted to jump for joy. He had not located Roarke, perhaps there was still time for her to find him.

"Where is he?" Decimus asked sharply.

"I have been informed that the man Roarke has continued on his journey."

"When did he leave?" Decimus asked.

The man appeared nervous when he answered, "I do not know."

Decimus looked ready to choke the man. "Did you not think to ask?"

The man hesitated. "I will find out," he said and was about to leave when Decimus set a glare on him that would chill a man down to his soul.

"You dare to leave my presence without permission?"

The man shivered and quickly sank to his knee in front of Decimus. "Forgive me, my lord, in my haste to correct my error I insulted you."

"I will not tolerate such a hideous mistake again."

The man kept his head bowed in submission.

"Stand," Decimus ordered.

The man quickly got to his feet.

"You will take one other man with you, and you will go find this Roarke and return him to me."

Mary could only hope they would not find Roarke and she prayed for his safety.

The man hurried to the door and stopped when Decimus said, "Do not return without him, or you shall suffer for your failure."

The young man squared his shoulders. "I shall not fail you, my lord."

Found or not, someone would suffer. Would it be Roarke or this young man? Mary knew then and there that there would be peace for no one until Decimus was dead.

You will be the demise of Decimus.

Mary finally believed the seer's prediction.

Chapter 22

Mary woke early the next morning annoyed that she had fallen asleep before she could warn Roarke. After leaving her bedchamber, Decimus had lingered outside her door. He was speaking with someone, and while she waited she had fallen asleep. Exhausted from her travel and her first night with Decimus, she had slept straight through until morning.

She hurried to find Magnus; he would know Roarke's whereabouts.

The keep was just waking and she was afraid Magnus might still be abed, but as she entered the great hall he was walking to the open front doors. Sunshine streamed in, flooding the hall with light.

"Magnus," she called out.

He turned and greeted her with a smile.

She hurried over to him. "We need to talk."

"I walk the small rise just outside the village almost every morning. Would you care to join me?" He offered her his arm.

She took it and they left the keep.

The village was a buzz of activity yet all took time to bid good morning to their liege lord.

They passed the last cottage and were near the small rise when Magnus said, "I am sorry to make you walk a distance after all the traveling you have done, but I felt privacy was called for."

"You are right," she said, glad they were away from the keep and away from prying eyes and ears. "It would be best that no one heard our discussion."

Magnus led them to an area where they could sit on the edge of the rise and look down upon the keep and the surrounding village.

While the view was beautiful Mary had no time to spare to enjoy it. She gave a quick glance over the land to see that Decimus's men were gathered for breakfast around their campfire. She had not spied Decimus and assumed he was still asleep, at least she hoped he was.

"Do you know where Roarke went?" she asked.

"He said nothing to me about his destination. He made mention that it was safer for you both if he left before anyone realized he was gone."

"I made a terrible blunder last night. I thought to protect Roarke and foolishly made matters worse for him." She told him what she had done and how Decimus had ordered two of his men to go after Roarke.

Magnus did not appear disturbed by her news. "I would not worry. Roarke can take care of himself. I suspect that he is a difficult man to track, let alone find. What presently concerns me are the plans that Decimus discussed with me last night."

"Our wedding." She sighed.

"At least you will wed here among friends. And two

weeks gives me time to see if other arrangements can be made."

"Death would be the only thing that frees me from Decimus."

"That can be arranged."

"I thought about faking my demise, but I believe somehow Decimus would know and that would make matters worse."

"I will do all I can, Mary."

"You have, Magnus, and I am so very grateful. Fate holds me in her hands now, and I pray she will be generous to me."

They heard someone approach and Mary wished it was Michael, though she knew otherwise. She would not have heard his approach; he would have merely appeared.

She wanted to cringe when she spotted Decimus, but she kept her disappointment to herself. His dark manner always made him appear angry, and he looked more so now as he approached them.

She turned away to look out over the village and keep. She did not feel like dealing with his arrogance. She was also annoyed with his dress. He donned garments that were impeccably tailored and fit for royalty. He favored dark colors right down to the deep red garnet and blue sapphire rings on his fingers. How he could adorn himself in such riches won off the souls of innocent people she did not know.

He stopped beside her; the bright sun glared over his shoulder. She looked up at him, shading her eyes with her hand.

"A beautiful day is it not?" she asked.

"I do not recall giving you permission to leave the keep."

Magnus stood. "I requested her company."

"You should have requested permission from me."

"Until she is wed, Mary is still in my charge," Magnus said in a defensive tone.

Mary did not wish them to battle over her, but it was not her place to step between them. She would undermine Magnus's authority and strengthen Decimus's power if she interfered.

Decimus seemed to consider for a moment and reluctantly said, "You are right. She is in your charge, though I expect proper action from her, which is *your* duty to foster."

Mary watched as Magnus fisted his hand at his side; that he wanted to punch Decimus was obvious. But she knew he would not demean himself. He would remain a warrior strong in command.

"And what is it that you wished to discuss that requires a distance from the keep?" Decimus asked before Magnus could respond to his chastising.

Magnus held out his hand to Mary and she took it, rising gracefully to her feet to stand beside him.

"It does not concern you," Magnus said firmly.

"*She* is my concern, especially what she discusses with another man."

"What I discuss with *Mary* is between Mary and me."

Mary held back her smile. While Decimus spoke of her with little regard, by not calling her by name, Magnus made a point of speaking her name aloud. He let Decimus know Mary was a person unto herself and not mere chattel to be bargained over.

"I warn you, Magnus, be careful. I do not tolerate insolence well."

"Then we have something in common." Magnus

held his arm out to Mary indicating that they would take their leave.

Mary took Magnus's arm.

"I wish to speak with Mary alone," Decimus said.

"Mary has much to do if the wedding is to proceed on time," Magnus said.

A grateful Mary remained silent. She had no desire to speak with Decimus. It seemed the more she spoke with the man, the more she disliked him.

"I will not detain her for long and I will see that she returns safely to the keep."

Mary sensed Magnus's reluctance. She knew however that to learn all she could about her future husband, would mean spending time with him, whether she cared to or not.

"I will be fine," she assured Magnus and slipped her arm out of his.

"As you say," Magnus said. "I will tell my wife that you will be with her shortly so that you may begin work on your wedding dress."

Mary nodded. "I will not keep her waiting." She appreciated Magnus graciously limiting her time with Decimus.

Decimus remained silent until Magnus disappeared in the distance.

"He cannot protect you for long."

Mary smiled. "I will have you, my husband, to protect me."

Decimus circled her like a prey intimidating its captor. "You will be well protected. I will *know* your every move. I will *decide* your every move. You will *obey* without question."

Mary wanted to choke on her own words, but she

forced them from her lips. "I will serve to be a good wife."

"You *will* be a good wife. I will tolerate nothing less from you."

"You have made yourself clear. I understand perfectly." Her tongue was slightly sharper than she intended, but his arrogant, self-righteous manner irritated her.

He grabbed her arm, his fingers pinching her skin. "Your mouth is much too quick and you much too foolish."

She yanked her arm from his grasp and stepped away from him. "I have yet to exchange vows with you, so it is you who speaks out of turn."

His nostrils flared, a warning she had learned quickly to recognize as anger, but at the moment she did not care how angry he was. She would surrender soon enough to him.

"You dare to be insolent to me?"

She silently reminded herself that she would gain nothing if she did not retain her composure, but it was difficult. He commanded in his every word. She had trouble tolerating his constant edicts—how she would tolerate it when they wed, she did not know. The sobering thought made her rethink her actions. If she were not careful she would worsen her situation.

She forced herself to apologize. "Forgive me, I was inconsiderate."

"*You* spoke out of turn."

He could not even accept an apology. How she wished she could tell him how very rude and obnoxious she thought he was. Instead she said, "I am learning."

"You have *much* to learn."

If she did not direct the discussion elsewhere, she would soon find herself lashing out at him once again.

"May I inquire what it is you wish to discuss with me?"

He crossed his arms over his chest and took a firm stance in front of her. "I have been informed that you love to sing."

Who could have told him that? Magnus was the only one aware of her penchant for singing.

"I raise my voice in song on occasion."

"Let me hear you."

She looked at him oddly.

"I wish to hear you sing. *Now.*"

She had always sung when she was happy and at peace with herself. Troubling times found her voice dormant, having no desire to raise it in song. And she certainly had no desire to raise it now for a man who would have no appreciation for the beauty of song.

She raised her hand to her throat. "My throat remains tender from your man's attempt to strangle me."

"You would not have incurred his wrath if you would have surrendered."

She shrugged. "As I said, my throat remains tender."

"Try anyway."

He was adamant but then so was she.

"I am sorry to disappointment you, but I cannot sing now."

"Did you sing for the Dark One?"

His question startled her. It was his tone more than the question itself. Or was she wrong to think she heard jealousy in his voice?

She rubbed her throat. "I raised my voice in song for no one."

He stared at her until she grew uncomfortable.

"I do not think you tell me the truth, especially about the Dark One."

Was he fishing for information about Michael? Did he hope she would unwittingly supply him with information? Was he using her to get to Michael?

"I have told you what I know of the Dark One."

"It seems that no one knows a thing about this mysterious shadow. He appears out of nowhere and vanishes without a trace. He must certainly practice the dark arts to be able to perform such magic."

"I would not know."

"You did not see him work any magic?"

He was searching for information to use against Michael if he ever caught him, and who better to get it from than the woman who would be his wife.

"I saw nothing out of the ordinary."

"You think him a mere man with no extraordinary powers?"

Michael was no mere man to her. He was strong, brave, and unselfish, surrendering his own life so that tortured and condemned souls could know freedom.

"You hesitate," Decimus said, gleefully, as if he had learned something from her.

"Of course I hesitate. How do I explain a man I know nothing of? We barely spoke since I had no voice. I simply followed him. As for extraordinary powers? I saw nothing that would make me believe he practices magic."

"Good," Decimus said with a single nod. "The Dark One is then an ordinary man and ordinary men make mistakes. I will be there when he makes his."

Mary felt as if she had just betrayed Michael. She should have remained silent offering Decimus not a word. Instead she felt the need to defend Michael for she loved Michael with all her heart.

Unfortunately her love could do more harm than good. She had to remember to hold her tongue when Decimus queried her about the Dark One.

He held out his arm to her. "We go so that you may see to your wedding dress."

He forever issued commands, never once asking but constantly telling what would be done. And she had no choice but to obey him; to refuse him would only cause anger and retribution.

She took his arm, keeping her touch light. By the time they reached the keep she was anxious to leave his side. The fearful looks he received as they walked through the village had upset her. How often would she see similar looks on other people? How could she tolerate a husband who caused such misery to so many?

Mary was quick to excuse herself.

"I will see you at supper."

Another command by him, another performance by her. Only one day and she was already tiring of the act. What was she to do?

She voiced the troublesome thought as she entered the tower room where Reena and Brigid sat with piles of material.

"He is more obnoxious and demanding than I thought possible."

"He is dangerous," Brigid said. "You must be careful."

Mary plopped down on the wool carpet where the women sat. "Decimus does not wish to hurt me. He wishes to tame me, bend me to his will, make me an obedient wife for all to see. Then he can bask in the glory of his achievement."

"How long do you think you will be able to continue your masquerade of a dutiful wife?" Reena asked, examining the material.

"She does not have a choice," Brigid reminded. "Her safety is at stake."

Mary picked through the various materials and colors without notice. "You are right and perhaps that is what is so very frustrating. I have no choice.

"There is still time," Reena said, attempting to offer hope. "Did you learn anything from him?"

"I think someone is betraying me though I cannot imagine who. Decimus implied that someone alerted him to my whereabouts, and then just moments ago he made mention of my penchant for singing. No one but Magnus knew of my love for raising my voice in song. And I know without a doubt he did not betray me." Mary shivered and rubbed the gooseflesh that raced along her arms. "It does make me wonder, though— who else knows these things about me? And how?"

"It would seem a ghost follows you," Brigid said, crossing herself.

"Nonsense," Reena argued. "Someone feeds Decimus information."

"But who?" Mary asked, pushing the material away from her.

Brigid shoved it back at her. "You must pick for your wedding dress."

Mary shook her head. "I have not the heart. You pick, I have heard talk that you work magic with a needle."

"There, you see," Reena said. "Mary has been here just past a day and already she hears of your sewing skills. People talk and offer information without even realizing it."

"I heard it in passing. Two servants girls were discussing sewing and one made mention of how she wished she possessed your talent with a needle."

"Could someone have overheard Magnus tell you of Mary's love for singing?" Brigid asked.

Reena shook her head. "We were alone at the time, no one was nearby."

"We are missing something here," Mary said.

"This color would compliment you," Brigid said, holding up a deep blue silk.

"That is too rich for me."

"Nonsense," Reena argued. "It is your wedding day."

"Not to the man of my choice. I care naught about my wedding dress. Do as you will, Brigid, but keep it plain. It is not a day of celebration for me."

"I will see to it for you."

"In the meantime we all need to ask more questions and listen to more conversations," Reena said.

They all agreed and Reena made haste to see if she could discover anything from the servants who had served Decimus's men. Brigid left after taking Mary's measurements. She intended to request sewing help from other women, hoping to see if she would learn anything useful from their gossip.

Mary remained alone in the tower room. She wanted to be away from everyone, alone with her thoughts and her aching heart. She missed Michael so very much, and try as she might not to think about him, it was not possible. He kept creeping into her thoughts reminding her of his touch, his kiss, his love, and she ached with want of him.

A tear fell from her eye, rolling off her cheek. She caught it with her finger and stared at the solitary droplet.

"Do you shed that tear for me?"

Chapter 23

"**M**ichael," she whispered and looked to the dark shadows in the room.

He drifted out of the darkness, swathed in his black shroud, and she jumped up and ran to him. He caught her in his strong arms hugging her tightly to him, melding them together as one, never to be parted.

How she wished never to be parted from him, and the aching thought made her cling more tenaciously to him.

"I have missed you," she said, "so *very, very* much."

"And I you."

She tilted her head and closed her eyes wanting him to kiss her.

He did not disappoint her. He kissed her like a man separated too long from the woman he loved, and she returned the same in kind.

Their lips were warm, the taste bittersweet, and the kiss pure magic. Neither wished to part, but time was not on their side.

Mary slipped her hand beneath his mask needing to

feel his face. He was warm and solid, and real. "You are not safe here."

"No one knows I am here."

"Decimus hunts you," she warned, fearful for him.

"He will not catch me. I know him too well."

"You cannot be sure."

"I will not leave you to him. You are mine. I love you and will see you safe."

She smiled and moved her hand to rest on his chest. "I feel protected when you are near."

"You are always safe with me by your side." He squeezed her to him and nuzzled her neck. "I wish there were more time."

"It is dangerous," she said, though she wanted desperately to make love with him.

"One taste of you has intoxicated me, and I will not be satisfied until I have tasted you again."

"I wish to quench my thirst with you as well, but I fear for you."

"Do not fear for me, I know what I do."

She suddenly remembered Roarke and hurriedly told him of what she had done.

"Worry not, Roarke is safe and will remain so."

They were startled apart by footfalls on the stairs.

"Go," she urged him.

"Tonight," he whispered as he returned to the shadows. "I come to you."

She smiled and shivered in anticipation.

A tap at the door had her calling out, "Enter."

A young servant girl entered the room cautiously, her eyes wide, her face pale. "Lord Decimus insists on your presence in the great hall."

The girl was obviously distraught and Mary wondered if something was amiss.

Mary hurried down the steps and entered the hall. Magnus and Thomas, along with their wives, stood near the dais.

"What is wrong?" Brigid asked worried.

"Decimus ordered Mary to the hall," Magnus said. "He is in a rage about something."

Mary placed a hand to her churning stomach. Had he discovered the Dark One's presence?

Decimus stormed into the hall and stopped abruptly when he saw the others surrounding Mary. He looked as if he had rushed, perspiration dotting his forehead.

"I demanded *your* presence, Mary. The rest of you are dismissed."

Magnus stepped forward, his expression stern. "I think not. I give the orders in my keep."

Decimus glared at him with furious eyes that looked heated with the fires of hell. "My power exceeds yours."

"Not in my home."

Decimus stepped forward. "You will—"

Mary hurried between them. "I am at your service, my lord."

"At least someone knows her place," Decimus said and grabbed Mary by the arm.

Magnus looked ready to reach for Decimus's neck when his wife walked up beside him and took his arm.

"You will make it worse for Mary," Reena whispered.

Magnus calmed and murmured. "All would be well again by killing the bastard." He reluctantly bowed to his wife's wisdom and stepped back.

"How dare you insult me," Decimus said in a fury to Mary.

"Insult you? I know not what you talk about."

"Your wedding dress," he said as though his words explained all.

She looked blankly at him.

"I heard talk the dress is plain."

"There is something wrong with that?" she asked, baffled by his concern with her dress.

"I distinctly told you to make certain the dress signified my high status in the Church. Only a peasant wears a plain dress for her wedding. I expect rich material and a dress adorned with many jewels." Decimus ranted. "I will not be insulted on my wedding day by a bride who dresses beneath her station."

Mary did the only thing she could to appease the frantic man. "I apologize and meant no disrespect to you."

"You do not take our wedding seriously."

Mary bit her tongue, wanting to rant herself.

"I am generous with you and here you disregard my offer of salvation."

She eased her arm from his grasp. "I do not need saving."

"All the wicked need saving."

She could argue with him but it would do her little good. His beliefs were heavily ingrained in him, and he would allow no room for new thought. She would not waste her time on the ignorant.

"I will see that the necessary changes are made to the dress." She looked to Brigid who nodded, letting her know she would take care of it.

"If there is nothing else, I wish to take my leave," Mary said, making an attempt to act the obedient wife.

"Where do you go?" Decimus asked.

As far away from you as possible. How she wished she could walk out of the hall and keep going. She would walk all the way to freedom no matter how long it took her.

"Reena and I need to talk with the cook in regards to the wedding feast."

Reena stepped forward. "She is waiting for us."

"I grant you permission to leave," Decimus said and marched out the door.

Mary turned to Reena. "I care naught about the food for the wedding."

"Do not worry, it is being seen to," Reena said. "You are free to do as you wish."

Mary nodded and walked to the front doors. She peered out searching for signs of Decimus. Not seeing him, she left the hall and made her way through the village.

She made her way past the cottages, smiling every now and again at those people brave enough to look her way and return her smile. Most of the villagers averted their eyes, pretending they did not see her. She understood their fear, not of her but of Decimus and his power. She kept her distance, not wanting to add to their concern.

She turned down a narrow dirt path that wound its way into the woods, and when she found a secluded spot she sat on the hard ground and braced her back against a thick spruce tree.

Forever.

The thought that she was committed to Decimus forever caused her stomach to churn. According to his beliefs she would be wed to him, not only in this lifetime, but when they passed beyond. They would be *forever one.*

Her stomach protested and she rested her hand on it.

She had not given as much thought to her wedding day as she should have, but for a good reason. If she dwelled on her wedding she would need to face the consequences of her wedding night.

Michael had reminded her before they had made love that she would face the consequences of her decision. She had not given much thought to her wedding night. She had not wanted to. The idea of sharing intimacy with Decimus turned her stomach, so she had ignored it.

If he ranted so badly over a wedding dress, how would he react to an impure wife?

Mary rubbed her temple, a slight ache starting. She felt so very alone and had for a very long time. It was not until Michael had entered her life that her loneliness had vanished.

She smiled. It was odd to think that a shadow had brought light and love into her life. She was so grateful to him and did not regret for a moment loving him, no matter the consequences.

She did not know what her future would bring. She hoped it would be with Michael, someday, somehow. But for now she had to take one day at a time and survive.

Mary raised her head at the sound of footsteps and suddenly Horace came bounding out of the woods to plop down next to her. The dog was a loveable one, big floppy ears and a mixture of colors. He loved to be hugged and rubbed. She wondered where he had been of late.

Horace barked once and looked to the woods. A man large in girth walked out, leaning on a walking stick as he took slow steps toward them.

"He knows I cannot keep up with him and always gets ahead of me." The man stopped in front of Mary. "I am Patrick, Reena's father."

Mary was about to get up.

"Nay, do not disturb yourself. I will join you. I need a rest." He lowered himself slowly to the ground beside her. "Horace has been staying with my wife and me. Decimus ordered him gone from the keep. Guess he is afraid of the animal."

Mary thought that odd. A man like Decimus afraid of a dog?

"I heard you were a storyteller," Mary said smiling.

"And you look like you need to hear a story."

Horace seemed to understand the word *story* and settled down between the two to listen.

An hour later Mary knew all about the Legend and Reena and the way she had saved her village from starvation, and how the pair had fallen in love despite Reena's efforts to have him wed her best friend, Brigid. And how in the end Reena suffered the torture of the rack while Magnus fought to free his love. So they lived happily ever after.

Until Decimus and Mary.

"What tale will you tell of me?"

"That is up to you," Patrick said. "Your tale has yet to be written."

They parted ways when they reached the keep, Patrick and Horace returning to their cottage and Mary reluctantly heading to the keep.

How would her tale end, she wondered? Would she be its author or would another?

It was close to supper when she entered the keep and she hurried to her bedchamber to freshen herself. She combed her hair, leaving the long blond strands to hang free and frame her face. Her cheeks glowed pink from the fresh air and her skin was warm from the sun.

Her solitary outing and storytelling time had served

her well. She was ready to face the evening meal with Decimus. But more importantly she could not wait to make love with Michael tonight.

Her heart ached to see him and her body pulsated with anticipation of his touch.

Mary entered the hall to see most everyone seated at the dais. The seat beside Decimus was empty, waiting for her. No one occupied the seat to her left. It had been purposely left empty so that her attention would be solely on Decimus. She would have him and him alone to converse with.

Magnus sat to Decimus's right, Reena next to her husband, Brigid next to Reena and then Thomas.

Mary approached the table with a smile. She would keep high spirits even though he segregated her from her friends. She had later this evening with Michael to look forward to, and no one could steal that happiness from her.

Decimus stared at her when she took her seat.

"Good evening, my lord," she said graciously, bowing her head.

He seemed a bit befuddled and about to say something when he shook his head and leaned his face near to hers.

"You think to bewitch me with your beauty?"

She was startled by his accusation and did not know how to respond.

"You will wear your hair plaited as befitting a righteous woman, one who does not wish to call attention to herself."

"As you wish," she said, but before she could slip from her seat he grabbed her hand.

"Where do you go?"

"To do as you direct."

He lowered his voice to a deep rumble. "Not now, just do not wear your hair that way ever again."

"As you say." She settled in her seat.

Bored with her isolation and with an upset stomach, she ate little of her meal. She heard peels of laughter coming from Reena and Brigid and wished she could join them. She never truly had friends; the cottage where she had lived was as isolated as she was now.

There had been a village a bit of a distance from her home, and she had made a few acquaintances but no true friends. She felt Reena and Brigid were her first true friends, and she wanted to spend time with them while she could.

She noticed that Decimus would send Reena and Brigid scathing looks when they laughed. He probably thought joy a sin.

Magnus finally broke her boredom, though this caused her a dilemma without her at first realizing it. He suggested she sing.

"Treat us to your angelic voice, Mary."

Decimus ordered her not to raise her voice in song, but Magnus made it clear that this was his home and his word was law. Could she tempt fate and sing? She would love to raise her voice in a joyous tune. Singing healed her soul, and right now her soul could use some healing.

She decided to take a chance. She stood and avoided looking at Decimus, knowing he would not be pleased with her actions. She walked around the dais to stand in front of everyone. Tables were filled with many of Magnus's warriors and Decimus's men as well. The hall grew silent.

She chose a gay tune she and her mother would often sing together, and as soon as she began smiles spread wide. She never thought her ability special, but all who heard it swore she possessed the voice of an angel.

Her voice was clear and smooth, and sweet echoes rang off the stone walls, making it sound as if a chorus of angels sang along with her.

Once she started she did not want to stop, and she went from song to song. Everyone cheered her on, except Decimus.

He sat back in his chair staring at her, and she could only wonder what devious plans and punishments he conjured.

She finished with a beautiful love song, her voice hitting notes surely only an angel could reach. Silence followed her song and tears could be detected slipping down cheeks. Then the hall exploded into applause, the warriors, honoring her, jumped to their feet.

Mary smiled with joy and bowed several times before returning to her seat.

Decimus said nothing to her, though he stared at her with heated eyes. Surely she would suffer for her insolence, but she did not care. Her singing had restored her soul. She felt nourished and complete.

Decimus would impose his punishment, though, and one that was much too costly to her. He kept her at the table while he spoke with Magnus about nonsense. One by one the others drifted off to bed, the hall emptied, and still he would not let her go, no matter how many times she requested to take her leave. He denied her until she herself drifted off to sleep in her chair.

Decimus woke her and she saw the hall was empty and they were alone.

"I give you permission to leave," he said.

She struggled to stand, groggy from being woken from her sleep. She bowed her head and walked off.

"Mary."

She turned to face him.

"Never go against my orders again."

She bowed her head and felt herself close to tears as she left the room. Decimus mattered not, but Michael did, and she feared she had missed his visit.

She climbed the stairs slowly, her body still heavy with sleep. She entered her bedchamber, locking the latch behind her and looking around the room.

"Michael," she called out softly.

Nothing emerged from the shadows, and her shoulders slumped in disappointment. She walked to her bed discarding her clothes along the way and stopped, her eyes misting with tears. There on her pillow, on a piece of cloth, lay a bunch of berries.

Michael had been there and had brought her berries just like he had done when they were together. And she had missed his visit.

She wrapped the cloth around the berries and held them to her chest. "I miss you and I love you so very much."

She crawled into bed with a heavy sadness in her heart, and with the cloth of berries snug in her hand, slept.

She dreamed Michael was touching her, kissing her, whispering words of love to her, and she did not want the dream to end. She fought against opening her eyes, fought against letting him go again.

"Open your eyes, Mary. The room is dark and I want you to know that it is me making love to you."

Chapter 24

Mary slowly opened her eyes, still afraid she was dreaming. The room was dark, the near-dying fire's light barely casting a glow in the room. Above her loomed a shadow.

"Michael?" she whispered.

"I told you I would come." He brushed his lips over hers.

"I thought it too late, that I had missed you."

"I could not go without seeing you."

"Go?" she asked anxiously. "You are leaving? How long will you be gone?" The thought that she might not see him for some time sent an uneasiness rushing through her, settling heavily in her stomach.

"I have work to do, Mary," he reminded.

"I can help."

"We will see. Now, no more talk," he whispered. "I want to make love to you."

"I have missed touching you." She walked her fingers slowly up his arms, over his chest, and then down his hard belly.

"Careful," he warned, "or this will be a short evening together."

They both laughed and kissed, their hands reaching out to touch and love each other with a fierce tenderness born of a solid love.

His lips captured her nipples and he enjoyed the taste of her so sweet and tender. He had little time until dawn, but he did not wish to rush. He wanted to linger and savor every inch of her before he took his leave with dawn's first light.

She moaned and he reminded her that she must remain silent. She quickly stifled her heated response, fearful they might be caught.

His hands roamed her soft silky flesh, coming to rest between her legs. He gently enticed her to respond, and she did immediately, stirring his own passion just as quickly. It had not been long since their last time together but it seemed like an eternity. And now he wanted an eternity to make love to her.

She climaxed with a soft sigh and he smiled, though she could not see it. He wanted to please her over and over, only then would he join with her.

Mary attempted to have her way with him, but he was in total control on this night, and she could do nothing but surrender to his love.

After several soft sighs spilled from her lips, Michael slipped over and into her. She grasped his arms as he brought her to the peak of ecstasy, and together they spiraled into oblivion.

It took a while for their breathing to return to normal and for their racing hearts to calm. In the meantime they remained locked in each other's arms, refusing to let go, refusing to allow this moment to end, refusing to say goodbye once again.

Michael rolled off her and shifted her to rest against his side. She went willingly, wanting to remain beside him as long as possible.

When his breathing finally calmed he asked, "How goes it with you and Decimus?"

"He is an ignorant, arrogant fool."

"He is no fool," he warned.

"You are right," she reluctantly admitted. "His beliefs are so strong that it makes him dangerous."

"Can you wed a dangerous man?"

"Do I have a choice?" She tapped his chest. "You are a dangerous man but I would wed you willingly."

"Do you propose to me?"

She walked her fingers over his chest, up to his mouth, to slowly stroke his lips. "Would you wed me if you could?"

He took hold of her finger. "I would wed you as fast as I could and forever keep you mine."

She locked her fingers with his and held them firm. "Then know this now, this moment, this day, I pledge my love to you. I will give my love to no other, my heart is yours, my soul is yours, and I am yours *forever and always*."

"We exchange vows then here and now, I pledge my love to you. My heart and soul are yours now and beyond time. I give them freely to you. I will keep your love safe in my heart and see that no harm comes to it, and I swear by our love that I will see no harm come to *you*."

They kissed to seal their vows and Mary felt at peace. It did not matter now what vows she exchanged with Decimus for she had already exchanged vows with Michael. In her heart Michael was her husband forever and always.

"Sleep," he said and held her tight.

She knew he did not wish to say goodbye again, and he would leave her in sleep as he did the last time. She wanted to ask when she would see him again, but kept silent. She was content at this moment and she would leave it so.

She snuggled against him and fell asleep with a peaceful heart.

Morning dawned with beautiful skies and Reena asked Mary to join her as she walked the woods to draw plants. Old Margaret the healer had asked Reena if she would record the plants and their properties so that she could teach others her skills.

Mary was thrilled to participate in Reena's project and glad to be away from the keep and Decimus. It would also give her time alone to talk with Reena.

Mary dressed in the plain skirt and blouse Glenda had given her. She felt comfortable in the clothes; they were who she was. The richer materials did not suit her, and she was uncomfortable wearing them.

Her wedding dress held no interest. She was grateful Brigid had the project well in hand.

After she slipped on her soft leather boots and grabbed her brown shawl in case the weather should change, Mary left her room and hurried down the steps to meet Reena at Old Margaret's cottage.

At the bottom of the steps she turned the corner and ran into Decimus. Their bodies hit, and Decimus reached out to grab her arms and steady them.

She almost recoiled from the sweet scent that permeated the air around him. She could not quite place the scent, though she had smelled it on him before, but not as strongly. The strength in which he held her reminded her of his power and how truly imprisoned she was.

The thought made her want to flee.

"In a hurry?"

Had he sensed her eagerness to be gone from him?

She kept her calm, not wanting to diminish her chance of joining Reena for her outing. "Aye, my lord."

"Where do you go?"

She should have known he would want to know her whereabouts. Would he question her plans? Not if he did not know them.

"I go to meet Reena."

"Good, you work on plans for the wedding."

If he said so that was fine with her.

"I wish to talk with you later."

"Have I done something to offend?" she asked, not wanting to concern herself with the reason for their talk.

"It is time for you to know exactly what I expect of you as my wife."

Mary nodded. "As you wish." It would be better for him to detail her duties, then she would know what to expect and how to behave, and how she could use both to her advantage.

She lowered her head, averting her eyes from his, and waited for him to dismiss her.

To her surprise he slipped his finger under her chin and lifted her head until their eyes met.

"Tell me, Mary, have you ever kissed a man?"

He played with her and she intended to win the game.

"My lord," she said, spreading her eyes wide. "It would not be proper to kiss a man who is not your husband."

His nostrils flared; she had won.

"Go, I will speak with you later."

"Have a good day, my lord," she said with a slight bow of her head and stepped around him, keeping her pace unhurried, though she wished to run. She did not want him to know she wanted nothing more than to escape his presence.

"Mary!"

His booming voice stopped her cold, shivers running through her. She turned reluctantly and he waited for her to return to his side. She walked over to him.

"My lord?"

"Why do you wear peasant clothes?"

Her hands grabbed at the sides of her plain brown skirt. Her mind thought fast. "Reena and I are foraging the woods for flowers and greenery appropriate for my headdress. I did not wish to soil or ruin my fine garments."

"You may go," he said satisfied with her explanation.

This time she hurried her steps, though not so anyone noticed, and once outside the hall doors she picked up her pace and made a dash for Old Margaret's cottage.

Mary entered the cottage; the front door was open, welcoming all.

"You look well this fine day," Old Margaret said.

Mary smiled. "How could I not on this beautiful day."

"I am pleased that you will be helping Reena record my plants."

"I look forward to learning as I help," Mary said, always eager to gain new knowledge.

"Good, go then and enjoy, though be careful of the storm."

"And here I thought the day would remain sunny," Reena said, handing a basket covered with a cloth to Mary and slinging a leather pouch over her shoulder.

"The tempest begins," Old Margaret warns. "And does not settle soon."

The two women took heed of her warning and walked to the door.

"Mary," Old Margaret said, "a moment of your time?"

Reena walked out the door leaving the two women to talk.

"Be careful, Mary, you glow with love."

Mary placed her hand to her heart. "It shows."

"I see what others do not, but your love is strong and will refuse to remain hidden. Others will soon see."

"Thank you for the warning."

"God be with you, Mary. Your task will not be easy."

Mary joined Reena and they spoke not a word until they entered the safety of the woods.

"Is everything all right?" Reena asked.

"I pray so." Mary did not wish to burden Reena with more problems nor chance her knowing anything that could bring her harm.

They set to work searching for plants. Reena would do quick sketches of the plant while Mary recorded the conditions surrounding it.

"It is good that you can write and read, few do," Reena said.

"My parents felt it was important for me to understand many written and oral languages."

"My mother felt the same," Reena said. "And while I protested when I was young, I am grateful for my knowledge now."

They stopped to eat, the basket packed with bread, cheese, and cider.

"You carry more of a burden than you tell," Reena said, the large tree branches shading the spot where they sat. "Did Old Margaret see something that upset you?"

"She is a seer?"

"More a healer, though at times she sees things," Reena said. "Perhaps she saw what is obvious. You look different this morning. Happier, more content."

Mary silently chastised herself for being foolish. She had felt happier this morning. Though Michael had been gone when she woke, his scent had remained on her pillow and she had hugged it to her. The memories of the night before brought a smile to her face that she could not shed. She had not thought that others would see a change in her, but there had been a change. She had made love with the man she loved, and it had filled her with joy and peace.

Reena reached out to her. "I keep a good confidence."

Mary trusted her; she needed to. She needed a friend to share her burden with. "The Dark One came to me last night."

"You love him very much?"

Mary nodded. "I have never looked upon his face, but it matters not, for I know his heart."

"You must be careful; he must be careful."

"I know. I worry that our love will place him in jeopardy. I worry that he will take chances that he should not take, and I worry that we will not be together."

"Too much of a burden for one to carry alone," Reena said.

"I have carried many burdens. I had hoped one day my load would be lightened."

"Miracles do happen."

"All the time," Mary said.

"I have been thinking," Reena said. "The information we have gathered has been insufficient in finding out how Decimus tracked you down, and it appears that you and the Dark One remained barely a few steps ahead of him in his pursuit. Is there anyone you know that may connect the Dark One, Decimus, and you?"

"I have met a few people who know both men, though they knew naught of me. And then there is Roarke, but again he did not know me. I thought Magnus sent the Dark One to help me, but how did he learn of my need?"

"We've learned a man overheard two others who spoke of your plight and contacted the Dark One. When the Dark One learned that it was Decimus who searched for you, he knew that Magnus was your protector."

"Who was this man who contacted the Dark One? And what interest did he have in me?"

Reena shook her head. "I do not know and the Dark One never told Magnus the man's identity."

"Perhaps this mysterious man is the link to my being betrayed," Mary said.

"And why now after all these years would someone betray you?"

"Perhaps he is more foe than friend," Mary suggested.

"Then that would mean another hunts you."

"Or that another looks after me?"

"There is only one person who can answer that question," Reena said.

"The Dark One," they said in unison.

Chapter 25

The storm clouds that had gathered overhead upon Mary and Reena's return dumped a heavy rainfall on the land just before sunset. Everyone ran for cover and the village settled in for the night.

Mary was tired, having slept little the night before. An early supper and sleep was the only thing on her mind. Could she escape for the night and cloister herself in her bedchamber without causing a problem?

Decimus had wanted to speak with her, though he had not summoned her since her return to the keep. She hoped to beg a headache and be left alone for the night. Tomorrow would be soon enough to talk with him, but then there was also the rest of her life to talk with him.

Reena helped to fashion her excuse intending to prevent anyone from disturbing Mary, if she could.

Mary had just tossed herself on the bed to wait for the light fare Reena was having sent to her room when a sharp knock sounded at the door.

"Mary! I wish to speak with you."

She rolled her eyes at Decimus's familiar voice.

"I am not feeling well, can it not wait?"

"Open the door."

She sat up quickly, shivers racing through her upon hearing his tightly controlled speech. He was angry and she wished to cause no problems for herself or anyone else.

She went to the door and opened it, keeping her head respectably bowed.

He grabbed the door from her hand and slammed it shut, the force sending the sound echoing throughout the keep.

"I will tell this to you now, and you will remember it well."

She looked at him, and there in his dark eyes that raged in anger she thought she saw loneliness. It was a brief sighting and one she was not fully certain she had seen at all, it so startled her.

"No locked doors will ever separate us."

There would be no place to escape him, ever.

"We will talk now," he said, letting her know he expected no reply, just obedience.

Though her head had not ached before, it did now. "Please, can this not wait? My head aches."

"I will not tolerate excuses."

She wanted to scream at him to leave her alone, to go away and never come back, but her silent ranting served no purpose other than to cause her head to throb more.

She held her hand to her head. "I speak the truth, my—" She suddenly felt dizzy and stumbled backward.

Decimus was quick to reach out to her, grabbing her arm. He had just lifted her up into his arms when the door opened.

Reena walked in with a tray of food and stood startled by the sight of Mary's head resting against Decimus's chest.

"You have a healer?" he asked, looking to Reena.

She nodded.

"Go fetch her at once."

Reena left the tray on the table and hurried out the door.

Decimus carried Mary to the bed and laid her down gently. "From this moment on you will do nothing without my approval and I care not what anyone says."

"Mary is still under my guardianship," Magnus said from the open doorway.

"She is no longer," Decimus challenged with authority. "She is my wife to be and, therefore, my responsibility."

Magnus attempted to protest.

"Do not make me go to the king to make it official," Decimus warned. "You may be in his favor, but he will not deny me."

Magnus could not argue. He knew Decimus was right.

Old Margaret entered the room and seeing the two men about ready to battle, ordered them out. "Be gone, both of you, while I tend to her."

"I will stay," Decimus said.

"You will not," Old Margaret said firmly. "I am the healer here and I know what is good for her. Now be gone. I will let you know when you can return."

Decimus looked down at Mary, her eyes were barely open, he then looked to the healer. "Treat her well or you will suffer."

"She is in good hands, my lord," Old Margaret said then turned her back on him.

Magnus waited until Decimus left the room then followed him out, closing the door behind them after Reena slipped into the room.

Old Margaret heated water over the fire and mixed a special brew after Mary complained about her head.

"You are not well," Reena said surprised, sitting by her side on the bed. "I thought it a ruse as we planned."

"My head began to ache when Decimus knocked on my door. Then I grew dizzy and my stomach felt upset."

"Has this happened before?" Old Margaret asked, returning to the side of the bed.

"Nay, it has not."

"Drink this. It will help you rest." Old Margaret handed her a cup of the steaming brew. "You will sleep well and your head will feel better when you wake."

Reena and the healer helped Mary get undressed and settled her in the bed before Decimus was told he could speak with Mary.

"Only a few moments," Old Margaret warned him before she left. "She needs to rest."

Reena sat in a chair near the bed and Magnus stood next to his wife.

"I will be alone with her," Decimus ordered.

Reena did not want to leave Mary alone with him. "I thought to sit with her in case she requires help."

"Wait outside," he ordered and looked to Magnus as if ordering him to tend to his wife.

Magnus took his wife's arm. "We will wait outside the door."

Decimus sat on the bed beside her.

Mary's eyes flickered open.

"I have made a decision, Mary."

She wondered if she dreamed that Decimus sat beside her. Her head felt light and fuzzy, and she did not know if she was awake or asleep.

"We will not wait to wed. By week's end you will be my wife."

She sighed. "You are not real. This is not real. Nothing is real."

"I am real, Mary," he said and slowly reached out to touch her face. "I am very real. And you are mine."

Reena returned after Decimus left and let Mary know that she was there and would remain so throughout the night.

"Nay, you must not," she whispered. "I must be alone, please leave me alone." She begged until Reena agreed and left her to sleep.

Mary dreamed all night, her aching head playing tricks on her. One minute she thought Decimus was with her and the next she was certain Michael was there, until she finally realized that she was alone in her bedchamber.

Only then when she was certain no one was with her did she close her eyes and whisper, "Michael, I love you."

Her eyes were heavy with sleep when she heard the faint whisper. She ignored it wanting to remain in the cocoon of peaceful slumber. But it was a persistent whisper and she had no choice but to heed it.

Mary.

She struggled to wake, struggled to open her eyes.

Mary, I have little time.

Michael? Did Michael call her? Was she dreaming again? She fought harder to shake the sleep from her.

"Mary, are you all right?"

"Michael?"

"It is me. Are you well?"

She tried to open her eyes but they were so very heavy. "So tired . . ." She could not get the rest of the words from her mouth.

"Say nothing. Rest."

She needed to ask him something, but she was not certain what it was. Her mind was too foggy to think. It was important, though; she knew it was. But what was it?

"Question," she murmured.

"Sleep," he urged her. "Stay well."

Important. The question was important.

Why could she not remember?

"I love you," he whispered.

The words *I love you* were strong in her mind, but she could not force the thought aloud. And she returned to her cocoon of peaceful slumber.

Mary woke to a clap of thunder the next morning feeling much better, though concerned—she was not certain of last night's events. Had Michael visited her? Had Decimus told her they would wed by week's end? She did not know her dreams from reality, but she intended to find out.

After dressing in her green shift and tunic and plaiting her long blond hair she hurried to the great hall ready to eat.

Reena and Brigid sat at a table near the large fireplace where no one else was in sight, a relief to Mary. At least she would be able to eat her meal in peace.

"We heard the news," Reena said.

Mary shook her head as she joined them. "So it is true, I am to wed by week's end."

"You did not know?" Brigid asked surprised.

"After I drank Old Margaret's brew last night, I was not certain of anything."

"But you feel well this morning?" Reena asked.

"I have not an ache in my head and I am famished."

Reena ordered a servant girl to bring food for Mary, then huddled with the women to discuss the situation. "We have not much time."

"There is nothing we can do to stop this wedding," Mary said, knowing it was time to face the inevitable. "Even if we discover someone had betrayed me, what difference would it make? Decimus has decreed he will wed me and his word is final."

"Perhaps this person can protect you," Reena said, struggling to find a solution.

"If this mysterious person had the power to protect her, would he have not stepped forward by now?" Brigid asked.

"She is right," Mary said.

"There must be a way—"

Mary placed her hand on Reena's arm. "There is nothing that can be done. It is my fate to wed Decimus. I would like nothing more than for that not to be true, but it is and I can run from it no more."

"You are brave," Brigid said with a tear in her eye.

"I am not brave. I am fearful of wedding Decimus and"—Mary choked back her own tears—"I am glad I have known true love."

The three women shared tears and promises to always be friends, and of course Reena refused to believe that something could not be done to save Mary.

"I will continue my search," Reena said.

"She is not happy unless she is searching and getting herself into trouble," Brigid said teasingly.

"Mary!"

The three women jumped and turned to see Decimus marching into the great hall, his clothing wet from the heavy rain.

"We talk," he said and directed her to follow him with a wave of his hand.

She hurried after him, noticing the strength of his strides and the rigid way in which he carried himself. He was a man with strong beliefs, and he expected all to follow him.

She had spent precious time attempting to find a way not to wed him. Now it was necessary to find out more about the man who was to be her husband. She would need to know him well if she was to protect herself from harm.

He took her to his bedchamber. She hesitated at the door, it being not at all proper for her to be there. His scathing look warned of punishment if she did not obey, and she reluctantly entered the room.

"Sit," he ordered, pointing to the lone chair by the table.

He stood near the fireplace warming his hands.

He was richly dressed. His tunic was the color of deep red wine and was trimmed with gold and as usual he wore his rings. A gold cross on a heavy gold, chain hung around his neck. He certainly did not mind adorning himself.

"You are well this morning?" he asked after she had sat.

"I feel much better this morning. Thank you for asking."

He rubbed his hands together, they looked strong though his fingers were narrow, and she could not help but wonder how many people those very hands had hurt.

"I want you to rest today. I will instruct the servants to tend to you."

"It is not necessary. I am fine and I prefer to do for myself."

He glared at her. "This is why I wished to talk. I will make your duties as my wife clear, and then you will know how to behave."

"As you say." She had the feeling that she would repeat those words often.

He began with, "You will not speak unless I give you permission."

He droned on, detailing every step of her life with him. He would control her every movement, her every breath, her every thought. There would be no reason for her to think for herself, he would do it for her.

"After all," he said. "Women are inferior to men."

She remained quiet listening like a dutiful, inferior woman, while silently swearing that she would teach him otherwise. She would learn his faults and use them to her advantage.

It was evident that his first fault was arrogance and that certainly did not serve anyone well.

He walked closer to her and stared as though he looked through her, and she shifted uncomfortably in the chair. Did he see something? Did he sense something? His dark eyes made her uneasy and she looked away.

"Are you prepared to do your wifely duties, Mary?" he asked roughly.

She had not anticipated that question. Making love was not a duty, and she was grateful she had learned that with Michael. When two people loved it was a beautiful joining of two hearts and souls.

She did not know if he expected an answer. She had

none for him. How could she, when the thought of being intimate with him turned her stomach.

"I expect you to do your duty."

She stared at him, not understanding what he wanted from her.

"It is every wife's duty."

Her look became more confused.

He lifted her chin with one finger. "We will wed and you will give me a son."

Chapter 26

Mary was grateful for the knock on the door that interrupted them and allowed her to seek solace in her bedchamber, while Decimus saw to an urgent matter with his men.

She sat on the bed giving thought to his words. The idea that she would bear Decimus's children horrified her. Was that why she had not given the idea thought before? And what of Michael?

She placed a tender hand to her belly. What if she already carried his child? She had not even considered the possibility, or had she not wanted to? It would be a joy to have Michael's child. But to have Decimus raise the babe?

A heavy sigh had her throwing herself back on the bed. How could she let Michael's worst enemy raise his child? If there was a child. If not, she had nothing to worry about.

But what if she was with child? A child conceived from the love she shared with Michael . . .

"A foolish thought," she admonished herself. Having Michael's child now would not be fair to Michael or the child.

A knock sounded at her door. "Mary, it is Magnus."

She went to the door and let him in.

"I have been meaning to talk with you," he said.

He looked burdened. "Come, let us sit by the hearth and talk."

Mary always thought Magnus was a handsome man, and she thought he was even more so now after seeing him with Reena. They seemed to fit so perfectly together, though he was large and she small, it made no difference. When together there was no doubt the couple were in love.

He reached out and took her hand. "You were always strong. When your parents died and I took you away, you complained not and you shed your tears when you thought I could not hear you. Through the years I watched you grow into a remarkable young woman and . . ."

It seemed hard for him to continue.

"I did not want this for you, Mary. I wanted you free to live your life and to love."

Mary squeezed his hand. "It is my turn to save you and yours as you once did for me."

"I did not rescue you so that one day you would rescue me."

"Perhaps you did. Perhaps this is what was meant to be all along. Perhaps my destiny has always been with Decimus."

"That is not a thought I wish to consider."

"Do not worry yourself, Magnus. I am resigned to my destiny. I could not have it any other way. To think that Reena, you, Brigid, Thomas, or anyone here at the keep would suffer because of me is not acceptable to me."

"I want you to know that I will never stop trying to free you of Decimus."

She smiled. "That is a good thought for then I will always hope."

"Reena has hope. She feels there is something more to you wedding Decimus than anyone knows." Magnus shook his head. "When my wife gets an idea in her head, there is no stopping her."

"We have talked and what she says does make sense. Why would Decimus hunt me all these years? How did he *suddenly* find me? And why wed me? There are many other sinners he can reform."

"Reena believes the man who contacted the Dark One holds the answer. Unfortunately we have not been able to discover his identity."

Mary threw her hands up in the air in frustration. "That is what I wished to ask him."

"Ask who what?"

Mary realized her mistake. Magnus knew nothing of her love for Michael. Reena had given her word that she would tell no one and had kept it, though Mary never doubted she would.

"There is something important you are not telling me."

Mary hesitated, wondering how wise it was for anyone to know of her love for the Dark One. It would place them in jeopardy, which she had already done with Reena. Could she chance doing the same to Magnus?

She chose her words carefully. "The Dark One visits with me to see how I fair. I thought to ask him the identity of the man who requested his help."

"The Dark One is a good man and was upset when he heard the news that Decimus demanded to wed you."

She smiled. "He wished to see me safe."

"He has guided many to safety with no regard to his own well-being. He visits you here in the keep?"

She nodded.

"He should be more careful sneaking in under Decimus's watchful eye. The man seems to see and know everything."

"The Dark One seems to know more."

"Still," Magnus shook his head. "There is always a chance of him getting caught. Decimus's men just requested a meeting. They appeared anxious over something. One of them could have spotted the Dark One and they, at this moment, could be setting a trap for him."

Mary stood. "We should find out."

"Not an easy task. They are well trained in keeping their own counsel."

"We can try," she said, intending to protect the man she loved from harm. If Decimus's men were out to capture the Dark One, she would see their plans foiled.

By evening nothing had been learned. Decimus's men remained tight-lipped, sharing nothing with anyone in the village nor were they overheard discussing any news.

Mary wanted the Dark One to visit again soon, and then she did not want him to visit at all. She was selfish in her desire for him, yet concerned for his safety, which meant it would be wiser for him to keep his distance from her.

Then there was her question. Who was the mysterious man who requested the Dark One's help with Mary? Was he friend or foe? And could he answer her many questions?

The next few days were a whirlwind of activities. Plans for the wedding took priority and everyone in the keep was busy preparing for the ceremony and celebration.

Decimus had given strict orders that the affair be a joyous celebration. Magnus saw no point in arguing that few saw the wedding as a cheerful occasion of Mary's good fortune. Mary was the reason he agreed to a festive celebration, and the villagers would attend out of duty, fear, and respect for her.

Mary did the best she could to keep her spirits up as her wedding day drew closer, but it was not an easy task. Her thoughts lingered on Michael, who had not visited with her since she had been ill. She wondered over his health and safety and if he was risking his life to help others.

When she could, she would sneak away to the woods and sit in the solitude of the trees and the blossoming spring growth. Spring was in full bloom. The trees and flowers were vibrant with color, the earth's soil rich and ripe with plants.

Here amongst nature's beauty she would settle, relax and sing a gentle tune. Her singing calmed her and brought her peace, and no one but the animals and birds could hear her.

She sat today, the spring air warm, the sweet scent of freshly bloomed flowers strong in the air, and her thoughts chaotic. In two days she would wed Decimus and be bound to him for life.

She had not thought to ask him where they would make their home and it concerned her. How would Michael visit with her if he did not know where she was? She thought to ask if she could visit with Reena and Brigid on occasion and then perhaps Michael could visit her there. She tended to believe, however, that Decimus would keep her isolated and that her life would be a solitary one.

The burden of her thoughts weighted her shoulders and she sat with her head drooped and her legs folded beneath her on the hard ground. She purposely wore her plain skirt and blouse, thinking this would probably be the last time she dressed simply.

It would be the last time she would simply be Mary.

In two days she would be wife to Decimus and lose her freedom.

Arms draped in black wrapped around her so quickly, yet gently, that she jumped.

"I have missed you," Michael said, squeezing her back tightly to his chest.

Mary firmly grasped the arm wrapped around her waist. "I had so hoped you would come to me again. But it is selfish of me for you may be in danger."

"Worry not," he whispered, his shroud-covered face pressed next to hers. "They are led on a wild goose chase."

"You have been well and safe, then?"

"And I will continue to be well and safe."

"I wed in two days," she said with sorrow. "And I know not where I will live."

"Listen to me well, Mary," he said with a firm gruffness. "I will always know your whereabouts and I will never be far from you."

"You have no idea how your words relieve my worry."

"And you," he murmured, "have no idea how much I wish to make love to you."

She sighed. "I had so hoped that we could love once more before I wed Decimus."

"We can, we will, we must," he said, turning her face to slip his lips over hers and kiss her with a contained passion that ached to be released. "There is a secluded spot a short distance from here, but you must—"

"Keep my eyes closed," she said with a soft laugh. "But someday," she warned with a poke to his arm, "I will discover your secret."

She felt his body stiffen.

"God help us both, when you do."

She turned in his arms. "I pray that God will help and that one day we will be together."

They walked to an area draped with vines and tree branches that had formed a secluded hut. Michael spread the branches apart and she entered. It was small with only a dapple of light shining through, a perfect haven for them to make love.

He took her in his arms. "With us so near to the village, I do not think it wise that we disrobe."

She understood the wisdom of his words, but she wanted so badly to feel the length of him against her.

"I know it disappoints you," he said, his hand stroking her face. "But your safety comes first."

"Your mask, at least?"

"Then I must—"

"Blindfold me." She nodded. "I trust you, Michael, I always have and I always will."

He gently covered her eyes with his cloth belt and tied it securely around the back of her head. She waited as he removed his mask and when his warm cheek pressed to her cool one, she sighed and draped her arms around his neck.

"You feel so very good."

He was clean-shaven, not a stubble on his smooth

face, and she did not want him to stop rubbing his cheek with hers. She did not however complain when his lips followed the path his cheek had begun. He kissed every inch of her face and her legs trembled from the anticipation of their joining.

He eased her to the ground and when she reached to slip her hand beneath his shroud, he grabbed her arm.

"Nay, you must not. Let me love you."

"But I wish to touch you, feel you, know your flesh once again."

"Not this time, Mary," he said with regret. "Our time together is short and I wish to love you in a manner you will never forget."

"I wish to love you in return," she argued.

"Another time."

"There will be another time? You promise me this?"

He nibbled at her lips. "I promise there will be many more times."

She acquiesced and let him love her.

He removed not a stitch of clothing. He released the ties of her blouse as he kissed her lips, softly and slowly, then fast and urgently. His fingers slipped inside her blouse to tease her nipples until they turned hard. He then trailed down her neck with his lips sending gooseflesh racing over her with each lick, nibble, and kiss.

He finally made his way to her nipples and when his mouth claimed the solid orb, his hand inched his way beneath her skirt to stroke her inner thighs.

Mary bit her lower lip, knowing she must not make a sound but aching to scream with the fiery passion he had awakened within her. His fingertips crawled slowly along her thighs, inching between her legs and she instantly grew wet with anticipation.

He captured her lips and they kissed deeply, quenching their thirst and love for each other.

"I wish there was more time," he whispered. "I want to love you all day."

"I do not want this to end," she cried, her tears contained by her blindfold.

"I wish, oh how I wish, Mary," he murmured and slipped over her, entering her slowly until he rested full-length inside her.

She sighed. "I love you, Michael."

His groan was barely audible. "I love you more than you will ever know."

With that he moved inside her and she joined his rhythm, so familiar to her and so very satisfying. They took their time, though knowing they had little left. And they climbed together in their passion, holding on to each other, urging each other, and loving each other, until as one, they exploded together.

The clung to each other, neither one willing to let the other go.

They both became alert when they heard a scurry of footfalls, then realized it was a small animal passing by.

Michael took the blindfold off her after securing his hood, and Mary quickly adjusted her clothing.

"I cannot say when I will see you again," Michael said, pulling a twig from Mary's long blond braid.

"As long as *you will* see me again," she said with concern.

"I made you a promise. I will not break it."

"Unless," she was quick to say, "you feel yourself in danger, then you must promise me you will stay away."

"I promise," he said without hesitation.

She sighed relieved, for Michael was a man of his word.

He took her hand in his, slipped it under his mask, and kissed her palm. "Know that my heart and soul will be with you on the day you wed Decimus."

She rested her hand to his cheek. "I will be thinking of you."

"I am glad to hear that, for then you know you are loved." He took her hand. "It is time to go."

"Wait," she said remembering the question she wished to ask of him as he spread the branches and stepped outside. She quickly followed him. "There is something I must know."

"We do not have much time, can it not wait?"

She shook her head and asked her question. "I need to know who requested your help in finding me."

"Magnus asked for my help."

"Nay, the man who first asked you to find me. Reena explained it all to me and I am curious as to this man's identity."

"Why?"

"Because something does not feel right, though I cannot say what it is that troubles me, a missing piece of sorts."

"And what purpose will this missing piece serve?" he asked.

"It will make the puzzle more clear, more logical."

A sudden sharp sound like that of a branch cracking caused Mary to turn and see if anyone was near. Seeing no one and hoping it only an animal, she turned to Michael.

He was gone.

She looked around hoping to spot him, but he was nowhere.

She brushed her clothes clean and made certain her

hair contained no twigs or leaves, then she began walking back to the keep.

She never got the answer to her question, but what disturbed her even more was that Michael had questioned her need for an answer.

Was he trying to protect her, or did he feel she would not like what she heard?

Chapter 27

Mary stood by the window in her bedchamber in her wedding dress, waiting to be summoned to the great hall for the ceremony. Reena and Brigid had just left her, letting her know that it would be only a short time before Magnus came for her. He would escort her to the great hall and give her hand to Decimus in marriage.

The dress Brigid had stitched for her was simply beautiful. It was a combination of blues, from deep blue velvet to soft blue silk. The bodice neckline was square and billowed out from beneath her breasts to fall to a flurry of dark blue velvet at her feet. Pale blue silk ribbon threaded along the bodice and around the upper arm. The sleeves fell to her wrists, the ribbon running around the edge like a cuff. And sapphires adorned the square neckline, beneath the bodice, and also trimmed the cuffs.

Her honey-blond hair was piled on her head, ivory combs keeping it secure. Blue and white wildflowers and bits of greenery were nestled in the curls. Old Margaret had fashioned a lovely bouquet of dried lavender and mint. It smelled heavenly.

Everything was set; she would soon wed Decimus, their destiny forever joined. The only hope she had to hold on to was the seer's words.

You will be the demise of Decimus.

She prayed the woman's prophecy would be true and that one day she would be free to love Michael.

A cloud drifted over the bright sun and dimmed an otherwise sunny day. Was it an omen of what was to come? Would her life with Decimus always be dim?

A knock on the door drew her away from the window and her troubled thoughts. She opened it and Magnus walked in.

He looked magnificent in his dark splendor, black leggings and a black tunic trimmed in silver thread.

He offered her his arm. "It is time."

She attempted a smile but it faltered and she turned away to retrieve her bouquet and gather her courage. She felt on the verge of tears, and she could not allow herself to cry. She would show Decimus no weakness, only strength.

She turned after taking a deep breath and fortifying herself for what she must do.

"I am ready," she said and took his arm. She did not attempt to force a smile. It was not possible to display happiness when sorrow filled her heart.

"Your parents would be proud of you, Mary. You have grown into a beautiful, courageous woman."

She choked back her tears and nodded, not daring to speak.

They walked out of the room to face Mary's destiny.

Reena and Brigid had attempted to make the wedding special, filling the great hall with baskets of flowers and branches of greenery. A plethora of white candles graced the mantel, the tables and the dais and platters of food waited for the celebration to begin.

Decimus had intended a bishop to wed them but when he changed the wedding date, he had had to make do with the local cleric. He vowed that they would repeat the ceremony with a bishop in attendance.

Decimus stood next to the brown-robed cleric waiting for her approach. His colors chilled her for he had chosen a blood red tunic over black leggings with a large black cross stitched across the front of the tunic. His shiny black hair hung straight over his shoulders, and his face appeared more sinister than handsome.

The great hall was filled to capacity. All the villagers had been invited, and dared not refuse, and all of Decimus's men as well. If there had been time, no doubt the king as well as high officials of the church would have come.

Magnus walked her slowly to Decimus as if he took every step reluctantly. And when they finally reached him, Decimus stepped forward.

Magnus took her hand and placed it in Decimus's. Then he raised his voice for all to hear. "Treat her well, my lord, she is a gift."

Decimus gave a brief nod of recognition, though his dark eyes showed displeasure with Magnus's warning. He turned with her to face the cleric.

The ceremony went on for some time, the cleric extolling the virtues of marriage and the duties of an obedient wife. Mary was relieved when it was done, and she was pronounced Decimus's wife. It was over; she now *belonged* to him.

The celebration began, Decimus and Mary taking their place of honor at the two center chairs at the table on the dais. Magnus sat next to Decimus and Reena next to Mary.

Food was plentiful but Mary felt no hunger. No matter how hard she tried she could not get her thoughts off later in the evening when she would perform her wifely duties. The idea of Decimus intimately touching her made her sick, and she did not know what she would do.

Reena leaned close to her. "You worry."

"It is not as easy as I thought it to be," she whispered.

"Feign illness."

Mary leaned closer. "And put off my duties for one day?"

"Two maybe three if the illness is good."

"A short reprieve."

"I can help, as will Old Margaret," Reena assured her.

"I think my appetite returns."

"It must, so we have something to blame it on," Reena murmured. "Eat food your husband avoids. I will see that a few others complain of being ill."

"Not hungry, wife?" Decimus asked, turning to her.

"Famished, my lord," Mary said and glanced over his plate before filling hers high.

Surprisingly Decimus did not protest when voices were raised in song. But when Magnus requested that Mary sing a song, her husband's nostrils flared. She looked to him for permission, for truth be told she wished to sing. It could very well be her last chance to raise her voice in song.

Everyone waited for Decimus to grant his wife permission, and when he finally granted it the hall broke out in a cheer.

Mary thanked him, stood, and walked around to the front of the dais.

"I will sing a song of love, for it is strong in my heart this day."

No one need know that the love she spoke of was not for her new husband but for another. And she intended to sing it from her heart.

She started softly, her words clear and crisp, the melody heavenly. Then soon she raised her voice higher and higher until she sounded like an angel from the heavens. She mesmerized everyone in the hall, tears filling many eyes.

And as she finished, she crossed her arms over her chest and bowed her head.

Silence filled the great hall for a moment and then the crowd broke into wild cheers and applause. Shouts that she sing again rang clear and feet were stamped to encourage her to continue.

They were soon silenced when Decimus stood.

Mary dutifully returned to the chair beside her husband and sat. The hall remained silent for a few moments and then whispers began and soon turned louder until celebrating voices returned.

Decimus turned to her after the voices grew louder. "Who is the love in your heart for, dear wife?"

"For many, my lord," she said without hesitation.

He leaned closer. "Will you find room in your heart for me?"

"Is it not my duty?"

He stared at her silently and then without saying a word turned away.

With Decimus's attention focused elsewhere, Reena urged in a whisper, "Eat a bit more."

Mary did, helping herself to a piece of pie that no one had touched. She had to force herself but then maybe it was best her stomach did feel upset. It would make it easy to feign her illness.

The day turned to dusk and night drew near. Mary knew there was little time left to her and that she would soon need to complain about not feeling well. She had grown quiet and lethargic resting back in her chair.

Reena patted her hand and nodded her approval.

All was ready for Mary to make her move when the front doors of the hall burst open and a man came running in to drop down on one knee in front of Decimus.

"An urgent message, my lord," he said.

The man looked as if he had been riding hard and long, dirt and sweat covering him from head to toe.

Decimus stood and walked around the dais, ordering the man to follow him. He intended for no one to hear the message.

They left the hall, Decimus's men quickly gathering together as if awaiting orders.

Mary grew nervous and Reena took her hand.

"Perhaps you will not need to feign an illness tonight after all, perhaps the heavens have intervened for you."

"Then my prayers will have been answered," Mary said.

Decimus entered the hall and looked to his men. "Ready yourself. We leave immediately."

Mary was too stunned to speak.

Reena was not. "My lord, she needs time to pack her belongings, perhaps you should see to your duties and return for her in a few days time. We will have her ready for you then."

"How considerate of you, but unnecessary," Decimus said firmly. "Mary has few belongings, and it should take her little time to get them together. And of course with your help there should be no problem."

Decimus turned to Magnus. "See that she is packed and waiting at the front doors immediately." He then turned and walked out of the hall.

There was little time to protest and less time to say goodbye. Her few clothes and belongings were quickly packed. She was rushed to the front door of the keep just as Decimus's coach pulled to a stop before the steps.

She barely had given Reena a hug when Decimus appeared and grabbed her arm.

"We leave now."

With a tug and a push she was deposited in the coach, and before she realized she had not bid Magnus goodbye the coach took off. This was not how she expected her departure to be. She wanted time to thank everyone for their generosity and support and to urge them to stay in touch with her so that Decimus could not fully isolate her from the world.

Decimus sat quietly alongside her, looking deep in thought as the coach traveled with haste along a rutted path. She was jostled and jarred and wondered how Decimus could appear undisturbed by their bumpy ride.

He remained silent, revealing nothing of their destination to her. And after almost an hour of silence she could stand it no more.

"Where do we go, my lord?"

He turned his head slowly toward her. "That is not your concern."

She remained silent knowing full well he would only remind her that she was not to speak unless spoken to. She allowed her own thoughts to keep her company. She hoped that it would take until daybreak to reach their destination, then fatigue would surely force him to seek sleep and not her.

Hours passed by and she grew tired, her head bobbing until finally she tucked herself into the corner of the coach and drifted off to sleep.

She did not know how long she had slept when Decimus woke her with a start.

"We are here, Mary, wake up."

He sounded annoyed and she wondered who would suffer his wrath this evening. Something important was obviously on his mind, and whatever it was it did not sit well with him.

Decimus exited the coach first and assisted her as she stepped out. Her eyes rounded at the sight of the looming fortress in front of her. It was large, the stones dark, and the many torches glared like the eyes of a hundred demons.

She shivered and instinctively stepped closer to Decimus. Surprisingly he placed his arm around her, but then it was his duty to protect her and he would do right by his husbandly duties.

She could not help but ask, "What is this place?"

"Hell," he whispered harshly.

Her eyes rounded like bright full moons and, as they entered the ominous structure, a chill ran down her spine. He had confirmed her worst fear. She had just stepped through the gates of hell.

Mary huddled closer to her husband's side when she thought she heard a horrifying cry. "What is that?"

His arm tightened around her. "It is none of your concern."

There were warriors everywhere in the great hall and the few who looked to be servants appeared fearful and cautious in their manners. It seemed like a lot of activity for so late in the evening.

A large man approached Decimus. He wore a leather apron, his head was bald and his face scarred. "My lord, they await you."

"Did you heed my warning, Edmond?"

The man dropped his glance to the ground. "I thought only to please you, my lord. I started on the woman."

Mary's stomach rolled, realizing this man tortured an innocent.

"My orders, Edmond?" Decimus asked with an anger that had the large man trembling.

"To wait upon you, my lord."

Mary trembled when she realized she was in the Fortress of Hell, temporary home to Decimus, and a place where heretics met their fate. She had heard tales about it and thought them just that. She did not think such an evil place could truly exist, but now she knew it did. Its true name was the Fortress of Redemption, but no one was ever released from the fortress; once inside you were doomed, and redemption only came with death.

"An order you failed to obey."

"I—I—but meant—"

"Be gone from my sight. I will deal with you later."

Before anyone else could approach him, he turned with Mary firm in his arms and hurried her to climb the stairs until she thought them at the very top of the structure. They entered a room sparse with furnishings and few candles, though a fire burned bright in the large fireplace.

Mary hurried to the flames to warm her hands and ease her concern. "Are we to live here?"

He shook his head. "This will not be our home. This is a place where pagans and sinners meet their punishment and fate. I will not have my wife subjected to such vile matters."

Her shoulders slumped in relief, but only for a moment. Decimus pulled his tunic and shirt off and she thought he readied himself for bed and their union.

Her eyes locked on his naked chest and then his broad back as he turned away from her. He was built magnificently, his body a work of art, tapering and expanding in perfect symmetry and strength. He was powerful in muscle and form and that made Mary all the more nervous.

She remained by the fire, rubbing together hands that insisted on remaining chilled. How would she ever get through this night? Was it too late to feign an illness?

Decimus opened a chest near the window and took out a black shirt and gray tunic. He slipped them on and walked toward her.

"I had hoped to consummate our vows tonight but that is not possible. I have important matters to attend to."

Mary's legs trembled when she asked, "You go to torture people?"

He grabbed her chin. "Listen well, wife. You will ask me no questions. I have been tolerant of you thus far, but today it changes. Today you are my wife and will now obey me in all matters. Know your place is not to question me; your place is to serve me."

He stepped away from her. "Sleep. Tomorrow we seal our vows."

Mary watched the door close and she dropped to the floor, her trembling legs not able to hold her up a minute longer.

She had wed to the devil and had descended into hell.

Chapter 28

Mary woke feeling unwell the next morning. She could blame it on all the food she had eaten the night before, but her unsettled stomach had plagued her for the last three mornings, dissipating by midday. She had tried to ignore the signs but they had continued, and she now feared she was with child.

It was barely a month and yet signs warned of an impending pregnancy. She rose from bed and was grateful for the dry bread and honey, though ignored the fresh milk. It seemed to upset her stomach even more.

She did not know what to do. If she did not consummate her marriage soon he would never believe the child his. Then she would place Michael's child at risk. As much as it abhorred her, she would have no choice but to be intimate with Decimus as soon as possible.

She slipped her husband's dark green velvet robe over her linen nightshift and sat alone at the table near the window, enjoying the bread and honey. It was a dismal day, rain fell heavily, and she was grateful for the blazing fire that combated the chill.

The door suddenly opened and she looked to see her husband striding into the room, wearing the same clothes he had worn the night before. Loud voices, shouts and cries echoed in the hall and down the stair-well behind him, though the sounds turned to muffles as soon as he shut the door.

Decimus walked over to her, his hand reaching out to stroke her face. Mary had to stop herself from recoiling.

"Are you all right? You look pale."

His concern startled her and the truth worried her. "A fitful night, that is all."

He nodded, accepting her simple explanation. "Rest today, I have much to see to."

"May I be of help, my lord?" she asked, hoping to gain valuable information whether for her or Michael.

"There is nothing you can do. You will remain in our bedchamber today."

She looked concerned.

"Prisoners have escaped and I must see to their capture."

She prayed with all her heart that those who had escaped remained free, and she prayed harder that the Dark One, if involved, remained safe from harm.

"Will you be long, my lord?" She suddenly wanted to seal their vows and have done with it.

"I cannot say. The servants have been instructed to see to your care. If they do not serve you well, let me know. You are to want for nothing." He walked to his chest and retrieved a black cloak.

"I am satisfied to rest and wait on your return."

He walked over to her and grasped her chin. "You learn your place quickly. That pleases me."

She looked up at him and he shocked her when he leaned down and brushed his lips across hers.

"Until later, wife." He then marched out of the room swinging his cloak around his shoulders.

She shivered and pulled the robe tightly to her chest. No one but Michael had ever kissed her, and she felt as if she had just betrayed him. Her stomach suddenly rumbled in protest and without warning she lost what food she had eaten.

Servants arrived to take her tray and see to her needs. They appeared upset when they realized she had been ill.

She assured them all was well, the food fine, that she was only a bit sick from her wedding celebration. They sighed in relief and asked if there was anything she needed. She explained that she wished to rest and not be disturbed until well after noon. They left assuring her no one would bother her.

Mary knew she was taking a chance, but with Decimus gone it would be her one opportunity to investigate the fortress. She did not know what she would find, but her search might prove useful to Michael. And she could not sit all day and do nothing.

She quickly dressed in a plain brown skirt and pale yellow linen blouse. She plaited her hair so as not to draw attention and to make herself appear a mere servant. Having not been introduced to most of the staff, and with the size of the fortress, she was certain no one would question her as long as she appeared busy.

With a pile of linens in hand she left the bedchambers and made her way through the halls and down the stairwell. What she hoped to find she could not say. But then Reena had taught her well about being aware and recording her findings, and being she did not possess Reena's talents for drawing, she would need to record her findings in words once she returned to her room.

She spent a good portion of the morning searching the ground level of the fortress. It held a great hall, a large cooking area, and a substantial pantry. The cook's helpers were busy salting meats and paid her no heed, though two young servant girls eyed her suspiciously as they strung mushrooms and onions on strings to dry.

Her search alerted her to possible escape routes and to the endless number of servants constantly at work. A stench drew her to heavy wooden doors that opened onto a stairwell. It descended down into what Mary was certain was the depths of hell, the torture chambers. She could not bring herself to investigate, not today. Her stomach already protested at the stench that drifted up. She was sure to be ill if she made her way down where the odor grew more offensive.

Tired and disheartened she hurried to her bedchamber. Only minutes after slipping out of her clothes and into her husband's robe, servants knocked on her door with the noon fare.

She bid them enter and had them leave the food on the table. Soft cheese, roasted pork, and cider filled the tray, but she ignored the delicious scent and sat looking out the window at the heavy rain.

She thought to be brave and help Michael, but she found she could not investigate the dungeons, the horrible smell forcing her to keep her distance. How would she ever live a life filled with such horror?

After sitting for a spell she picked at the food, and finding herself not hungry she went to the bed to rest. It was well into the afternoon when she woke with a start.

She heard shouts and loud voices and instantly assumed Decimus had returned.

She hurriedly dressed in the dark green tunic and shift, her hair still plaited and her eyes still droopy with sleep when she descended the stairs to the hall. She heard the bravado in the warriors' voices. They obviously were pleased about something, and she hoped it was not because they had found the escaped prisoners.

Mary entered the hall and came to an abrupt halt. There on his knees before a circle of warriors was Roarke, beaten and badly bruised and bleeding. She almost rushed forward and demanded that they release him, but she held her tongue knowing her actions would prove more disastrous than beneficial.

Roarke appeared to think the same for he caught sight of her out of the corner of his bruised eye, almost swollen shut, and shook his head.

"My husband?" she questioned the warriors, though no one in particular. They all seemed too concerned and pleased with their capture of Roarke.

"Delayed," one man answered as if she were unimportant.

"How long?" she queried.

"As long as it takes," another barked. "He hunts the Dark One and will soon have him."

Mary looked to Roarke with eyes that begged him to tell her Michael was safe.

He mouthed a word that none noticed but her. *Never.*

They would *never* capture the Dark One and the thought relieved her, though Roarke's capture worried her. She could not let him be tortured and made to suffer unspeakable cruelty. She had to find a way to set him free.

"My husband ordered you to wait upon him." Mary spoke with a firmness that startled the warriors. "Remember well his orders; he does not condone disobedience." She hoped his orders were consistent with what had transpired last night. It seemed that nothing was to be done to prisoners until his arrival.

She hoped her reminder would cause them to leave Roarke alone in a cell, maybe then she could find a way to free him and keep him from suffering before Decimus returned.

One warrior spoke up. "We know well our duties."

"Then see that they are done," she said sharply.

The men were uncertain how to react to her authoritative manner. They did, however, know what Decimus expected of them, and the dire consequences of any action that did not meet with his approval.

They hauled Roarke off to the dungeon with mutterings and murmurs that they did not wish her to hear.

She returned to her room to think, and every step of the way wished she could contact Michael. Once in the chair by the window she shook her head. It would not be wise for Michael to enter the fortress, though no doubt he had on other occasions. The man simply could enter and exit any building at will. She often wondered how he did it.

Decimus was bound to return soon, once he realized that the Dark One had escaped him yet again. He would probably be in a rage and who better to take his anger out on than a man associated with the Dark One.

She had to set Roarke free.

That would mean descending into the dungeon, but Decimus's wife would not be granted permission to enter.

But a servant lad baring food for the guards would.

She could don a cap to cover her blond hair, wear a loose shirt and jacket to hide her breasts, and smudge dirt on her face. But where to get the clothes?

When she had been down in the cook area she had wandered out a door and noticed horses stabled close by. There were bound to be stable boys who made their home with the animals. She could find the garments she needed there.

But first she would need to make certain the servants would not look in on her. If they discovered her gone, the fortress would be in an uproar.

A servant girl returned for Mary's food tray just as she finalized the plans in her head. Would her idea work? She could not dwell on her plan failing. She had to take the chance or Roarke would suffer, or perhaps die.

"I am feeling rather poorly," Mary said with a heavy sigh.

The young girl looked nervous. "Should I send the healer?"

Mary had not thought the fortress to have a healer. People suffered here, they did not heal.

"It is not necessary," Mary assured her. "Little sleep is the cause and I can see to taking care of that. I intend to sleep. Please make sure no one disturbs me. When I wake I will send for you."

The servant obliged with a nod. "I will let no one disturb your rest."

"I appreciate your help," Mary said, relieved part of her plan was going smoothly.

Mary waited, giving the servant girl time to return downstairs, then she opened the door and seeing no one there, she slipped out. She had to walk through the kitchen and she did not know if the servant girl would be there. She could not take a chance and be recognized.

In the great hall, she picked up a jug and carried it high so that it partially hid her face. She then took a deep breath, told herself to be confident, and entered the kitchen. She made her way around servants, all of them busy preparing food. With the size of the fortress there were many mouths to feed and that meant all day preparing food.

She was grateful for the frantic activity. She slipped by without notice and once outside, she placed the jug in the corner. She would return for it. It contained mead and the guards would certainly enjoy a swig.

The stable was busy, several young lads attending to the returned warriors' horses. She kept to the dark corners of the stable, much like the Dark One did when he was in a room. She did not want to be noticed; this was not a good place for her to be.

She made her way carefully to a small room to her right just beyond the entrance. Once inside she was grateful to see that it contained clothes, boots, caps, and cloaks for the lads use.

She wasted not a minute in gathering what she needed and made her way out of the stable. With all the activity no one noticed her, and she scooped up the jug of mead as she hurried to a large door around the side and to the back of the stable.

She had discovered the location of the door that morning and saw that it exited into the inner courtyard of the fortress. Where she would go from there, once she freed Roarke, she was not certain. But together they would figure something out.

She changed in the shadows, rolling her own clothes into a bundle to leave by the door. She would change again on her return. After tucking her braid firmly beneath the knit cap and smudging her face and hands with dirt, she grabbed the jug of mead and headed for the dungeon.

No one paid her mind and she was pleased. Her disguise worked well, giving her more confidence in her plan. Doubts itched at her, though, when she descended into the dungeon; and the stench turned her stomach and it refused to settle.

I will not be sick. I will not.

She chanted the words over and over in her head.

It was a dark and dismal place, torchlight being her only guiding step. She heard the rattle of chains and the clang of a hammer on metal. She swallowed back her fear and proceeded down the dank hall until it suddenly widened considerably and cells appeared on both sides of her.

Small openings with metal bars that sat high in the doors were the only way of seeing the prisoner within.

"What business have you here, lad?"

She turned, startled by the strong voice and even more startled to see Edmond, the man her husband had spoken to upon their arrival. He was more wide than tall. He looked as if he did nothing but eat, so large was his size. His nose was flat, his head bald and his face dripping with sweat. He held a metal bar in one hand, the pointed tip glowing red with fire.

"Mead," she said in a low gruff voice, holding the jug out to him.

He eyed her suspiciously.

She had expected reluctance. Decimus had trained his men well. They were not to trust under any circumstances.

She stood tall, her big jacket concealing her breasts. "I will be a warrior for Decimus one day, and I came to see where I will bring the sinners I will capture."

Edmond braced the metal rod against the wall and reached out to take the jug from the lad. "You sound a strong one."

"I am, nothing will prevent me from succeeding with my plans."

"Good," he said and wiped his arm across his mouth after having taken a swig. "Have some." He held the jug out to her.

Mary took the jug, held it to her pursed lips, and let the mead flow down her chin. She returned the jug to him and wiped her chin on her sleeve.

"You are a good lad."

"Where are the warriors?"

"Celebrating with the women," Edmond said with a grin and took another swig.

Mary had no doubt Decimus would frown on such a sinful celebration, so they enjoyed themselves in his absence.

This was something she had not expected but could work to her advantage.

"They do not include you?"

He was swigging hard on the mead, the liquid dribbling down his thick chin. "Someone needs to watch the prisoner."

"There is only one?"

He nodded. "The others escaped, but not this one. He will suffer." He pointed to the metal rod and smiled at the still glowing tip.

Mary thought she would retch. The man actually appeared as if he took pleasure in torturing people. She had to get Roarke out of here. Edmond looked eager to set to work on the new prisoner.

"I will watch the prisoner for you."

Edmond glared at her. "How do I know I can trust you?"

"I am to be a warrior for Decimus." She spoke as if he insulted her. "I will serve my lord well and do him proud."

Edmond gave a firm nod. "You will make a fine warrior."

"Then give me this chance to prove myself and for you to enjoy yourself." Mary grinned as she hoped a man would.

He laughed and snorted. "A good lad you are. Let no one near him." He pointed to the cell at the end and to a key ring hanging on a peg on the wall beside the cell. "I will not be long."

"I do not mind guarding the prisoner."

Edmond grinned, his look pure evil. "I get my pleasure in many ways, the best being from the screams of the prisoners." He laughed, the jug firm in his hand as he walked off and disappeared into the dark corridor.

Mary forced back the bile that rose in her throat and hurried to grab the keys on the wall. She fumbled with them, her hands trembling horribly.

"Roarke," she said, "I am here to free you."

Chapter 29

"Mary?" Roarke asked emerging from the dark cell.

"Hurry, we do not have much time," she urged and reached out to take his hand.

He looked more bruised and battered than when she had seen him only a couple of hours ago.

"Are you able to walk?"

"I will walk, do not fear." But he clung to her, and she squeezed his hand to let him know she was there for him.

"We must get out of here before Edmond returns."

"What of Decimus?"

"He searches for the Dark One," she said slipping her shoulder beneath his arm and helping him to walk.

"A useless search," he said and leaned on her.

His injuries concerned her. She did not know how serious they were or if they would hamper his escape.

They climbed the staircase more slowly than she cared to.

"You are in pain?" she asked.

"No pain that will keep me from doing what is necessary."

She took him to a dark corner of the great hall and sat him down to rest. "Wait here, I will return in a moment."

Mary hurried to where she left her clothes, changed quickly, making a bundle of the clothes she had worn. She was glad for the flurry of activity in the fortress for it kept everyone busy with their work. She appeared a servant who raced about as everyone else did.

She left the smudges of dirt on her face, then hurried to return to Roarke.

"Put this on," she urged Roarke as she handed him the knit cap she had worn and the jacket. She took smudges of dirt from her face and wiped them on his.

He did not protest and did as she instructed, though he voiced his concern. "You may suffer for this."

"Only if I get caught."

"Michael would be proud," he said with a smile and grabbed his side.

She again supported him with her shoulder. "We need to get through the kitchen and out the back. There we must find a way to get you out of the fortress's inner courtyard. We must appear a couple ready to sneak off to enjoy ourselves."

Roarke nodded.

They clung to each other, smiling and laughing as they walked through the hall into the kitchen.

They kept to themselves, hugging each other, and several smiles were sent their way, a few men nodded at Roarke. They were out of the kitchen and down the path to the door behind the stable in no time. Once through it they braced themselves against the stone wall, even though the rain fell heavily upon them.

Mary could tell that Roarke was exhausted and would not make it much farther.

"You need to rest before you continue your journey," she said, thinking where he would be the safest. "Is Magnus's land far from here?"

"A few hours by horse."

"Then I need to get you a horse."

Roarke looked alarmed. "You will not place yourself in danger for me."

"I will see you safe."

"You have done enough, Mary, leave the rest to me."

She shook her head. "You are in no condition to do anything but mount and ride to safety."

"And how do you propose that I ride out of here without drawing attention?"

"A diversion."

"You are as brilliant as Michael."

She smiled though it faded quickly. "When you see him tell him I miss him."

"I am sure his message is the same for you."

It did not take much to create the diversion, she simply began yelling from the dark corner of the fortress that the Dark One was here.

Panic ensued and she was quick to harness a horse and take it to Roarke.

"Everyone is in a panic and rushes about. You will disappear in the chaos."

They joined in with the chaos in the courtyard. It seemed as though everyone was in fear. The animals seemed uncontrollable, which served Roarke well for his horse became agitated and he fought to control her as he nudged her to the exit.

Mary hid in the shadows and yelled out that she saw

the Dark One enter the fortress and everyone scurried about calling for the warriors, who emerged with a flourish from the hall.

Mary helped Roarke guide the agitated horse out of the fortress and into the woods just as the drawbridge slammed shut.

"Ride fast and hard to Magnus," she urged, helping him to mount. "He will see that you are safe."

"What of Decimus?"

"He will not hurt me. He has plans for me, and besides no one can prove I did anything. It was a young lad who freed you. Now go before they send warriors out to search."

"God bless you, Mary," he said choking back tears and guiding the horse into the thick darkness of the woods.

The rain pelted her as she watched Roarke disappear. Magnus would see to his care and he would be safe there. She only wished that she were going with him. She took her time returning to the fortress, hoping she would be able to sneak back in and wondering what excuse she could use if she were caught.

She approached the drawbridge, which had been lowered, and hesitated, bracing herself against the stone wall. Riders were coming and she did not wish to be seen.

Her breath caught when she saw her husband, his black cloak flying out behind him, his wet dark hair plastered to his head, and his eyes glowing red-hot with anger. He was in a fury, the two riders behind him keeping their distance.

The horses' hooves pounded upon the wooden drawbridge as they crossed it in a frantic gallop.

Decimus had returned.

Mary snuck her way across the drawbridge, lurking in the protection of the dark shadows. She was wet to the bone, her clothes soaked through, her hair sopping wet. But it did not matter; Roarke was free.

Decimus was screaming at his men as Mary moved along the shadows of the fortress wall, inching her way closer to the entrance that would allow her to enter the kitchen and make her way to her bedchamber.

"You capture this Roarke and then he escapes? And how do you explain the escape of the other prisoners?" He looked down at his men from where he sat on his horse as if judging and condemning them all.

The warriors cowered around him.

Decimus looked from one man to another, his dark eyes searing each one of them. "I think there is a traitor among you."

They all protested mightily, swearing they were all loyal to him.

"Then tell me how this Roarke escaped?"

They all turned to look at Edmond.

The large man trembled and stuttered as he spoke. "A young lad—he—he offered to—to watch the prisoner."

"What young lad?" Decimus asked, the rain pouring down on him and his men.

"I—I—I did not get his name."

"You left a prisoner with a young lad who you did not know?" Decimus dismounted and walked over to Edmond.

The large man stepped back, fear evident in his eyes. "He told me he was to be one of your warriors."

Decimus looked to his men. "Gather all the lads in the fortress and bring them to the hall. Edmond will identify our traitor."

A shout rang out from the door to the fortress.

"Lady Mary is not in her room."

"Damn," Mary mumbled. Now what was she to do?

"Search the fortress and the grounds," Decimus ordered. "I want her found."

Mary hurried along the stone wall, unplaiting her hair and pulling her blouse out of her skirt. She had to appear different from the woman who had been seen hugging a man. She returned through the kitchen and entered the great hall at the same time her husband did.

Silence filled the hall and his warriors stared at her, some with their mouths agape. Edmond stared but she realized there was no recognition in his eyes.

"Your whereabouts, wife," Decimus demanded. His smoldering eyes warned he was on the verge of erupting.

She had thought of an excuse, though she knew it not an adequate one. "I went exploring the fortress and found myself lost."

"Did I not order you to remain in your room?" he asked approaching her.

"I grew bored." She remained firm in her stance, showing no fear, and caught several of his men snickering at her.

"You dare to disobey me?"

His anger was about to erupt and she was not certain what he would do. She backed away from him.

"*Do not* move away from me."

She stood where she was.

"You will learn obedience."

"Aye, my lord," she said, bowing her head in submission. He was much too angry to attempt reason. Acquiescence was her only choice.

"When I order you to do something you will do it without question. I care not how bored you grow, my word is law and you will obey."

Silence was her only defense.

"I will not tolerate blatant disobedience."

"I am sorry, my lord," she said attempting to appease him.

"Sorry means nothing if it is offered without truth."

He accused her of lying. He did not trust her and that could prove dangerous for her.

"I am sorry," she reaffirmed more strongly. "I have yet to learn the ways of a good, obedient wife. I ask your forgiveness and patience with me. I will attempt to do better." She bowed her head once again.

"Your apology will teach you nothing," he said. "Punishment will."

Her heart stilled for a moment, fearing his punishment may be severe enough to harm her unborn babe.

Mary waited for him to dismiss her, but instead he ordered her to sit in a chair near the hearth. She was grateful for the fire's warmth. Her soaked garments chilled her to the bone and she had begun to tremble. She huddled close to the fire, the heat helping to calm her shivers, though not her concerns. What punishment would Decimus inflict on her? Would it harm her unborn babe? Her disturbing thoughts grew along with her fear.

Young lad after young lad was marched before Decimus and Edmond, and the large man shook his head at each one, until he finally cried out.

"This is him, this is the lad who tricked me."

Mary turned wide eyes on the young man and noticed that his clothing was similar to the clothing she had worn.

"You are sure?" Decimus asked.

"Yes, and if you give him to me I will get a confession from him."

Good lord, she could not let the horrified young man suffer for what she had done.

"I have done nothing," the young man said trembling. "I have tended the horses. One is ready to birth and I have seen to her care."

"You lie." Edmond spat at him. "You were in the dungeon."

Another young man stepped forward. "John speaks the truth, my lord. He has been with the mare all day. He has never left her side."

Decimus turned to Edmond. "You will know more pain than is possible if you lie to me and accuse an innocent young man to save yourself."

"He looks like the lad," Edmond said contritely.

"You may go," Decimus said to the two young men, and they scurried out of the hall as fast as possible.

He ordered his men to continue searching the grounds and the fortress, though he told them that he believed Roarke long gone. He ordered Edmond to wait in his solar and then he pointed Mary toward the staircase.

"Our bedchamber."

Mary was led up the stairs, trying desperately to calm her worries. She had the unborn babe to consider, and she must do whatever necessary to keep him from being harmed.

After closing the door, Decimus descended on her with a rage. "Did you have anything to do with this man Roarke's escape?"

Chapter 30

Mary placed her hand to her chest as if in shock. "My lord, how can you ask me that?"

"Do not play games with me." He grabbed her by the arms. "You are soaking wet."

"And chilled." She kept her demeanor calm.

"Take your clothes off," he ordered sharply.

He released her, went to the bed, pulled the blanket off, and returned to her.

Panic rose inside her. Did he intend for them to consummate their wedding vows now? She was cold, exhausted, and had little strength left to protest, not that she could. It was her wifely duty; she had no choice. With slow, trembling hands she tugged at the ties of her blouse, praying for courage.

He shook his head, dropped the blanket, and rid her of everything but her nightshift. He stared at her, his eyes so heated they should have warmed her but instead a shiver raced through her. He wrapped her in the blanket, securing her arms in a tight cocoon.

She was unable to move, her arms taut against her sides. She felt trapped and vulnerable like a prisoner with no chance to defend.

"You think to make a fool of me? You think I believe your lies that you were exploring the castle? Do you wish to be punished?"

She remained firm in her lie. "I speak the truth."

"I think not," he raged. "I think you helped the prisoner to escape."

Fear prickled her skin, but she refused to cower to his anger. She had to remain strong and convince him she had nothing to do with Roarke's escape. "I did no such thing. Why would I?"

"Because you are a fool," he said with a near shout.

"You are the fool for believing me capable of such a task."

"Capable?" He all but laughed. "It takes strength, courage, and fearlessness to escape and you have proven to me that you possess all three. You did, after all, escape my prison."

"With help," she reminded him.

"Exactly," he said with a smile that chilled her. "You were helped, so now you help another. Is that what the Dark One taught you? To risk your life for someone of no importance?"

"I did not risk my life."

"You risked more than you know," he said, his tone threatening. "You think I will not punish you?"

He pushed the chair closer to the fire and with a push and a shove forced her to sit. "Think on what your foolishness will cost you."

He stormed out of the room slamming the door shut behind him.

She shivered, then loosened her arms and hugged the blanket tightly around her. What had she done? Had she placed her unborn child in harm's way? Would Decimus feel it necessary to punish her to save face in front of his men? She could not even use her pregnancy to prevent torture for then he would know she had been with another man.

Good lord, what had she done?

"Mary."

She turned and quickly searched for Michael.

"Where are you?" she asked anxiously.

The dark figure stepped out from the shadows.

"Are you all right?"

She ran to him, throwing herself into the safety of his strong arms.

He embraced her fiercely.

"Oh, Michael. I have been so foolish," she said, holding on to him and never wanting to let go.

"Tell me what is wrong."

"I helped Roarke to escape. I had to. He would have suffered greatly if I had not set him free."

He eased her away from him but held her arms firmly. "You should not have taken such a dangerous chance. I would have helped him."

She shook her head. "He was badly hurt. He needed to escape then or he would never have survived."

"And what if you were caught?"

"I gave it no thought," she said. "It was something I had to do and now . . ." She pulled away from him, her eyes round with fright. "Oh, Michael, I am a fool. Decimus threatens to punish me and I fear for the safety of our unborn babe."

He made no move, nor spoke one word. He stilled in silence and remained so for several moments.

Mary grabbed his arm. "I am sorry to have told you like this, but we must do something to protect our babe. I cannot bear the thought of losing your child and I cannot convince Decimus it is his since we have not been intimate. I know not what to do. I only know our child needs protecting. You must do something," she pleaded with trembling lips. "You must save our babe."

He yanked his arm free of her and with a flourish that caused Mary to take several steps away from him, he grabbed hold of his black robe and with one full sweep he pulled it off him and tossed it aside, his gloves following.

Decimus.

She choked on the name that refused to spill from her lips. Decimus stood before her in his rich finery, his glittering rings and his dark eyes glaring.

"You tricked me," she said, believing herself ten times the fool for not realizing that her new husband was a devious and spiteful man.

"Mary—"

She backed away from him. Her hand stretched out in front of her to keep him at a distance. "Do not touch me. You are pure evil."

"Mary," he said again, his voice gruff.

Her eyes turned wide. He sounded so very much like Michael.

"It is *me—Michael.*"

She shook her head, confused. "Michael? Decimus?"

He approached her slowly. "We are *one* and the *same.*"

She shook her head harder. "I do not understand."

He made no move to reach out to her, for the nearer his approach the farther she moved away from him. "Michael, the Dark One, is Decimus. We are one."

The back of her legs hit the edge of the bed and she gratefully lowered herself down to sit. Unable to prevent the tears that filled her eyes from falling, she wept.

Michael was instantly at her side, on his knees, grasping hold of her hand. "I am sorry I upset you with my threats. But I was angry that you risked your life when I should have been here to help Roarke. I worried even more when I thought that you might be with child and it was not only your life in jeopardy."

She could not stop shaking her head. It made no sense to think all along she had been with Decimus. He had rescued her, protected her, and loved her. "I do not understand any of this, nor do I know if I should believe you."

He squeezed her hand tightly. "Close your eyes, Mary, and listen to me."

She stilled her head and stared at him.

"I know it is difficult for you to understand. I have placed a heavy burden on you and one that could prove harmful, but I ask for your trust."

She looked upon the eyes of a man she thought vile and yet she heard the voice of the man she loved with all her heart.

"I know not what to do. I hear Michael, yet I see Decimus." She shivered.

He held her hand firmly. "I understand your apprehension, but give me a moment to explain my necessary deception."

"How do I know you do not continue to deceive me? How do I know that your deceit is nothing more than a trap?"

He brought her hand to his lips and kissed her palm softly as Michael had done so often. "Because I love you with all my heart and soul."

His familiar voice caused her to ache for Michael, but her eyes could not shed the image of Decimus kneeling before her.

"Trust me, please, Mary," he begged. "Give me a chance to explain."

She warned herself against being foolish, but what if . . . ? What if Michael and Decimus were one?

"It is so hard for me to think of you as—" She stopped and turned away from him.

"Just listen to my voice. Do not look upon me, and after you have heard my story then you may decide."

She turned back to him. "And if I do not trust your word?"

He hesitated. "I will see to your escape and you will be free."

She closed her eyes slowly. "I will listen."

He heaved a sigh of relief and quieted his own apprehension before beginning his story. "I lived in a village in Scotland, a quiet place where man and beast lived in peace. We practiced the old ways and beliefs, my mother an exceptional healer and my sister—"

He stopped and swallowed the lump in his throat and the ache in his heart.

"My sister was special, trusting all and believing only in good. The clerics came and called us pagans and attempted to reform all who did not believe as they did. They turned neighbor against neighbor until chaos reigned and the innocent suffered.

"My father was the first accused of heresy, he was punished and killed, leaving me responsible for my mother and sister's protection. My mother urged me to take my sister and leave, hide before it was too late, and one day seek revenge on those who destroyed the family. I foolishly thought I had time, and it was when I was away seeking help from a nearby clan that they came for my sister and my mother."

Mary felt her chest grow heavy with the pain he must have suffered.

"If it were not for Roarke, I would be dead. When I discovered how my mother and sister were made to suffer before they died, I lost all reason. I wanted nothing but revenge. Roarke, who had been my friend since I was a young lad, reminded me of my mother's words. He urged me to hide and seek revenge not by killing those who had harmed my family but by freeing the innocent.

"What better revenge than to continually rob from your enemy what they wanted most? And to help those, the innocent, who needed it the most. I changed my identity and infiltrated my enemy's camp. I quickly worked my way up and reached a position so powerful that no one dared question me or prevent me from doing as I pleased. And I have saved hundreds of innocent people from suffering and death. My mother had been right, her death was not in vain."

Mary stared at him with wide eyes. "But you have killed people—"

"Only those in the Church who have proved a serious threat to me, only they have found themselves at Decimus's mercy. All others have left here alive, though thought dead by the church leaders."

Mary began to cry. "My parents?"

He took her hand and squeezed tight. "I was not the one to order your parents' capture and when I heard of their fate, I attempted to return so that I could free them and you. I was not in time; my journey was delayed and I knew they would suffer horribly, but then Magnus saw to them and to you, for which I was grateful."

Mary gasped. "Now I know where that familiar scent comes from. The scent I smelled around Michael when first we met. It belonged to a man who often visited with my father late at night. He always remained in the shadows and they would talk." Tears spilled down her eyes. "It was *you*."

He brought her hand to his lips, choking back his own tears. "I had promised your father that I would see him, your mother, and you free. He knew of my true identity and that placed him in jeopardy. I was securing your escape when your parents were captured."

"How did he know who you were?"

He shook his head. "He amazed me when we first met, for he told me that he knew I was not an evil man but a messenger and redeemer for God. And he would help me in any way he could."

A sudden realization had Mary saying, "There was no man who questioned my safety and brought you to Magnus. It was you. That is why you never answered me when I asked you the man's identity."

"I had no choice but to get you out of where you were."

"You knew where I was all these years?"

"Of course," he said. "It was the only way of making certain you remained safe. I knew Magnus could protect you for the time being, but there would come a time he could not."

"And that time came?"

"Church leaders insisted that you be found, fearing that you had matured and would begin spreading your father's teachings. They wanted you purged of your sins, which meant they wanted you dead."

"You convinced them you could reform me?"

"The Church edict forced me to look at other ways of assuring your safety. If you were my wife, no one could touch you. I feared that no matter where I sent you, you might be found, whereas if you remained by my side you would forever be protected."

"But why rescue me if you intended to marry me all along?"

"The Church made mention of your name as a possible problem. That was when I informed Magnus that you were in trouble. I thought he would move you until I determined the Church leaders' intentions. Unfortunately Magnus had his own problems, leaving me no choice but to see to you myself."

"You found out the Church wanted me dead after we were together?"

"Just before I rescued you, and by then I had promised Magnus I would see you safe. I had not yet decided to make you my wife."

"When did you decide?" she asked.

"Why would be a better question. I attempted to convince myself it was for your benefit, but it was for a selfish reason." He squeezed her hands tightly, afraid to let go. "I fell in love with you. You released me from the darkness and shed light on my isolation. I began to feel again, to remember what it was to love."

She eased her hand out of his and reached out slowly, hesitated then finally touched his face. "I know you and yet I do not. I know Michael is there inside you, but when I look upon you I see Decimus, the man who I have hated these many years."

Her hand did not remain long upon him and he ached

at the loss of her touch. "I could not chance you knowing who I was. I had to make certain you thought me repulsive, evil, and not to be trusted. Even now you look at me with doubt."

"You did not trust me to know your true identity?" she asked sadly.

"After a while I feared for you to learn of my true identity." He sighed heavily and shook his head. "I have warred with my feelings for you. Do I tell you? Do I not? Is it safe for you to know? Would you love Decimus as much as you love Michael? I feared losing your love."

Mary stared at him, uncertain of who he was. "It is difficult for me to accept that Decimus and Michael are one and the same. Decimus hunted me while Michael saved me and loved me. How do I bring the two of you together?"

Decimus gently cupped her face with his hand. "With love?"

Tears slowly slipped down her cheek.

He moved his hand to rest on her flat belly. "Love for us both?"

"Oh, Michael," she cried and rested her forehead on his. Mary closed her eyes and trailed his face with soft kisses until she found his lips and then she kissed the man she loved, the man who owned her heart and soul.

He took her face in his hands and returned her kisses. "I love you, Mary. God, I love you so very much that it hurts."

She kept her eyes closed. "You are not alone anymore, never fear losing my love, it is forever. It will take me time to grow accustomed to your face—"

"Not too long, please?" He sounded as though her

words pained him. "I want to love you in the light so that we may look upon each other."

"It will take time. Michael is whom I trust and love. I must learn to trust and love Decimus. I see you as the same, but it is difficult to comprehend. . . . With time—"

"We do not have much time."

She opened her eyes and tried to keep firm in her mind that it was Michael she spoke with, no matter that it was Decimus she looked upon.

"We have the rest of our lives together."

"Nay, Mary," he said sadly.

Her heart quickened and her stomach fluttered. "What do you mean?"

"You carry our child and I will not see either of you in danger." He squeezed both her hands in his. "I will make plans for your escape, then see you settled in a safe place—away from me."

Chapter 31

"**S**end me and your child away?" Mary asked, stunned. "You cannot mean it."

"I will see you and my child safe," Decimus insisted.

"Without a husband and father?"

He stood and looked down on his tearful wife with a pained heart. "You think I want this? You think that I do not want to be there with you when you give birth to my child? That I do not want to watch him grow? That I do not want a life with you and him?"

Mary stood and took a step toward him then stopped, staring at him.

Her hesitancy hurt but he understood it. She felt safe with Michael, not with Decimus. He stretched his hand out to her, giving her a choice.

She waited but a moment, staring at him, and then allowed her eyes to drift shut as she reached out and took hold of his hand.

He pulled her close, wrapping her in a tight embrace. She felt so very good, the warmth of her, the strength of her; he wanted to hold her to him forever, to never part, always love . . .

But that was not meant to be.

She looked at him with sorrowful eyes. "We can do this together, you, me, and the babe."

He gave her a gentle kiss. "How I wish that were possible. But look at where you now temporarily reside—in the Fortress of Hell. It is no place for you and it is definitely no place for our child. And I will not have you spend your life in service to me."

She had to smile. "You seemed to enjoy convincing me otherwise."

"I had the perfect excuse," he said with what appeared a hint of a smile.

Mary had never seen Decimus smile; she did not think him capable. The thought that she had touched his heart, and it had begun to heal, touched her own heart.

"You needed to think badly of me," he continued. "I treated you poorly so that you would hate me."

"You could have trusted me and confessed the truth."

"It was not you who I did not trust—it was me."

She looked at him confused.

"It would not have been easy to keep up the charade if we both were aware. My heart would have betrayed me. And as for you? From the very first time we met, you looked at Decimus with disgust. If you had known I was the Dark One, would you have looked at me the same?"

She was about to debate the issue with him but thought better of it. "You are right. My eyes would have spoken the truth no matter how hard I attempted to hide my love for you."

"Then you see why it is impossible for you to remain here as my wife. It will be more difficult for you to hide your feelings toward me, and knowing my true identity could place both of us, and our child, in jeopardy."

She stepped away from him, angry that they should be parted when they only found each other. "You have surrendered much of your life seeking revenge. Have you not avenged your family's deaths enough? Can you not walk away now knowing you have accomplished what you intended and have a life of your own?"

"I have freed many who otherwise would have died brutal deaths, but more continue to be persecuted. How do I walk away from the innocent when they need someone to help them?"

"Let someone else help them," she said angrily. "I need you and"—she placed her hand to her stomach— "your child needs you."

He walked over to her and rested his hand over hers. "I wish . . . I wish things were different."

"Then make them different," she begged. "I do not want to spend my life without you."

"We will discuss this matter no more," he said adamantly.

Her eyes rounded when she caught the familiar tone of Decimus, but she feared him no more.

"We will discuss it until you *are* in agreement with me," she protested.

"Will we?" he asked, his voice a bit too gentle and his hands beginning to roam up her arms.

"You will not sway me in this."

"I have no doubt of that. You can be stubborn," he said and ran his fingertips ever so lightly beneath the sleeves of her nightshift, sending gooseflesh rushing over her. His fingers found their way to her neck and he stroked her soft skin, kissed her warm lips, and silenced her stubbornness.

"I want to make love to you. I want you to look into my eyes and see me, know it is me, know that I love you."

She stumbled on her words not certain who she was to love. "Mic—De—who are you?"

"You need to know me as Decimus, and it is time for us to consummate our wedding vows."

Her smile was gentle. "I had feared this time, but no more."

"You will only know love this night and for all the nights to follow until we say our last goodbye."

"I will have memories to keep me warm," she said sadly.

"And for me to fill my endless days and nights without you."

"Then let us begin making memories," she said, taking his hand and walking to the bed.

He rushed out of his clothes, she slipped out of hers and climbed into bed, pulling back the blanket, inviting him to hurry and join her . . . and he did.

He lay beside her, bracing his elbow on the bed and resting his head on his hand so that he could see all of her naked beauty. He wanted to watch her as he slowly touched every inch of her, starting with her face.

His strokes were feather light, tantalizing her soft flesh. She sighed and moaned and squirmed, and he grew hard watching her respond so passionately to his touch.

"You are so very beautiful," he whispered and kissed her lips.

She wrapped her arms around his neck and drew him to her until he slipped completely over her. He had thought to take his time with her, but she had a different idea and he responded to her need.

Their loving turned fast and furious as if they could not get enough of each other, as if both were starved with a hunger that could not be quenched. She climaxed quickly and wanted more and he obliged. When he thought her spent, she pushed him off her to climb on top of him.

"You are not tired—"

"Shhh, let me love you," she whispered before biting his lips playfully, then settling herself comfortably over the full length of him, tossing her long hair back over her shoulder, and riding him with an energy born of love.

He grasped her waist and helped her to keep a steady rhythm, but help was unnecessary. He fit her well and she relished the feel of him, hard and powerful and throbbing deep inside her.

She leaned down over him, her long blond hair forming a tent around his face and, nibbling on his lips, she said, "I cannot get enough of you."

"Take what you want of me," he urged and she did until he felt her body slow its rhythm and he knew she grew tired.

He eased her off him and joined with her once more, taking full control and finishing their lovemaking with an explosive climax. Together they soared past time and space, united as one in the heavens only to drift gently back to earth.

He moaned his satisfaction, she sighed hers, and they rested together in each other's arms content, if only for this moment.

When a chill began to creep over their damp, naked bodies he reached down and pulled the soft wool blanket over them, tucking it around her. They snuggled together, content and at peace.

"We will be left alone this night?" she asked and hoped.

"I saw to what was necessary. The rest can wait until morning."

"What of Roarke?"

"You tell me."

She rested her hand on his chest as though her gentle touch would keep him calm, when she said, "I had to help him. He had already been tortured and would suffer more. And why was he so close to the fortress?"

"Roarke has been my partner since the conception of the Dark One. I could not have accomplished so many successful flights to freedom without him. This time was no different."

"The night we arrived here you were busy making plans to free the prisoners. It was the reason for our hasty departure from Magnus's keep?"

He nodded. "It was imperative. There were two young lads and one was badly hurt when captured. I did not think he would survive the night."

"Did he?" she asked, reciting a silent prayer for the lad.

"He did but could not journey as fast as the others. Roarke remained with him until help could be sent. By then my men were close on their trail, and to keep them from finding the lad and his rescuers, Roarke led them away and was caught. I feared I would not arrive in time to stop his torture."

"I arrived in time," she said proudly.

"You could have been caught." His admonishment could not hide the pride in his voice.

"But I was not and Roarke is free, though in need of care."

Decimus sat up. "Is he hurt badly?"

"He was only able to walk slowly, so I secured him a horse. He is on his way to Magnus's keep."

He sat up, looked to where his clothes lay discarded on the floor, his body tense with flight—then looked to her.

"Go, he needs your help," she said, sensing his concern for his friend.

"I will see him safe and then return," he said jumping out of bed and dressing with haste.

"And what am I to say if asked of your whereabouts?"

"I will return before anyone knows me gone, and no one would expect Decimus to keep his wife apprised of his whereabouts." He leaned over and kissed her soundly.

"I cannot escape," she said, a thought coming to her that might be useful.

"You must," he said with sorrow and shook his head. "We have no time to discuss this now, we will talk of it when I return."

She grabbed hold of his arm. "It cannot be an escape, Mich—Decimus." It was imperative she remembered to call him Decimus and no other name for fear of making a mistake in front of someone. "The Church would forever hunt me. I must die and be laid to rest."

He plopped down beside her on the bed. Her words were an added burden to his already heavy mind and heart. "You are right."

"Then it is good that I am with child. I will grow large and a few months before I am to give birth, I can die due to problems with my pregnancy. No one would question my demise."

"That is a good plan and one I had not considered. We will talk on it when I return."

"I will miss you." Her gentle words were a plea from a loving heart.

He reached out to raise her head to his. He captured her mouth with a kiss that stole her breath. "That will keep me strong in your memory until my return." He eased her head back on the pillow and tucked the covers around her. "Sleep well, wife, know you are safe and know that I love you."

He left and Mary lay in the quiet of the night, the crackle of the fire the only sound in the room. The startling discovery that Decimus and Michael were one remained fresh in her mind. If she had been more aware of the subtle hints that connected the two men, she might have realized Decimus's charade.

How could one man always manage to outsmart another? Never had the Dark One failed in his rescue attempts. And he had found ways into supposedly impregnable fortresses and keeps. Black magic had been whispered along with the Dark One's name, for no common man could call the darkness friend.

But it was with patience, intelligence, and illusion that Michael achieved his goal. While the Dark One was hunted, he stood before their very eyes and no one knew.

She empathized with him over the loss of his family, recalling her own pain in losing her parents. There comes a time, however, when revenge can do no more and it must be laid to rest and life must go on.

The idea of spending her life without Michael was not a thought she cared to consider. She would not allow him to abandon her and their child out of duty.

Time at least now was on her side. She had a few months reprieve to fashion a plan of escape, not only for her but for her husband as well. She would need help for there was much to consider and prepare for, and who better to assist her than Reena and Brigid. That would mean confiding in them the truth of Decimus's identity. Could she trust them?

Without a doubt, though the knowledge could prove dangerous to them. It would have to be their choice.

She yawned and stretched, feeling more content than she had in weeks. It had been two months since her harrowing escape had begun. Summer fast approached and the fields would soon be lush with crops, the meadows a plethora of wildflowers, and she would be growing heavy with child.

Fresh, new beginnings all around and that meant for Decimus as well.

They would start anew, she would make certain of it.

It was her turn to play a charade and free him as he once freed her, and she would do it with confidence and determination.

He would expect her to shed tears and cry thinking of their eventual parting, and she would need to play the role well. It would not take much since just the thought of saying goodbye to Michael forever filled her with dread. She would not lose him. She would not let Decimus rob her of Michael. She would have her husband even if she had to bury Decimus to do it.

After all, the seer had spoken; she *would* be the demise of Decimus.

Now she understood, and she would see that the prophecy rang true.

Chapter 32

In public Mary played the obedient wife to Decimus extremely well, and the heartbroken wife to Michael, often appearing tearful over their eventual parting. Her true self was the scheming, independent woman who intended to have things her way, and she was proud of her.

Mary had asked for a note to be sent to Reena and had written it in a Celtic script that few could read or write, though she knew Reena would understand the words. Her message, she hoped, would bring a visit from Reena and Brigid and, of course, their husbands since the men would not allow their wives to travel alone.

The visit would give her time to confide the Dark One's identity in the two women and formulate escape plans. She was taking a chance, a dangerous one, but then her husband was worth the danger.

She sat on a narrow wooden bench in a small flower garden behind the fortress. Loving hands tended this garden, forcing a tiny bit of beauty to grow in hell. Summer was but a week away and many flowers were in full bloom while others abounded with ripe buds aching to burst open.

"My lady," a servant girl gasped, coming to an abrupt halt after rounding the corner of the fortress.

Mary smiled hoping to calm her unease. The girl appeared worn out, her brown hair hanging limply around her pretty oval face. Her hands, which she hugged in front of her were red and raw, perhaps from too much scrubbing in hot water. She was reed-thin and had the loveliest pale blue eyes.

"Is this your garden?" Mary asked.

The girl looked on the verge of tears and Mary hurried to assuage her concern.

"It is beautiful. You tend it with great care."

"I—I—" she stumbled nervously over her words. "No one kn-knows of it."

"A secret garden, how wonderful. May I share in it with you?"

The girl looked stunned, and at a loss for words, she nodded.

"Your name?" Mary asked.

"Jenna, my lady."

Mary was not accustomed to being referred to as "my lady." She did not feel the title appropriate or necessary. She would have much preferred for Jenna to know her as Mary.

"Jenna, a lovely name. Will you not sit with me and tell me about your garden?" With so much chaos of late it would be nice to talk of so simple a thing as a garden.

Soon Mary found herself on her knees weeding the flower patch with Jenna, who was surprised that a lady knew so much about plants.

"What are you doing?"

The harsh voice startled them both and when Mary looked upon Decimus, for an instant, she forgot he was Michael and cringed at the sight of him.

He was dressed completely in black except for a touch of gold trim. The furious glare in his dark eyes and his hands planted firmly on his hips almost made her tremble in fear. That is until she looked over at Jenna. The poor lass looked absolutely terrified.

Mary immediately sought to defend the cowering girl. "My lord, Jenna was nice enough to let me help her with this beautiful garden she planted for your pleasure."

Jenna's trembling did not cease, though her hand inched closer to Mary's and rested against hers as if in appreciation and protection.

Decimus took a sharp step forward and Mary grabbed Jenna's hand, holding her firm before she could fall back in fright.

"My wife will not tend a garden. That duty is meant for a servant."

"And Jenna does her duty well, which I was thinking . . ." Though the thought had just come to her. "You promised me a personal servant to tend to my needs."

He looked about to strangle her.

Mary smiled. "You are so very generous to me, my lord, and I would appreciate it if Jenna could be made my servant and *mine alone*."

For a brief instant she recognized a glint of Michael in his dark eyes, and her heart filled with joy. She did so love that man and immediately felt guilty for toying with him.

"I would be most grateful, my lord," she said with a bow of her head.

"You would serve my wife well?"

"Yes, my lord," Jenna answered, though her voice trembled. "It would be an honor to serve your wife. There is nothing she would want for. I would see to her every need."

"And not let her tend this garden?"

Mary was quick to catch his eye and saw his own teasing nature surface.

"My lady may enjoy the garden while I do the work. She will not toil in the soil; it is unbefitting to her station."

"Good, then as of this moment you are my wife's personal servant. You will answer to me or my wife and no one else. Is that clear?"

"Yes, my lord."

"You will be given a room near our bedchamber. Go gather your belongings."

Jenna bowed her head and jumped up, then stopped abruptly and extended her hand to Mary. "My lady."

Mary smiled and took her hand but when she stood, her head suddenly turned light, her stomach grew nauseous, and the world around her dimmed.

"My lady, are you all right?"

Mary was unable to answer, and with panic in her eyes looked to her husband.

Decimus caught her in his arms before she collapsed.

It was a strange sight, and all who saw it stopped and stared. The man who ordered tortures and condemned many to death rushed through the fortress with his wife cradled in his arms.

A young servant girl followed in his wake.

Whispers followed the trio and then tongues began to wag.

"A wet cloth," Decimus said to Jenna as he laid his wife on the bed in their bedchamber.

Jenna was a step ahead of him, rinsing a cloth she had dipped in the water bucket and hurrying to his side.

Decimus applied the wet cloth to Mary's face and worried over her, especially if she should call him anything other then Decimus. It would be better if Jenna were not here.

"My wife may need sustenance. I do not think she has eaten at all today. Go and get her food and drink."

"Aye, my lord," Jenna said and hurried out of the room, closing the door behind her.

He pressed the cloth gently to her pale face. "Wake up, Mary. You are safe. I am here with you." He kept repeating the reassuring words to her until they turned more forceful and became a demand. "You must wake up now, I insist. Do not frighten me like this."

To his relief her eyes fluttered open.

"What happened?" she asked in a bare whisper.

"You fainted." He patted her face with the cloth until her eyes were open wide, then laid it aside and took her hands in his. "Do you feel all right now?"

"I am a bit nauseous," she admitted. "And my head fuzzy."

"Did you eat this morning?"

She frowned. "I was so eager to seek the outdoors, the day so beautiful, that I gave no thought to food."

"I thought that, plus the babe, might be the reason for your faint. I sent Jenna for food."

Mary realized she was on her bed. "You carried me to our bedchamber?"

He nodded. "To everyone's surprise."

"Oh dear," she sighed. "Tongues surely must be wagging now, and with us being here only three weeks there will be talk that I was with child before we arrived."

"No one would even dare voice the thought and chance sending Decimus into a fury. Your faint actually works well for our plans. If you appear sick throughout your pregnancy then your death will be easily accepted."

Mary had thought differently and another plan began forming in her mind, one she would share with Reena and Brigid when they arrived. It was a plan that would benefit all.

"Are you suggesting I faint more often?" she asked with a giggle.

"Absolutely not," he said adamantly. "I forbid you from ever fainting again."

"I do not think the choice will be mine."

"Then the babe better listen to me well," he said smiling.

Mary loved seeing him smile. It was so very rare to see him do so, and it never failed to fill her heart with joy.

Decimus splayed his hand on her stomach. "You will not faint again."

The door opened and a wide-eyed Jenna stood balancing a platter in one hand. From her horrified expression she must have heard Decimus's order and thought he was issuing it to his wife.

Decimus quickly stood and followed through on keeping his image of a wicked and uncaring soul.

"I do not expect my wife to be an ill and weak-willed woman. See that you remain strong so that you will give me fine sons." He turned to Jenna. "Make certain she eats and rests and takes walks. I hold you responsible for her well-being."

Without another word to Mary, he stormed out of the room.

Jenna hurried to her side, her eyes filled with tears. "My lady, you must stay well or he will surely send me to the dungeons for torture."

"Do not worry, all will be well," Mary said. She would have no choice but to see Jenna free. If her plan succeeded and Jenna was left behind, she could possibly be made to suffer. So although Jenna did not know it, in a few months time she would be starting a new life.

The days passed pleasantly enough, at least when she was alone with Decimus. He remained a strict, heartless man in front of others. No one dared to question his orders, any directive from him met not an ounce of opposition.

She watched people tremble with fear when confronted by Decimus. And she attempted to listen to the gossip that circulated throughout the fortress, but whispers turned to murmurs in her presence. Everyone feared she would confide in her husband what she had heard and punishment would follow.

Jenna was careful with her remarks, always praising Decimus and reminding Mary of her husband's orders.

Mary continued to play her part well and to plan. She had hope of their successful escape and she intended to hold that hope strong in her heart and see that it became reality.

Decimus was roused from bed late one evening by one of the guards. He tucked the blanket around Mary and told her to sleep, he would return when he could.

He returned angry, several hours later, bolting the door behind him.

Mary shook away the sleep and sat up to see her husband pacing in front of the fireplace. "What is wrong?"

"Jenna was caught stealing food."

Mary jumped out of bed and hurried to her husband's side. "Stealing food?"

He stopped pacing and slipped his arm around her waist. "She was caught taking the leftover food from your tray and giving it to her younger brother, who waited in the woods."

"What is wrong with that?"

"It is not permitted. It is considered stealing and punishable by severe torture."

Mary's legs grew weak. "You cannot be serious."

He shook his head. "I issued the orders myself when I first came here. I had to make certain they all feared me beyond reason, so that none would question me. I needed complete obedience if I was to be able to come and go from the fortress without question."

"No one has ever stolen?"

"No one has ever been caught."

"Except Jenna."

He nodded. "I found out that Jenna had been sharing her own food with her younger brother who lives in the woods. When she became your personal servant, she began giving him your leftovers. The boy is just as thin as his sister. They were orphaned a few months ago and Jenna had no way to feed them, so she came here to work."

"Is that how you get most of your servants; they have a choice of either starving or working here?" Mary asked.

"I suppose working in hell at least allows for a chance of an everlasting life in heaven."

Though fearful, Mary asked, "Are Jenna and her brother now prisoners?"

"They huddle in a cell together. I knew they needed each other's strength so I made it appear as if they would suffer their fate together. The young lad appears maybe six years, though Jenna claims his age is eight."

Mary grabbed her husband's arm. "What will you do? Everyone will expect you to punish them." Tears clouded her eyes. "Can the Dark One save them?"

Decimus stepped away from her, the look of anguish in his eyes tearing at Mary's heart. "I would need Roarke's assistance."

"You have me."

He raked his hair with his fingers in frustration. "I cannot risk your safety."

"Is that not my choice?"

He looked at her as if she were daft. "I will not place you and my child in danger."

She walked over to him, her blue eyes pleading. "They are two innocents, Jenna and her brother. Why should they suffer for being hungry? Roarke is not here; I am. I can help, just tell me what to do."

He shook his head and walked away from her, turning back with angry eyes that had her recoiling. "How do I justify involving you? I wanted to keep you as far from harm as possible."

"I understand, but right now two innocent children are our concern. There must be something we can do."

He marched over to her and grabbed her by the arms. "I have no choice if I want Jenna and her brother to survive."

"Then let us not waste another minute."

His hands turned gentle and he drew her slowly to him. "You promise me you will be careful?"

"I will take no unnecessary chances."

He hesitated, then nodded his consent. "The Dark One cannot be involved in this escape. I will need to keep the men distracted while you free Jenna and her brother. You will then need to take them to safety. Do you feel well enough to walk a distance?"

"I am fine and Jenna will be with me."

"And your return?" he asked with concern. "I cannot venture out and bring you back. I must convince everyone here that you are ill and must remain in bed, and that only I will tend to you."

"Will men search for us?"

"I will keep them away as long as possible, but eventually there will be a search. There are other men— men to be trusted, once prisoners themselves who now help in freeing others. They will guide Jenna, her brother, and you, and will show you a return route that is safer, accompanying you a short distance. But there will be at least half a day that you will be on your own." He shook his head. "This is madness; you cannot be walking the woods alone."

"I have done so before."

"Not as my wife you have not." He sounded determined that she would not do this.

Mary thought otherwise. "I will not see Jenna and her brother suffer when I am capable of helping. I will return before you realize I am gone."

"I think not. When I lay in bed without your warm, soft body next to mine, I will worry."

She placed a gentle hand on his arm. "Nothing will happen to me. I will see them safe and be in our bed before dawn tomorrow. Besides, I am experienced with a bow and can use one if necessary."

"A bow? Who taught you how to handle a bow?"

"The bowman in the village I was brought to. I was barely eleven and angry over my parents' deaths. Vengeance filled my heart and the thought of piercing my enemy's heart with an arrow filled me with determination to learn how to use a bow."

He placed his hand over hers. "You did pierce my heart, though it was love's arrow that felled the mighty Decimus."

She smiled proudly. "I am an excellent bow woman."

He laughed and kissed her with a gentle haste. "I am glad to know that, though I will not worry less about you. There is no time to spare if we are to do this. We must move immediately to free them. How did you slip past the guards when you freed Roarke?"

"I borrowed clothes from the stables and wore a cap to hide my long hair. Dirt smudges on my face helped greatly."

"I will get you what you need and wait until you are ready. Then I will call the men from the dungeon so that there will be no one to stop you, but you have only minutes for they know I will not leave the dungeon unattended for long."

She saw the worry in his dark eyes and thought to assure him. "I will be fine."

He wrapped his arms around her. "You better be, for I will never forgive you or my own foolishness for letting you risk your life like this."

He kissed her but there was no time to linger. They had to act now before the young pair would suffer.

In no time Mary was dressed once again as a lad, and before she tucked her blond hair beneath the wool cap, Decimus kissed her again.

"I love you."

"And I you with all my heart," she said.

"Travel safe and be careful, I already wait impatiently for your return."

Holding her hand, Decimus checked the hall to see that they were alone. Together they sneaked down the curving staircase. Mary hid within the shadows, a bow clasped tightly in her hand and a sack of arrows strapped to her back as Decimus summoned his men.

The escape had begun.

Chapter 33

Mary managed to free Jenna and her brother William from the dungeon with little difficulty, and within hours met with the men in the woods who would take them to safety. She did not, however, advise anyone of her fatigue.

Jenna had been shocked and relieved to learn that Mary would help them escape, though she made her concern for Mary known. She worried that Decimus would take his wrath out on his wife if he should learn that she freed them, and she urged Mary not to return.

"I cannot do that, Jenna." Mary tried to explain. "I would place myself in even more danger. I must return; I have no choice."

"But you are free," she cried and wiped at her tears. "For the short time I have known you, you have been so very good to me. Now William and I have a chance to live a better life because of you. Please join us."

"It is not possible, and I must be on my way. My husband thinks me ill and confined to my bed. He is busy with the escape, but there will come a time he looks in on me and will see that it is not his wife beneath the blanket but pillows."

"I do not know how I can thank you," Jenna said, clinging to Mary's hand.

"By living a good life with your brother," Mary said, then hugged the thin girl and bid her farewell.

Two men took her to the woods and one looked uncertain about leaving her on her own.

"The terrain is not easy, the path not always clear. Are you certain you can manage on your own?"

"Your directions are clear. I will be fine," she assured him, though worried that her fatigue might catch up with her before she reached the fortress. But she had no choice; she had to return as quickly as possible. She could rest all she wanted to once in the fortress.

She took to the woods in bright daylight, but knew that it would be near to dawn before she reached the Fortress of Hell. She had walked quite a distance before she rested, and no sooner than she sat did she hear a noise. She was quick to her feet and quicker to take bow and arrow to hand and wait, the trees shielding her.

Decimus delayed his men from beginning their search as long as he could then released them, praying Mary and the two young ones were well gone.

It was near to nightfall and he hoped that Mary was safe and close to home, though he knew it would take her the night to reach the fortress. He had walked the familiar path many times.

The darkness was a friend to him; he only hoped Mary would feel the same way and she would find the shadows and sounds of the night her protectors.

Later that night in their bedchamber he paced the

floor waiting for her. He attempted to sleep if only for an hour or so but sleep eluded him. He could think of nothing but his wife and unborn child alone in the woods, prey to man and beast.

He thought several times to go in search of her, but he realized he could not leave the fortress for then he would need to leave someone in his ill wife's care and that was not possible.

He stood by the window, looking into the dark night and praying for his wife's safe return. His heart was heavy with worry not only of her safety, but also of the thought of having to let her go. He had briefly considered escaping with her when the time came and leaving all the madness behind him. Then his senses returned to him and he knew he could not forsake his duty to the innocent. He had to continue his work and help as many people as he could.

The thought did not ease his heartache, nor would it comfort him when he lay in bed alone without his beloved wife. But he was a man of honor and he had no choice in this matter.

He would take what time he had with her and love her with all his heart. That was why she had to return to him.

By dawn.

Decimus stood by the window and watched the sun rise. Mary was to return by dawn but was yet to be seen. His worry and fear mounted with each passing hour. Then he was informed that someone approached and his heart wrenched with worry.

He waited at the entrance to the fortress. Could it be Mary? Had someone found her? Was she ill?

The wagons and riders approached and in the lead was a man in an iron mask on a sturdy black steed.

The Legend had arrived at the fortress.

Reena was quick to slip off her mare but approached Decimus with caution. "We thought to visit with Mary, if you approve of course."

Decimus stared at her. He was no fool, Mary had sent for the lot of them when she had sent the note he had learned about. She was up to something and, if he had her here right now, he would find out what she was up to.

"You are welcome to visit *briefly.*"

"How kind of you," Reena said with a pleasant smile. "Where is Mary?"

Decimus had no chance to answer.

"Mary!" Reena yelled and hurried past Decimus.

He turned to see his wife walking out the door dressed in proper attire, not a smudge on her pale face. He had to restrain himself from rushing forward and scooping her up in his arms. She looked near to collapsing.

"Are you all right?" Reena asked with alarm.

Mary stepped forward on trembling legs. She was bone tired and hungry, and though she was thrilled to see Reena and the others, she wanted nothing more than her husband's loving arms around her.

She managed a weak smiled and looked to Decimus before answering Reena. "I am—"

She was suddenly lifted up into her husband's arms.

"Did I give you permission to get out of bed?" he said, his nostrils flaring and his eyes blazing with an angry heat.

"You have been ill?" Reena asked, close on Decimus's heels.

"Mary has not felt well for days and needs rest." Decimus was firm in his retort.

"I will look after her," Reena offered, though it sounded more like a demand.

"That is not necessary. Wait in the hall while I see to my wife."

There was no doubt that he meant to be obeyed, and Magnus reached out and grabbed his wife by the back of her tunic.

"Do as he says. You will talk with Mary soon enough."

"She does not look well at all," Reena said concerned.

"We will make certain she is well before we leave here," Magnus assured her.

"That we will," Reena said, folding her arms firmly across her chest. "For I will not leave here until I am certain of it."

Decimus wanted to scream, shout, and cry out his joy that Mary had returned safely, though she appeared completely exhausted. And that worried him.

"I should have never let you do this," he said, placing her gently on the bed.

Mary rested her hand on his cheek. "Jenna and her brother are free and I am but tired. Freedom heals them and sleep will heal me."

He kissed her palm. "You took longer than I expected; I worried that something had happened to you."

"I came upon your men," she said quietly. "I thought only one at first and was ready with my bow and arrow. Then I spied another and knew I needed to hide and wait for them to pass. It delayed my return."

Her near capture filled him with dread, and he silently swore he would never place her in such danger again. He would see her safe and free of harm. "Rest," he urged and placed her hand on her stomach, his hand covering hers.

"I understand now." Her eyes drifted closed.

"What do you understand?"

"Why the Dark One does what he does."

"And why he must continue his work," he said regretfully.

"Everything changes yet it stays the same."

Decimus had to lean closer to hear her, her voicing drifting off to a mere whisper as she fell asleep. He did not understand the pertinence of her remark, but then she was tired and probably not making sense.

He waited by her side until he was certain she was asleep. When a soft knock sounded at the door, he hurried to see who dared disturb them.

Reena stood with her hands on her hips, Brigid behind her. He had to admire Reena, for a small wisp of a woman she had courage.

"Is Mary all right?"

"She is with child and has not been well." He saw no reason to keep that information from them and it was time her pregnancy was known, time for their escape plan to begin.

Reena went to walk past him but he blocked her with his arm across the doorway. "She sleeps."

Reena looked perturbed, but Brigid handled herself well.

"Would you like someone to sit with her in case she should wake and need assistance?"

Reena was more direct. "We heard that her personal servant was accused of stealing and had escaped before punishment. It *must* have upset her."

"It was no concern of hers." He had often wanted to cringe at his own arrogance, but it was necessary to keep up the façade. He was however grateful to Brigid for offering to sit with his wife. He would feel more at ease if someone he could trust remained with her.

He stood aside. "Do not disturb her."

He forced himself not to smile when he saw Brigid grab hold of Reena's arm. The tiny, thin woman looked ready to lunge at him. He was glad to know Mary had good friends. She would need them.

They walked to the bed and after seeing that Mary was asleep, Reena pulled a chair near the bed for Brigid to sit.

Decimus noticed then that Brigid was round with child and a sudden sadness rushed over him. He would have to send Mary away when she was heavy with his child. He would watch her walk out of his life never to see her or to know his offspring.

He wanted to scream and lash out at someone but he could do nothing, just as he had not been able to do anything about his family's suffering. What good was love when it only brought more pain and sorrow?

He turned and hurried out the door. A scurry of footsteps caught up with him as he descended the staircase.

"Since Mary has not been well, I think it wise she return with us so that she may get proper care."

Decimus stopped so abruptly that Reena smashed into his back. He turned, grabbed hold of her arm, and marched her down the remainder of the steps.

"Mary stays with me." He felt his fury boiling. He had only a short time left with his wife and he was not willing to relinquish a moment of it.

"Take your hand off my wife."

Reena froze along with Decimus. She had not heard her husband use that vicious tone often, but when he did there was not a soul who did not obey him.

Decimus released her slowly. "Your wife speaks when she should not."

"A trait I admire in her," Magnus said and held his hand out to his wife.

Reena took it and stood to his side.

"Your reason for being here?" Decimus asked bluntly.

"We came to visit Mary," Magnus said, recalling how one day his wife burst into his solar and insisted they go see how Mary was fairing. She wanted to leave that day, that very minute. It was obvious she had been worried, then Magnus found out that Reena had received a note from Mary, requesting help. Help with what she had not specified. They left the next day.

"We can set up camp in the woods if we are not welcomed here," Magnus said, receiving no immediate response from Decimus.

"You may stay," Decimus said, his own thoughts on the note Mary had sent to Reena. "I will have rooms made ready for you."

"Thank you for your hospitality," Magnus replied, though he sounded just as grieved as Decimus. It appeared they both felt the same; Magnus did not want to be there and Decimus did not want him here.

One of Decimus's men rushed into the hall and, after a respectful bow to Decimus, said, "The men are returning, my lord."

He waved him away and summoned a servant working in the hall. "See that food is brought to our guests and rooms prepared." He looked to Magnus. "I must see to my duties. Do not get in the way of my men or the workings of this fortress, or you will pay the penalty."

Magnus waited until Decimus left the hall before he turned to his wife.

Her words prevented his own. "Mary is pregnant." She lowered her voice. "And I do not think Decimus is the father."

While Thomas and Magnus set up camp for their men outside the fortress, Reena decided to see what she could learn on her own.

An hour later with a food tray in hand, she joined Brigid. The two women sat at the table near the window and talked in whispers, not wanting to wake Mary.

"I find few who are happy here, and those who claim to be speak out of fear," Reena said. "One woman wishes she could take Jenna's place as Mary's personal servant. Jenna had often spoken of how kind and considerate the lord's new wife was and many had been jealous. Jenna had also defended Mary against gossip."

"What gossip?" Brigid asked.

Reena looked to the bed where Mary lay sound asleep. She kept her voice low just the same. "There is talk that Mary was with child before coming to the fortress."

Brigid shook her head. "But then that would mean that Decimus is not—" Brigid gasped then quickly covered her mouth with her hand and cast an anxious glance to the bed.

"Mary sleeps deeply, probably exhausted by her worries and all she has endured."

"The father could only be . . ." Brigid looked around the room suspiciously. "The walls have eyes and ears, one can never be too careful."

"True," Reena agreed, casting her own suspicious glance. "We will need to be cautious."

"Do you think the babe is why Mary summoned us?"

"What else could it be?" Reena kept her voice to a murmur. "We must help her get away from Decimus before it is too late."

Chapter 34

Mary woke to a faint flicker of light from the fireplace. Though summer was near upon them, the stone fortress retained a chill and a low fire was kept in the fireplaces.

She was grateful for the spark of light, unafraid of the shadows that lurked in the corners and around the edge of the bed. The darkness meant she had slept the day away. She had no sense of time and felt as if she could sleep several more hours. Her stomach, however, was the culprit that woke her. She was reminded that she had not eaten in nearly a day.

Unfortunately she did not feel like moving. She was warm and snug beneath the soft, light wool blanket. She yawned more loudly than she intended and her stomach grumbled right afterward.

"Hungry and tired?" The familiar voice asked from the shadows.

Mary smiled as Decimus stepped into the light. Perhaps it was the old familiar voice that made her feel at ease with a face that was yet not recognizable as the man she loved.

"I thought myself alone." She reached her arms out to him.

He sat on the bed and slipped into her arms, lifting her up to meet him and hugging her as if it had been months since last he held her.

"I would not leave you alone," he chided.

She laughed softly at his rebuke.

He poked her in the side where he knew it tickled. "You no longer fear the all-powerful Decimus?"

She captured his finger in her hand, holding it prisoner. "I no longer fear Decimus." She lowered her voice. "I know his secret."

He leaned closer and whispered. "What is it?"

She touched her lips faintly to his. "He has a loving and caring heart."

"That's a dangerous secret to know." He returned her kiss.

"I would go to my grave with it."

He stopped, about to kiss her once again. "You will do no such thing. If ever you should find yourself in danger of protecting my identity, you will save yourself."

"How can you ask that of me? And besides, I would be put to death for consorting with you no matter what information I surrendered."

He stood and grabbed hold of his head as though he prevented it from exploding. "I cannot bear the thought of you suffering for loving me."

"I would suffer more if I did not love you."

His browed wrinkled and he looked confused. "Sometimes you make no sense."

"That," she said, attempting to sit up and he hurrying to assist her, "is when I make the most sense."

Decimus braced pillows behind her back. "We shall discuss this and other matters while you eat, then you can rest again."

"Is it late, everyone abed?"

"All retired at least two hours ago, the fortress rests." He walked over to the fireplace and after a few moments he returned with a tray. "I have kept this goose pie hot for you."

Mary licked her lips and rubbed her hands together.

He placed the silver tray on her lap and placed a cloth upon her chest.

"Tell me why you would suffer more if you did not love me."

Mary took several spoonfuls before offering an explanation. "To have never known such a wonderful love existed would have caused more suffering in my life. I would have forever wondered about love and why I could never find it."

"You would have found another love."

She shook her head. "You are my destiny." The seer was right. Decimus was her destiny and she planned on seeing to his demise, so that Michael could live.

"Destiny makes the choice for us then."

"Destiny presents us with choices; it is up to us. Destiny presented us to each other; it is our decision what we do with our love."

"We have no choice in this matter," he insisted.

"But we do."

"You know I cannot walk away from those who need my help," he said, frustrated by his own reasoning.

"Everything changes yet remains the same."

He shook his head. "You said that before falling asleep and I wondered what you meant."

"You fight for the innocent who suffer, but the innocent continue to suffer. No matter how many people you free, there will always be more people who need freeing. Thus, things change, yet remain the same. Only until man opens his mind and heart together, will ample change take place. You should be aware of this since you spoke with my father and know of his teachings."

"Some teachings are easier to learn and practice than others. But tell me, could you have allowed Jenna and William to suffer?"

"Not when I had it in my power to see them free."

"Then how do I walk away knowing countless people will suffer because I was not there to save them?" he asked.

"There will always be countless people you cannot save, perhaps it is time to change your fighting tactics." She hurried her hand to her mouth to cover the huge yawn that attacked her.

"You need more rest," he said and reached for the tray, most of the goose pie gone.

She snuggled down under the blanket. "You will join me?"

He placed the tray on the table and returned to the bed to kiss her cheek. "I will join you shortly."

One tired eye widened. "I had forgotten. We have visitors."

"Someone in particular who is determined to see you well and gone from this fortress."

"Reena." Mary smiled. "I look forward to speaking with her. And Brigid, she is well?"

"She sat with you while you slept."

"It is so good to have caring friends." She yawned again.

"Sleep," he urged her. "You will visit with them tomorrow."

Her eyes were already drifting shut and her words a mere mumble. "I love you."

He sat watching her sleep, thinking of his love for her and the tiny babe that nestled safely in her stomach. He would protect them both with his life never letting any harm come to either of them. That was the very reason he was sending her away, to keep his family safe. He had been unable to protect his family once; he would not see it happen again even if it meant he could not be with them.

But her words had made sense. How long could he continue leading this double life before someone discovered his secret? How many could he save and how much of a difference did it make?

Was there a way for them to be together?

Did he dare hope that they had a chance?

He shook his head and walked to the window, leaning against the wall and looking out on total darkness. He had lived in the shadows for over twenty years and was barely thirty and four years. How much longer could he exist in darkness?

Had not his path been defined for him after losing his family? Had he not made a pledge to avenge their deaths? Had he not kept it?

He had placed his family in danger once before because he listened to others' opinions. He could not be persuaded again to make a foolish choice. He had to know his wife and child would be safe, and they could only be safe far away from him.

As much as it hurt him to let Mary go, he had no choice. He would make plans and see that Roarke took her to safety, and he would say his last goodbye to her and his unborn child.

* * *

Mary woke to a delicious scent and found Reena and Brigid sitting at the table in her bedchamber whispering and eating.

"Save some for me, I am starved," she said and threw the blanket back to hurry out of bed.

The three women squealed with delight and hugged each other. Reena fussed over Mary, finding a black velvet robe, though the sleeves too long, for her to wear. Reena saw to freeing her hands, folding the velvet sleeves back several times, then the three gathered around the table to share the morning meal and talk.

"First, we must know you are well," Reena said. "You looked so very pale yesterday and then Decimus told us of the child you carry."

"I am fine."

"Are you sure?" Brigid asked, placing a protective hand on her rounded stomach. "You do not want to take a chance with your or your child's life."

Mary rested crossed hands on the table and prayed the choice she was about to make was a wise one. She had no doubt that she could trust the two women; it was that she would be placing them in danger that made her reconsider.

"Your note was clear," Reena reminded her. "You need help and that is why we are here."

"The help comes with a steep price. It places you both in *extreme* danger. I have no right to ask you to take such a risk."

"We are friends." Reena said, covering Mary's hands with her own.

"Brigid, you are with child and I understand if—"

Brigid added her hand to theirs. "You are with child as well, and as Reena said we are friends."

Mary nodded and spoke before she could change her mind. "I helped two prisoners escape the fortress and was only returning from a day's walk when you arrived."

The two women stared at her in shocked silence for a brief moment.

"You took a risk being with child and being Decimus's wife," Reena scolded out of concern.

"I risk much more than an escape," Mary said and looked to each woman.

Reena spoke low. "There is gossip in the fortress about the babe's father."

Mary grabbed hold of her goblet of cider and rested back in her chair. "What is being said?"

"That you were with child before reaching the fortress," Reena confirmed. "Since all knew you arrived on your wedding day, and due to Decimus's firm belief in Church doctrine on celibacy before marriage, it is thought he is not the father."

"Decimus will learn of the gossip soon enough," Brigid said. "What then?"

Mary thought the timing perfect. The gossip would serve her plan well and lead to the conclusion of the ideal solution to her problem, though she required help in implementing it.

It had to be carried out precisely, leaving nothing to chance and making certain that in the end the Dark One had no choice but to follow her plan. Was it fair of her not to give him a choice? But then he was not giving her one. He insisted they could not stay together. She thought otherwise and intended to prove herself right. She had to; she refused to live life without him.

"Mary," Reena said, drawing her out of her musings.

"Decimus will show no mercy if he should discover you helped prisoners escape. And I hate to think of the consequences when he discovers the truth about the child you carry."

"I have a plan."

"Will it free you?" Brigid asked hopefully.

"I will need to go away and never return," Mary said with sadness, knowing she would miss her friends. "There is no other way."

"We will do what must be done to free you," Reena said firmly, choking back a tear.

Brigid refilled their goblets with cider. "Does the Dark One know?"

"Aye, the Dark One knows that I carry his child."

"And what says he?" Reena asked.

"He insists that I go away never to see him again. He claims he must continue with his work here, and that I and his child would be safer far away from him."

"He saves many lives," Brigid said, "the numbers too numerous to count."

"He has sacrificed enough of himself. It is time for him to live," Mary said, angrily. "There will always be someone who needs saving. He cannot save them all. The people must begin to save themselves." She sounded selfish and she was, for her husband's sake. "And he is bound to be caught eventually. Who will free him then?"

"He chose to take that chance," Reena said. "Can you not convince him that you and the babe need him more?"

"I have tried, but he is stubborn and I fear for his life. You may think me selfish, but I want him with me. I do not ask that he surrender his battle, just that he change how he battles. All good warriors change tactics from time to time. How else does he avoid capture by his enemy?"

"What you are telling us is that the Dark One is not a willing participant in your escape plan, which makes for a more difficult success," Reena said then grinned. "Though not necessarily a failure."

Mary wiped away her last few tears and smiled. "You will help me?"

"That was my intention since I first received your note, and when I read it to Brigid, she agreed."

"I told Reena that we must come at once. Your note seemed urgent."

"The Dark One's plans have me remaining here until I am heavy with child. I wish to leave as soon as possible." She realized when she helped Jenna escape that she would be wiser to hasten her own plans. When she was swollen with child it would only make for a more difficult travel. Now she was still agile and able to move freely, the babe but a tiny seed inside her.

"A wise choice," Brigid said. "I have not yet grown full with child and I already find myself moving more slowly. It is best you go now when you have no added burden."

"We will need to begin very soon," Reena said. "If we delay there is always a chance of someone discovering our plans."

"What of our husbands?" Brigid asked. "Will we require their help?"

"I think we will need them," Mary said. "We will need strong men to carry the bodies."

"Bodies?" Reena asked alarmed. "What type of plan have you devised?"

"A permanent one. I want everyone to believe that the Dark One and I are dead. I do not want to live in fear that one day someone will find us. I want there to be no doubt that we are dead. Tongues must wag, the gossip grow and spread far and wide."

"It is a dangerous plan," Reena said. "Decimus will want to view the bodies and make certain there is no breath left in them."

Mary took a deep breath and looked at her friends. "When I was with the Dark One he took me to a village where many of the people he had helped lived. They assisted him in helping others to escape. I met a seer there and she predicted my future."

Mary took another breath. "She told me I would be the demise of Decimus, that he was my destiny."

Reena grabbed Mary's hand. "You cannot mean to kill Decimus. It is too dangerous."

Brigid agreed. "He sees everything, knows everything. He will surely find out."

"*Extremely* dangerous is what I told you my plan would be."

The two women looked ready to argue, but Mary spoke up.

"It is not the danger you think and what I am about to reveal you must swear never to speak of, not even in a whisper."

The two women shivered and nodded their heads.

"The seer's words made no sense and frightened me until I discovered the Dark One's true identity. The Dark One and Decimus are one."

Chapter 35

Reena and Brigid were stunned, neither woman able to speak. They sat and stared with wide, bewildered eyes at Mary.

"I was just as shocked," Mary said. "I actually thought that Decimus had played a trick on me when he pulled off the black shroud to reveal himself. It took little time for me to realize he spoke the truth, though it has not been easy to merge the two men as one. Decimus continues to appear the cruel, unforgiving torturer of innocent souls and yet within him is the Dark One, the man who fights for and frees the innocent."

"So with Decimus's demise, the Dark One lives," Reena said, Mary's plan making more sense.

"Michael lives," Mary said with a smile. "He is who I know and love."

"And his plans for you are?" Reena asked.

"That I appear ill throughout my pregnancy and just before the babe is born, I die. Decimus would see to the burial arrangement and the Dark One to my escape, saying his last goodbye to me when he turned me over to the safety of his friend Roarke."

"Roarke healed well and left with us, though we separated along the way," Reena said. "He expressed the need to return and help the Dark One."

"I will need Roarke's help as well."

"What is your plan?" Reena asked.

By the time they finished discussing what Mary had in mind, it was decided that Magnus and Thomas would not be told of anything until the very last minute. The women feared the husbands would attempt to dissuade them or change the plan to one they deemed more suitable and safer for the women.

Mary entered the hall to find Decimus speaking with Magnus and Thomas. They all wore frowns, and she could only imagine what her husband discussed with them.

"Your visit will be short. I have work to do," Decimus said and turned, almost colliding with his wife. He grabbed firm hold of her arms. "Should you be out of bed? You have not been well."

"I am feeling much better," she said, her head bowed in respect.

"Visit with your friends now for they will not be staying long." Decimus released her and marched off, expecting his orders to be obeyed.

Magnus approached her. "Are you all right, Mary?"

"I was feeling ill when you arrived, but a sound night's sleep, though it was more like a full day's sleep," she said with a laugh, "has seen to reviving my health."

He stepped closer to her. "Reena advised me of your note and request for help. What is it we can do for you?"

"There are some things that I will need of you, though I cannot discuss them with you now."

"We will be here for you," Magnus assured her.

"I appreciate your help and patience in this matter."

Thomas stepped forward. "I stand beside my lord in all matters."

She smiled. "You are true friends and we will talk soon, but now I must see to another matter that needs my attention." She thanked them again and left the hall.

"Something more goes on than she tells us," Thomas said to Magnus.

"I agree and I think it involves your wife and mine."

Mary hurried out of the fortress to see if she could find her husband. He was chastising a group of his men in the center of the courtyard. She approached slowly, keeping her demeanor that of an obedient wife.

Decimus turned, his tongue sharp. "I am busy, wife, what brings you to me?"

"A private question, my lord." She trembled to show fear, though the act was not difficult. His dark, penetrating eyes could put the fear in anyone. She had to remember he was the man she loved.

He dismissed his men with the wave of his hand. And while he kept his expression stern he spoke in a soft whisper that only she could hear.

"You are feeling well?"

"Aye, my lord," she said, bowing her head to keep up appearances.

"I am sorry to send your friends away, but the longer they remain the more careful I must be, and I selfishly want what time I have left with you, without worry of discovery."

"I feel the same and I ask that they be allowed to remain here until the end of the week."

He waved his hand as though he dismissed her remark and said, "I see no problem with that."

"One other thing," she said, softly. "Reena told me that Roarke had returned part of the way with them and then left to find the Dark One. Have you heard from him? I wish to know that he is well and safe."

"He waits for me in the woods, where we will begin to formulate a plan for your death and escape."

"May I go to him?" She intended to find him whether given permission or not. But she did not want Decimus to know that.

He hesitated a moment. "Take Reena or Brigid with you so that it looks like you are taking a walk in the woods."

"I will see you later," she said and bowed her head.

"Be gone," he shouted. "I have no time for nonsense, take your walk and leave me be." He turned and walked over to his men without another glance.

Mary found Reena but left Brigid who was already busy securing the items necessary for the escape.

"Roarke will not speak to me in front of you," Mary said, when they had almost reached the area where he waited for Decimus.

"I will wander off on my own," Reena assured her, making it known in a raised voice that she went in search of feathers for quills and that Mary was to relax and enjoy the beautiful summer day.

Roarke stepped out from behind a tree as soon as Reena had disappeared into the woods. "Reena knows you meet me. She did not need to leave."

"You are too perceptive," Mary said with a smile.

"But I needed to talk with you alone and Reena understood."

"She and Brigid took good care of me," he said and reached out his hand.

Mary took it and he helped her to sit on a fallen tree, and joined her.

"They are good friends, like you."

Roarke's handsome face brimmed with a smile. "You want something from me."

She nodded and looked out on the beauty of the woods, so alive with new summer growth, the bright sun shining down and a gentle breeze wafting around them. It was peaceful here and that is what she wanted for Michael and herself—peace.

"Have you spoken with Michael since your return?"

"Briefly," he said. "He told me you are aware of his identity and I hear congratulations are in order."

She placed her hand to her stomach. "He will be a father come winter."

"He is pleased, though . . ." Roarke did not finish.

She saw he was upset and she prayed he felt the same as she. "He deserves a life, Roarke."

"I have told him this time and time again. His family, especially his sister, would not have wanted him to surrender his whole life for them."

"But he feels they surrendered theirs for him, does he not?"

"No matter how much I tell him it was not his fault, he believes otherwise," Roarke said.

"So he continually surrenders himself for others, with the dream of saving his family over and over. Yet now, with his child inside me, he continues the family, what his mother and sister would wish for him. Their persecutors cannot rob Michael of his bloodline."

"He feels committed to save as many people as he can."

"Do you think he has not saved enough? Do you not think it is time for him to fight in another way? Do you not think it is time for him to live?" She sounded as though she pleaded her case, but it made no difference, she was pleading for the life of the man she loved.

"He is a stubborn man and I have often told him that he cannot go on forever living a lie; he will be caught."

"Do you not tire of this life yourself?" Mary asked. "Would you not like a wife and family?"

Roarke rocked back and glanced up at the heavens. "Peace, I would love some peace in my life."

She reached out and touched his hand. "Then help me free Michael and finally lay his revenge to rest so that his family may rest, and you may know peace yourself."

"You are a courageous woman, Mary."

She grinned. "I am a woman deeply in love."

"Michael is a lucky man."

"He may not agree with you, especially after I tell you what I have planned."

"Your plan will free him of Decimus and the Dark One?" he asked.

"Only Michael will live."

"Tell me what you have in mind."

They huddled in discussion with Roarke making a few suggestions that would help secure the plan's success. They plotted date and time, Roarke agreeing it must be done immediately or they would risk someone learning of it. He also agreed that Michael might be angry with her at first.

"I am prepared for his wrath; I am not, however, prepared to live my life without him," Mary said stubbornly. "In time he will come to realize the wisdom of my actions."

"When he holds his newborn in his arms, he will be grateful to you."

Mary sighed softly. "As I will be grateful to see him hold his son or daughter and know that his family continues on within the tiny babe."

They heard heavy footsteps and Reena talking to herself much too loudly.

"Reena lets us know of her approach," Roarke said with a laugh.

"She will be pleased that you help us." Mary waved to Reena to join them when she caught sight of her.

She hurried over.

"He joins us," Mary said with joy.

"Good, now all that is left is for us to finalize the plans and choose a day," Reena said, relieved.

"We have chosen a day," Roarke informed her. "We carry out the plan the day after tomorrow."

"Brigid and I will tell Magnus and Thomas that morning."

"I think it wiser if I discuss the plans the night before with them. Timing, actions and illusion will be vital to the success of this plan. They must be fully aware of what they must do. We cannot waste a minute nor hesitate. Decimus must be taken by surprise."

"From what Mary has planned I think he will be stunned," Reena said.

"Giving us all the time to do what we must." Roarke smiled. "Do you wail well, Reena? It is a vital role you will be playing."

"For my small size I have a loud wail," Reena said with pride.

The three laughed and parted ready, yet nervous that if all went well, in a day's time Decimus would be no more.

Mary rolled over in bed that night to hug her husband, her hand roaming down the length of him teasing him into attention.

He responded immediately growing large in her hand.

"You have not been well, I thought not to disturb you."

She squeezed him hard and he grabbed her hand.

"Be careful, you make me want you with a need so strong—"

She squeezed him harder, her need as desperate as his.

In a flash he had her on her back and he was slipping over her and into her as he ravished her mouth with demanding kisses. She responded with the same demand and hungry need, welcoming him into her and holding tightly to him as they loved strong and hard.

Their joining left them breathless, their bodies damp, and their hearts beating wildly. They held hands, lying on their backs and staring at the ceiling as their breathing calmed and their bodies cooled.

Neither spoke, their minds on opposite thoughts.

Decimus felt the heavy weight of their future parting on his heart. Each day they spent together was one day closer to their last day. How would he ever let her go? How would he be able to live without her?

His mind reeled with the tormenting thoughts, but he would not let her know. He had to see that she and his child were safe and free from harm and able to live a good life. And that meant he could not remain with them.

He loved her with all his heart and she would take

his heart with her when she went, for he would never love again.

Mary thought of the day after next and how they would be free to live and love. She would not let her plan fail. She was even more determined now after making love with him. She could not think of a future without him beside her. Whether making love, snuggling together in bed, holding hands as they did now, she could not bear the thought of their binding love not continuing.

She thought him admirable for wanting to continue to help the innocent but not at the cost of their love. He could do more by living his life, having a family, and teaching the innocent to defend themselves.

He rolled onto his side and stroked a finger along her face. "Never forget how much I love you."

"You need not worry that I would ever forget you or your love." She smiled and gently touched his face while silently adding. *I take both with me.*

Chapter 36

Mary entered the hall early the next morning to find it a buzz of activity. The servants rushed about and Decimus's men ate with a hurried flourish. One look at Reena and Brigid and she knew there was a problem.

Decimus walked up to her before she reached the dais. "I will be leaving after the noon meal."

Mary ignored the decorum of a proper wife and demanded, "How long will you be gone?"

Her husband turned a sharp tongue on her. "Do not question my actions, wife."

She continued to defy him, needing to know if it was but hours or days that he would return. "I have not been feeling well and you, my husband, should be concerned and not ride off for days."

Decimus glared at her and she knew he attempted to warn her to hold her tongue. "Whether days or weeks, it concerns you not."

"It does," she said with a shout and fled the hall.

Decimus followed her to their bedchamber slamming the door shut. "What is wrong with you, challenging me like that in front of my men?"

"I do not want you to go away," she said, anxiously ringing her hands. "How long will you be gone?"

He walked over to her and took her trembling hands in his. "A week at least, perhaps longer. I have been summoned to address a church council."

That was not good. They could not wait a week to carry out the plan. Decimus had already made it known that Magnus's visit was to be brief. And without everyone's help, the plan was not possible. If she did not free Michael now, she did not know when she would get another chance.

He looked concerned. "Are you not feeling well, Mary?"

She shook her head. "Just anxious about your absence. I wanted us to have all the time together we could."

"I will do my best to return as soon as possible." He kissed her cheek. "Rest and visit with your friends, but they must be gone before my return."

His words settled it for her. It was today or never.

She wrapped her arms around him, held him tight, and whispered in his ear, "Remember, no matter what, I love you."

A knock at the door interrupted them.

"I love you too," he said softly and with a worried look he stepped away from her and raised his voice. "You will obey me, wife, and I will hear no more of your foolish tongue." He flung open the door and one of his men stood there. Decimus stormed out of the room, leaving the stunned man to close the door behind him.

Reena and Brigid arrived at her bedchamber shortly after Decimus left.

"We do this today," Mary said before anyone could speak.

"What of Roarke?" Reena asked.

"Someone will need to go and tell him the plan has been changed and that it is urgent we implement it before Decimus can leave."

Reena volunteered since she knew where Roarke could be found in the woods. Brigid was left to inform Magnus and Thomas.

"They will have no choice but to help us," Reena assured her friend. "And do not let them batter you with questions and demands. Tell them what they must do and if they refuse, or attempt to dissuade or change the plan, then remind them that all of our lives will be in danger."

"Decimus told me they leave after the noon meal, so that is when we attack," Mary said. "His men will be gathered in the hall to eat before departing. The servants will be about, we will have a good crowd to witness my husband's and my confrontation."

"We finish here in the bedchamber," Brigid confirmed. "I will make certain the blood is available and all evidence cleaned away afterward."

"Where will you go?" Reena asked, close to tears.

"I do not know. I only know that Michael and I will be together." Tears pooled in her eyes. "If I do not get a chance to thank you or bid you both farewell, know how much I appreciate all you have done for me."

The three women hugged and rushed off knowing little time was left for them to set the plan into action.

It was not long before Magnus burst into her bedchamber and forcefully shut the door behind him.

"You cannot be serious about this plan," he said, walking up to her.

Dressed all in black and his eyes aglow with anger, he looked like a demon about to descend on her. But Mary held her ground, her chin high and her stance firm.

"I will not lose the man I love. I will set him free with or without your help."

His eyes lost some of their heat. "You should have come to me and I—"

"There is no time to think of what I should have done. I made my choice, and now you must make yours. Do you help me or not?"

"You know I will help you," he said exasperated. "How could I not?"

"When this is done you will have fulfilled your promise to my parents. You will finally see me safe. No one will ever hunt me again—I will be dead."

"If all goes well." Magnus sounded doubtful.

"You must have faith."

"I would have more faith if Decimus, the Dark One, Michael, whomever he is, had been made aware of this plan so that he could play his part as well as everyone else involved."

"He would have protested."

"Do you not think the choice his?" Magnus asked. "I was shocked to learn of Decimus's true identity and more shocked to realize how much of a chance the Dark One had taken all these years. Do you expect him to simply walk away from it all?"

"I am not asking him to completely forsake his vow to help the innocent. I but ask that he change his battle plan so that he may save more than merely a few. When he realizes the wisdom of my plan, I think he will be less likely to judge me foolish."

"I have had little time to digest all Brigid has told me, but in an attempt to understand your reasoning I see that this choice comes from the heart. Have you thought this through clearly? Are you certain this is best for you both?"

"Minds and hearts often war with each other when decisions are necessary. I can only tell you I feel this is the right choice for us both. And since you know true love yourself, could you live life without Reena?"

Magnus did not hesitate. "I will do all I can to make certain this plan of yours succeeds."

Mary hugged Magnus, grateful for his support, then stepped away to wipe the tears from her eyes. "I cry too much of late."

"You have been through much. You have the right to shed tears." He took her hand. "Tell me where you plan to settle with Decimus."

She shook her head. "I do not know, though it must be far enough away, where Decimus will not be recognized."

"His reputation extends far and wide."

"But not all have seen him, they have only heard of him."

"Far to the northwest there is an island few know of," Magnus said. "The clan there remain much to themselves and accept few outsiders. But I know them well and, if I advise them of your predicament, I do not think they would mind if you and Decimus joined them."

"You are generous and I hate to ask more of you—"

"Ask me, Mary, I wish to help."

"There is a small village the Dark One had brought me to. The people were very kind. I fear for their safety once the chaos of Decimus's death settles."

"Ask no more. I will see them all safe," he promised.

She hugged him again. "Thank you. You are a wonderful friend." She grasped his arm. "You will let no one touch the bodies? It is so very important no one is allowed near them."

"No one will come near any of you, I give you my word," Magnus said with a strength that made Mary smile.

"I think I have covered everything," Mary said, running through the mental list of all that she had planned. "I will meet with Roarke when he returns with Reena and finalize the details, then there is nothing more to do but wait and act our parts."

"You have been a good friend, Magnus. May you and Reena know much joy."

"I wish you and Michael much luck and a long life together."

They hugged and parted, knowing that they might never see each other again. Mary was grateful that the Legend had been in her life.

Noon approached and Mary stood in her bedchamber looking around, making certain all was in readiness. She had tied back her long blond hair with a ribbon and had donned a pale blue linen dress, knowing the blood would appear more horrifying against a light color.

Everyone had to believe her dead and with blood pouring from her they would not want to look too closely. She gave the room one last glance and left knowing the next time she returned here, she would leave a dead woman.

The noon meal was a hurried affair, Decimus making it known he wished to be on his way as soon as possible. He lovingly squeezed Mary's hand beneath the table, letting her know he cared.

She squeezed his in return, praying that Decimus's demise would go well.

One of Decimus's men rushed into the hall and Mary knew the plan had been set into motion. She looked to Reena and she nodded, letting her know that Brigid, Thomas, and Roarke were ready for them.

"The Dark One has been spotted entering the fortress."

Decimus stood with a jolt, sending his chair toppling backward. "I will have his head this time. He will not escape or—someone else's head will roll."

Mary knew he was confident that it was someone's foolish imagination that made him think he saw the Dark One, and he used it to his advantage. She was about to do the same.

She stood with a flourish, her eyes wide and anxious, and turned on her husband, screaming, "No, I love him."

Decimus was stunned silent.

"I *will not* let you hurt him," she wailed and pounded on his chest. "I carry his child. Not yours." She moved away from him as if he were a vile creature, her hand extended out to keep him from approaching her. "Do you hear me, Decimus? It is the Dark One's child I carry."

The hall turned dead silent as they all waited for Decimus to make his move.

Decimus regained his senses and grabbed her arm. "Whore!" He shouted, and glared at her with confusion as he dragged her from the room and up the stairs.

"What are you doing?" he asked angrily as they climbed the stairs.

"Giving us a future," she said as he opened the door to their bedchamber.

He looked bewildered and even more so when he entered the room to see Thomas, Brigid, and the Dark One waiting for them.

He pointed to the dark shrouded figure. "What goes on here?"

"Forgive me, Decimus, for I must take your life so that Michael may live," Mary said and stepped away from him, knife in hand.

He stared at her shocked. "You cannot do this." He caught a movement from the corner of his eye and easily deflected Thomas's fist while landing a solid punch to the large man's jaw, sending him stumbling backward.

"It is a chance for us," Mary pleaded.

"I have a duty—"

"To me and your unborn child."

"To people who suffer and die needlessly. But your elaborate plan will serve us well," he said with anger. "It will be an unfaithful wife who dies this day."

She grabbed his arms. "No, I will not lose you."

"You never had me," he said coldly.

She glared at him as though he had struck her. "Afraid, Decimus?" She all but spit the name. "Afraid to love instead of hate. Hate is so much easier. It demands nothing of you and gives nothing in return, whereas love gives endlessly and returns endless love. Your mother knew that when she urged you to leave and fight. She did not expect hate from you for she knew, as your sister did, in love there was power. They understood the power of love. Can you not see what you can do by loving instead of hating?"

He laughed with an anger that chilled. "Do you not hear how foolish you sound? You think love will prevent the torture and suffering of innocent people?"

"The *absence* of love is what causes the torture and suffering of innocent people."

Her words struck him like a fist to his face.

"My father taught me that in knowledge there is power. Teach the people how to survive in the absence of love. You will save many more lives than you do now."

Decimus remained speechless, words failing him.

"I intend to survive with love," Mary said softly and with a tear of courage slipping down her cheek, she gave a brief nod.

Decimus turned ready to deflect Thomas's blow, but Roarke quickly stepped in and grabbed Decimus's arm. The hasty intervention gave Thomas just enough time to land a solid blow to Decimus's jaw and he collapsed to the floor.

"Hurry," Mary urged, fighting the need to make certain her husband was all right. "We have wasted precious time."

Everyone sped into action.

Roarke did a good imitation of Decimus's voice, screaming vicious threats at Mary. She matched his screams, claiming over and over again her love for the Dark One.

Those in the hall did not know what to do and some of the men inched closer to the staircase ready to fight if their lord should need them.

Magnus and Reena pushed past them to keep them at

bay a bit longer and to be the first to reach the room when the signal was given.

In the meantime, Brigid and Thomas set to work staging the triple murder. Decimus lay on his side, his garment ripped to look as if he had fought and had been stabbed in the heart, the bloody knife lying nearby. Mary lay on her stomach, blood pouring out from beneath her as though she were stabbed in the stomach. The Dark One's hood had been pulled back to reveal Roarke and blood covered him everywhere so that no one would look too closely and see that no wounds actually existed.

When all was ready, Brigid went to the door, stepped outside the room along with Thomas, and let out a bloodcurdling scream. Reena and Magnus rushed up the steps, Decimus's men following close behind.

After making certain Decimus's men saw them, Thomas and Brigid hurried back to the room before Magnus and Reena. Thomas immediately bent down beside Roarke to protect him, his huge body making it nearly impossible to see anything but his face.

Brigid kneeled beside Mary, sobbing uncontrollably.

Reena entered and began wailing as soon as she saw the bodies. She threw herself down opposite Brigid to flank Mary's body and to let no one near.

It was Magnus's duty to see to Decimus, and he kneeled beside him as the men poured into the room. After making it look like he had examined the body thoroughly, Magnus raised bloody hands as if in proof. "Decimus is dead."

Reena wailed her sorrow, rocking back and forth on her haunches, the blood beneath Mary catching the hem of her dress and growing into a large stain.

One of the men pointed to Roarke and shouted, "Look,

the man who escaped the fortress, he is the Dark One."

"Take his head, Decimus wanted his head," another shouted.

Thomas hovered protectively over Roarke.

Magnus knew time was of the essence. Any moment Decimus could regain consciousness. He had to be moved immediately. And they needed to get Roarke away from the angry men.

Magnus barked orders. "There has been enough blood shed this day. No more will be spilled. Go see to a wagon. We will take the bodies and bury them in the woods."

"Decimus deserves a decent burial," one of his men said.

"His reputation is known far and wide. Do you not think some would want to do harm to his grave and perhaps his body? His wife has been in my care before he wed her. I will see her properly buried on my land. The Dark One's grave also needs anonymity."

"We keep the Dark One's head to show the church council that he was caught and he will trouble us no more," one man demanded.

Magnus stood tall. "He will be buried with his head and his grave will be known to none."

The man's hand went to the hilt of his sword.

"Try it," Magnus challenged. "And you will be dead before your sword leaves your sheath."

"He is the Legend," the man behind the challenger warned.

"Go prepare a wagon now," Magnus ordered, stepping toward the men.

They scurried like frightened rats and Magnus shut the door behind them.

Mary raised her head. "Is Decimus all right?"

"He is still unconscious and pray he remains so until we are away from the fortress," Magnus said. "We will wrap the three of you in blankets and Thomas and I, along with a few of my men, will take you into the woods for burial." He turned to his wife. "Gather our things as fast as you can and be ready to depart when we return."

Magnus bent down in front of Mary. "We cannot chance meeting with you again. You must flee immediately. Roarke has directions to the island I spoke of. Be safe, Mary, and be strong."

"Thank you, Magnus, I will never forget you."

"We must hurry," Reena reminded, tears spilling down her cheeks.

"Keep up your wailing, Reena, while we are carried out and placed in the wagon, in case Decimus should come awake," Roarke said from where he lay on the floor. "My thanks and Godspeed."

The two made fast work of wrapping the bodies, though leaving enough room for them to breath. Decimus was the most difficult, being unconscious. Magnus sent Brigid to get a few of his men to help carry the bodies out. He would take no chances with Decimus's men, though he expected opposition, which he got as soon as his men entered the hall carrying Decimus's wrapped body.

"We carry our lord," one demanded and a dozen men stepped forward in support.

Magnus was about to protest when he realized it would be good for them to feel the dead weight of his body. It would leave no room for doubt.

"You are entitled that honor," Magnus said and signaled his men to hand Decimus over.

Reena wailed louder as they transferred the body and

prayed that Decimus remained unconscious. It was only a short distance to the wagon, but anything could happen. The dead trio would not be safe until they were far away from the fortress.

Decimus's men did not rush and took care when placing their lord's body in the wagon. They backed away reluctantly, fear of the Legend making them less inclined to argue over his burial.

Roarke's body was added next and laid beside Decimus's, and Mary was laid on top of Decimus. This had been agreed upon in case he should wake; she could urge him to be silent until all could be explained.

Reena ran to the side of the wagon wailing, and as she took a heavy breath she thought she heard a groan. She grabbed the side of the wagon and wailed like a banshee screaming in the night.

Magnus rushed to her side and she threw herself into his arms and whispered between her sobs, "I think he wakes."

Magnus signaled Brigid, who rushed to Reena's side, and when she learned of the problem she joined Reena in wailing as loud as she could.

Thomas hurried to join Magnus on the wagon seat and Magnus's men mounted their horses, following the wagon that pulled away from the fortress at a steady pace. As much as Magnus wished to rush, he could not. People lined the courtyard, in homage or gratitude that the devil was finally gone, he was not sure. He could not ignore their presence, so the pace was steady but slower than he preferred.

"Keep silent," Mary urged in Decimus's ear when she felt him stir. "It is time to trust *me*."

He could barely move or see; he only heard his wife's urgently whispered warning. That she lay on top of him eased his concern, for at least she was with him; otherwise he would not have remained where he was.

The roll and sway beneath him could only mean that he was in a wagon and, wrapped as he was, he could only assume it was a death cart he rode in, which meant Decimus was thought dead along with his wife.

Mary had gotten her way. He was not certain whether to be angry or relieved. But then it mattered not, for the deed was done and could not be revised.

He thought about her words to him. She had not expected him to completely give up his work to help the innocent, she merely wished him to change the way he helped. Was it possible? Could he teach as Mary's father had taught? He could help many remain free and he would . . .

See his child born.

The thought was a jolt to his heart and he suddenly felt an overwhelming sense of relief and joy. He would have a life with Mary and their child, and more children would now be possible. He would be able to resume use of his name and his bloodline would endure.

He wanted to wrap his arms around his wife and hug her tightly, let her know that her strength and wisdom was much appreciated.

She had courageously set them free.

Decimus listened as Magnus instructed his men to guard the trail and make certain no one followed them. One by one he heard the men ride off. Then after what seemed like an hour of riding along a bumpy road, the wagon drew to a halt.

Mary was lifted off him and he felt another body beside him that was quickly removed. He was lifted out last and unwrapped from the blanket. His wife stood before him, Magnus and Thomas flanking her.

Magnus was the first to speak. "She did this because she loves you."

Decimus stepped forward and stopped abruptly, catching sight of the blood that soaked her stomach.

She hurried up to him and pressed her hand to his fake heart wound. "Goose blood."

He grabbed hold of her and hugged her tightly to him. "You took such a chance."

"I had to," she said, tears rolling down her cheeks. "I could not live without you. And the seer told me it was time for Decimus to die."

He looked at her oddly. "The seer?"

"The old woman, in the village you took me to, she was a seer. She told me that Decimus was my destiny and that I would be his demise. I did not understand her words until I discovered that you and the Dark One were one. Then I realized what she meant. With Decimus's demise, my destiny with you would be secured."

He cupped her face in his hands. "And you had the courage to meet our destiny. I am proud to call you my wife."

They kissed and Magnus and Thomas grinned.

Roarke stepped into view. "Almost lost my head because of you."

The two men grabbed each other in a bear hug.

"You took an extreme chance for me, Roarke."

"Not only for you, Michael, for me as well. I have grown tired of running and hiding. Now that it is done, thanks to your wife, I am grateful."

"There will be time for talk between you three later," Magnus said. "You must hurry and be on your way.

Decimus's men may have attempted to follow. You need to get yourselves as far from here as possible, as fast as possible."

Thomas had retrieved two sacks from beneath the front seat. He placed them on the end of the wagon and opened one.

"Brigid and Reena saw to packing clean clothes," Thomas said. "It would do you no good to be seen with blood-ridden garments. They also managed to pack a sack of food."

"Kiss them for me," Roarke said and reached for clean garments.

Mary took her clothes and walked into the woods to change quickly while the two men saw to shedding their bloody garments. In minutes the trio looked like ordinary peasants, except for the sapphire and garnet rings on Decimus's fingers.

He took them off and handed them to Magnus. "Do what you will with them, I care not." He then slipped his arm around Mary. "I have a gem worth much more."

With handshakes, hugs and waves the group parted.

"I am going to scout ahead a few feet to make certain no one is about," Roarke said and walked on.

Decimus took hold of Mary's hand and they began to walk. "You will tell me when you grow tired."

She smiled and grasped his hand tightly. "I feel wonderful. We are free. Free to love and live and that makes this a glorious day."

"I agree," he said with a huge grin. "And know, wife, that I love you with all my heart."

"And know, husband . . ." She paused and frowned at him. "Who *is* my husband? I want his real name."

"It has been so long since I have spoken it."

"Then it is time for you to speak it once again, for your child shall carry your name."

He smiled with pride and looked upon his wife. "I am Ryan of Emlygrennan."

Mary grinned. "And I am Mary wife of Ryan of Emlygrennan."

Ryan kissed her, slipped his arm around her waist, and together they took their first steps into the future as husband and wife.

Discover Contemporary Romances at Their Sizzling Hot Best from Avon Books

Avon Romantic Treasures

*Unforgettable, enthralling love stories,
sparkling with passion and adventure
from Romance's bestselling authors*